Monkey Bridge

LAN CAO

VIKING

VIKING
Published by the Penguin Group
Penguin Putnam Inc., 375 Hudson Street,
New York, New York 10014, U.S.A.
Penguin Books Ltd, 27 Wrights Lane,
London W8 5TZ, England
Penguin Books Australia Ltd, Ringwood,
Victoria, Australia
Penguin Books Canada Ltd, 10 Alcorn Avenue,
Toronto, Ontario, Canada M4V 3B2
Penguin Books (N.Z.) Ltd, 182–190 Wairau Road,
Auckland 10, New Zealand

Penguin Books Ltd, Registered Offices:
Harmondsworth, Middlesex, England

First published in 1997 by Viking Penguin,
a member of Penguin Putnam Inc.

1 3 5 7 9 10 8 6 4 2

Grateful acknowledgment is made for permission to reprint an excerpt from "The
Waste Land" from *Collected Poems 1909–1962* by T. S. Eliot. Copyright 1936 by
Harcourt Brace & Company. Copyright © 1964, 1963 by T. S. Eliot. Reprinted
by permission of Harcourt Brace & Company and Faber and Faber Ltd.

PUBLISHER'S NOTE
This is a work of fiction. Names, characters, places, and incidents either are the
product of the author's imagination or are used fictitiously, and any resemblance
to actual persons, living or dead, events, or locales is entirely coincidental.

LIBRARY OF CONGRESS CATALOGING IN PUBLICATION DATA
Cao, Lan.
Monkey bridge / by Lan Cao.
p.   cm.
ISBN 0-670-87367-5
1. Vietnamese Americans—Fiction.   I. Title.
PS3553.A5823M6   1997
813'.54—dc21   96-52418

This book is printed on acid-free paper.
(∞)

Printed in the United States of America
Set in Adobe Garamond and Weiss Italic
Designed by Francesca Belanger

To my mother

(1925–1992)

To my mother
(1925–1992)

(Come in under the shadow of this red rock),
And I will show you something different from either
Your shadow at morning striding behind you
Or your shadow at evening rising to meet you;
I will show you fear in a handful of dust.

The Waste Land
T. S. ELIOT

ACKNOWLEDGMENTS

To my father, for his love, wisdom, and most humbling example of unconditional devotion and moral courage. General John Fritz Freund has been an unwavering presence in my life since we met when I was six, and Mrs. Margaret Freund gave me hope and love when they mattered the most. In memory of my brother, Anh Tuan Cao, whose love of life and family live on in Shannon Kiet Cao; to my nieces and nephews, Natalie, Patrick, and Stephanie—may they remember their family legacy and celebrate their present. Himilce Novas, for her writing, which inspires mine, but most of all for firm roots, faith deep, and boundless love unbroken over time. Khoi Nguyen, my childhood friend and more, for his most uncommon understanding of friendship, family, fidelity, and for love given before it is even asked. With astonishing ease, Christine Wolf shows that wonder, surprise, and intellectual spark can flow from pure chance. Thank you for your gift and rare alchemy of fire, ice, and laser insight. You turn prose into poetry and poetry into transcendent light. Arthur Pinto, my trusted friend and confidant, for his wit, eloquence, firm hand, and steadying presence; I look forward to and rely on our conversations on a daily basis. Anthony Sebok pointed me in a new direction, and his generous suggestions helped me achieve a wonderful career change in teaching. My agent,

Ellen Geiger, believed in this novel when it was in its formative stages. She pictured its completion when it was far from finished, encouraged me to continue writing, and helped move the book forward with each successive reading. My editor, Carole DeSanti, for genius, generosity, and faith in me—and a lot of enthusiasm and hard work. I am fortunate to have had the benefit of her sharp and sensitive editing of the novel. And to Joan Schmidt, with gratitude for precious time, for love, friendship, and grace in all the rites of passage.

Monkey Bridge

The smell of blood, warm and wet, rose from the floor and settled into the solemn stillness of the hospital air. I could feel it like an unhurried chill in my joints, a slow-moving red that smoldered in a floating ether of dull, gray smoke. All around me, the bare walls expanded and converged into a relentless stretch of white. The bedsheet white of the hallway was an anxious white I knew by heart. White, the color of mourning, the standard color for ghosts, bones, and funerals, swallowed in the surface calm of the hospital halls.

A scattering of gunshots tore through the plaster walls. Everything was unfurling, everything, and I knew I was back there again, as if the tears were always pooled in readiness beneath my eyes. It was all coming back, a fury of whiteness rushing against my head with violent percussive rage. The automatic glass doors closed behind me with a sharp sucking sound.

Arlington Hospital was not a Saigon military hospital. Through the hydraulic doors, I could see the lush green lawn that stretched languidly across an immense parking lot. A few feet beyond, a spray of water blossomed upward, then rotated in a soundless circle wide enough to reach the far outcropping of grass. The American flag, flown sky-high from a sturdy iron pole, still swelled and snapped in the wind. I knew I was not in Saigon. I was not a hospital volunteer. It was not 1968 but 1978. Yet I also knew, as I passed a wall of smoked-glass windows, that I would see the quick movement of green camouflage fatigues, and I knew. I knew the medic insignia on his uniform and I knew, I knew, what I would see next. His face, not the face before the explosion, but the face after, motionless in a liquefied red that poured from a tangle of delicate veins. "Oh God, oh God, oh my God!" people cried. The doctor, the medic, and the operating-room crew killed in a cramped, battered room reinforced by rows of military-green sandbags. The calm of Saigon had always been unreliable, narcotically unreal. Who could have known before the man was cut up that an unexploded grenade, fired from a launcher—not a dead bullet—had lodged in the hollowness of his stomach?

"Look," Bobbie said. "See how it pops in your hand?" Bobbie was my best friend from high school. She was squeezing a rubber toy shaped like a bowling pin with a round mouth and two round eyes that bugged out with each squeeze like a pair of snake eyes. A toy that doubled as a physical therapist's rehabilitation tool, it could make my mother laugh, and at the same time would exercise her left hand. "Good for a weak hand," she proclaimed.

Bobbie had no subverted interior and would never see the things I saw. I could feel the sharp, unsubdued scent of chemicalized smoke settle in my nostrils as I watched her meander among a collection of toys. The very idea of a gift shop in a hospital, with stuffed rabbits and teddy bears and fresh roses and carnations, was new to me. Despite the immediacy of illness, an American hospital, after all, was still a place where one could succumb to the perplexing temptations of hope.

This is Arlington Hospital, I reminded myself. There, beyond the door, was the evenly paved lot, its perimeters unenclosed by barbed wire or sandbags. Visitors mingled in the lobby; I had been taught to avoid the front portion of buildings. In Saigon, it would have been a danger zone, as was any zone that a hand grenade could conceivably reach if thrown from a passing vehicle.

My mother was still in her bed, a cranked-up baby bed reinforced with piles of pillows pushed against the fully extended metal railings. She lay with one arm diagonally shielding her face, breathing hard. I avoided looking too closely at it, her red blotchy face that had been burned by a kitchen fire years ago. As she told it, she had been preparing caramelized pork when flames from one of the burners had caught on a silk scarf loosely wrapped around her neck. This web of tender skin that she referred to as The Accident had been diagnosed as permanent, and, worse still, she seemed to accept it as such without question. French night cream I bought was simply put away on the bathroom shelf, behind my moisturizers and cleansing lotions. Cucumber and tomato treatments I prepared remained in the refrigerator for days, until they soured and thickened and had to be discarded. I knew the wound could flare into a lurid red, because it was at those moments that strangers adopted an attitude of polite abandon and courteously dropped their eyes, as I too dropped mine.

She had once been beautiful, in an old wedding picture years ago, her skin the smooth, slightly flushed alabaster of a mere fifteen-year-old bowing happily before the family altar. Even now, the delicate feline features showed, in spite of the singed and puckered flesh.

The nurses moved in and out, coaxing a needle into my

mother's thick, unyielding veins, whispering. Their white canvas shoes made soft shuffling noises against the linoleum tiles, maintaining a constant and instinctive distance of several feet from my mother's bed.

"She's talking in her sleep again, calling out to Baba Quan," Bobbie said. The expanse of white blinded my eyes. In spite of the darkness in her curtain-drawn room, the walls and the tiles and the stark white of my mother's twisted sheets and pillows emitted a flurry of bright, funeral-white lights.

Since she was first admitted to the hospital almost one month before, after Mrs. Bay, our neighbor, found her slumped on the bathroom floor, she had been calling out for my grandfather.

"Baba Quan. Baba Quan," she repeated, his name coming out of her throat as a long infernal moan, like none I had heard come out of her before. Although partially paralyzed and restrained by a band tightened across her chest like one giant tourniquet, my mother could still move, even if only with the random force and strength of a trapped and frustrated eel.

I knew my mother to be the sort of daughter who had always been devoted to her father. She had never truly recovered from the mishap that left him without the means to leave Saigon. For some unknown reason, they had missed each other at their place of rendezvous on the 30th of April, 1975, and the preapproved car that was supposed to take both of them, along with a few other Vietnamese, to an American plane, had had to leave without him. Because I was already living in America with Uncle Michael, as I called him—the American colonel we befriended in Saigon—my mother left her father, her only remaining family member, behind. From that day on, my grandfather's absence glistened just beyond the touch of our fingertips. During those moments when my mother sat alone by the window, I could almost see her hand trying to make contact with the moment when her father had failed to appear. The memory of that day continued to thrash its way through her flesh, and there were times when I thought she would never be consoled.

"Do you remember your grandfather?" Bobbie asked. Bobbie seemed to think I was a baby and not a teenager when I left Vietnam, so young that memory could not possibly have taken hold.

"Yes," I said, "although I could count on my fingers the number of times I actually spent with him at family gatherings and holidays." My grandfather was born in Ba Xuyen, a rice-growing province in the Mekong Delta. He was a traditional man, a devout Confucian who did not like to travel away from his village home. According to my mother, he was always preoccupied with tending the spirits of his ancestors, their burial grounds. "The spirits stay with the ancestral land," my mother had explained.

I leaned over the railing and rubbed moisturizing cream into my mother's skin. My house in Saigon had been stocked with mementos from her village in Ba Xuyen. Coconut halves, smoothed and hollowed into bowls and filled with brown earth and a handful of well-worn pebbles; a rusty iron scythe that hung like a half-moon on the walls of my mother's bedroom; and a fountain my grandfather kept filled and replenished with water from a fast-moving brook by the outer edge of the village. A patch of earth and a sprinkle of water from the province of Ba Xuyen in the Mekong Delta. That is what "country" means in Vietnamese—"earth" and "water" combined.

"We must all maintain a loyalty to our beginnings," Baba Quan had told my mother once. "We tend to our souls, not our bodies." And to me he whispered, "Burn a candle for your grandmother, little granddaughter, and ask for her blessings from the world beyond."

My grandfather was a farmer. He brought the fertile blackness of the earth with him. When I looked at his face, I could almost see the rice fields I had never seen. I could say the words "plows" and "water buffaloes" as if they were as unsurprising as "notebook" and "Citroën." Even then, when I was a mere seven-year-old, but certainly more often now, I wondered about his history, and the fables and myths of our ancestral land. "Take me with you to Ba Xuyen," I had begged. I had adored him with a fierceness that distance made completely possible.

"I want to meet him. The way Mrs. Bay talks, he sounds like the flashiest guy in town," Bobbie said.

Mrs. Bay was my mother's best friend, her sole friend in Virginia. They were both widows whose husbands had died around the same year in Vietnam. We lived in the same building in Little Saigon, on the same floor, our apartments facing prosperously in the same lucky direction. She and my mother had lived in the same village. Mrs. Bay's parents and my mother's parents had both been tenant farmers to Mr. Khan, the most powerful landowner in Ba Xuyen, with holdings so vast that, as the saying goes, a stork would have to stretch the full majestic length of its wings to fly the expanse of his land.

Baba Quan, according to Mrs. Bay, had been considered odd by the villagers, a man more concerned about staking out his one-hectare leasehold with lions he carved from mahogany and infused with fierce protective spells, than about tending and harvesting the land. He was simply more flamboyant than most of the farmers of Ba Xuyen, Mrs. Bay would explain. "He wore the strangest clothes for a farmer," she said, "colorful pants and shirts with various patterns and designs, while everyone else would be wearing black or brown." And after a moment's pause, she would say, with a wink and a definitive nod, "He was certainly an eccentric." I interpreted this to mean that my grandfather had many talents. I could see him in his work shed, his hammer and saw hung neatly on nails tacked to the walls, his screws and bolts, and a few cans of paint, scattered by the foot of a sawhorse.

"Someday maybe we'll have airplanes that go from Saigon to Washington," I said. "And maybe my grandfather will be able to fly over here, just like that."

"That's what we're hoping for, right?" Bobbie replied. One way or another, Bobbie and I would find a way to bring my grandfather to the United States. Or at least that was our plan.

I turned toward my mother. Her firefly eyes clicked open and closed, and along her forehead the horizontal grooves had deepened into sharp narrow ruts. Slowly, she extended the full length of her arm, a straight profile of skin and bone, and sliced the air with long diagonal slashes. Her body had become a battlefield, she a war wound fastened to a bed in a suburban hospital more equipped to deal with cesarean sections and other routine operations.

I took her hand and pinned it under mine. A salty smell of pickled plums Mrs. Bay brought from the Mekong Grocery rose from her mouth. She had gone from eating by tubes to sipping liquid and recently to pureed baby food and finally, last week, to pickled plums and pho, a Hanoi beef-noodle soup. I could smell the fierce immediacy of cinnamon, anise, and fish sauce on the tips of her nails. My mother was getting better.

The sleeping pill must have worn off, because she plucked her hand from my grasp and started poking around, jabbing, punching the remote-control buttons with faltering fingers. She was getting excited, waving her hand, her good right hand, in rapid movements, her parched purple lips chewing air, mumbling, sputtering—a furnace flinging hot grease.

"You've been calling out to Baba Quan again," I said.

She shrugged. Her body went rigid, her arms slapping and flailing the bed. She pointed to the mustard-colored plastic pitcher on the stainless-steel table by the bedside. On cue, I poured water into the paper cup and left it within easy reach near the edge of the night table. "You pick it up yourself," I said. A month ago, I would have handed it over to her with perfect Confucian etiquette—clasped in both hands. The right hand would have been too flippant, the left hand an insult, but both hands were perfectly, exquisitely polite.

"That's what the nurses said. Let Mrs. Nguyen do everything herself," Bobbie piped up. They had issued their warnings: my mother was capable of doing many more things than she let on. "Force her to use her hands, especially her left hand," they had commanded. "They're full of threats," Mrs. Bay had complained in turn. If she doesn't do this, if she doesn't do that, her muscles will dissolve, she won't be able to move, she'll forget she has a left side. How could they have known it was not muscular but karmic movements and the collapse of Heaven that frightened my mother?

I took her hands, thick with calluses gone soft, and positioned them toward the Dixie cup. She stared at me with importunate eyes, and I could see frustration, nostalgia in the looks she gave me, beneath the fault line of rage that threatened always to crack open and explode. In the eerie silence of the room, I could practically hear the sound of old memories ripping their way through her face. I stood back and watched. Even the unruly thatch of black hair could not completely cover the splotches of very old burn on her cheeks that still occasionally ignited into a fresh, rampaging red. It wasn't summer, and yet the threat of heat from the radiator had been enough to seduce old wounds.

The television screen flipped from sitcom to sitcom. A few months in the hospital and already my mother was switching channels like a native-born American child. She laughed along with the artificial laughter on screen.

"What are you looking for, Ma?" I asked.

"Jaime . . . Jaime Sommers." She looked around the room. The Bionic Woman delighted my mother. Jaime could very well materialize out of drawers, ceilings, and walls. They both shared bionic ears. Hers, my mother believed, empowered her to hear things no one else could. Like the Chinese, the Vietnamese believed a set of long ears was a sign of longevity and luck. The Buddha, for example, had ears that spanned half the length of his face, and every painting or statue, my mother used to say with pride, depicted him with gracefully long and perfectly enlightened ears.

The Bionic Woman was a little bit of Shaolin kung fu mixed with American hardware, American know-how.

"I'll get it for you, Mrs. Nguyen," Bobbie whispered.

The television screen became a rectangle of icy aquamarine. Against the bleached electronic glow, the Bionic Woman crouched, then stretched her body, propelling it off the ground onto a tall building while supersonic vibrations accompanied each sequence of movements in the background.

A look of satisfaction registered on my mother's face. These were her sustaining sounds, the Dopplerized sound effects and metallic vibrations that signified Jaime's superhuman abilities. She pushed a button, cranking the bed to a more upright position. This appeared to be a particularly good episode. Jaime was especially alert tonight and was not making any move that would lead her down the wrong path.

A rattling cough raked through my mother's chest. "Baba Quan, Baba Quan," she suddenly gasped, drumming her right fingers against her left wrist, tying a ferocious knot with the sheet corners, carrying on in her usual convoluted language about karma I could not make out. "Karma," that word alone, whose sacred formula I could not possibly know, had become her very own singular mantra. This was alien territory, very alien, even for me. I checked Bobbie's eyes. To her, it was simply another foreign language, the thick, guttural sounds, the rises and drops in the voice, all simply a bit more exotic than her high-school French.

"I'm trying to reach him for you, Ma," I promised. "I've written." I flashed a coconspirator's glance at Bobbie. "We'll figure something out."

For the past three and a half years, my mother and I had lived quietly with the tragedy of my grandfather's disappearance, and I, in moments alone, had tried to piece together the missing minutes that led to his absence. The muffled stillness of that day continued to cast a long, heavy pall over our lives. What had happened to my grandfather? This question continued to linger in our midst and shroud our lives in a ravenous expanse with no discernible seams or edges.

Now my mother looked at me with urgent, inquisitive eyes, dull one minute, glowing the next, drifting in and out of consciousness, my grandfather's name reverberating through her chest. I eased her head onto the pillow. By the hospital's standards, my mother was behaving abnormally. But what was abnormal was not the behavior, only that it had been so public.

We each had our own way. My mother had hers, I had mine. My philosophy was simply this: if I didn't see it at night, in nightmares or otherwise, it never happened. I had my routines: constant vigilance, my antidote to the sin of sleeping and the undomesticated world of dreams. I reached for the pills, my kind of comfort—verifiable peace in every hundred-milligram pellet of reliable, synthetic caffeine. What harm could there be in that?

It was almost midnight. Alone in our apartment, I looked out the window. There was nothing but darkness outside, a fierce silence fractured by the occasional sound of black ghosts making their marks. Even the bare winter branches, tidy and muted like dry bones, had become a disturbance of tangled nerves. I closed my eyes. Simplify. Simplify. Everything will be all right.

There, in front of my eyes, were the sutures stitched zigzag across my mother's head. A stroke that struck as she stood on a stool and reached toward the ceiling to change the bathroom light, and she was now in a hospital with a blood clot in her brain, hallucinations and nightmares about a missing father, and "complications," as the hospital personnel referred to it.

"She's getting better, slowly, every day. We have great hopes that, with rigorous rehabilitation, she'll have full control of her right side very soon. The left side will need more work. But over all, she'll more or less be able to do most of what she used to do—as long as she sticks to her physical-therapy routine, of course," one of the nurses had told me.

Of course. My mother had had a hemorrhage, after all. I willed my mind blank and tried to keep a calm, steady gaze. "One wrong move," as my father used to say, and the force of too many things abruptly rammed inside my brain. I was already back there, in the military hospital in Saigon. This had been how the war entered the capital city. Pulsing flesh, exposed cartilage and bone fastened to mattresses shoved against hospital walls. With a notepad and a pen in hand, I had walked the halls, acted as a scribe, writing down battlefield memories and dying declarations from those war-wounded who were too weak to write letters. A fierce explosion: shards of metal flying from a large gaping wound. Too late to shove anything back now. One wrong move and something had tipped one notch too far and everything was pouring inside out, a live current of nervous wires connecting me to disorder, to insanity. A sliver of metal. Pinched arteries. Singed eyelids and exploded pupils, dislodged and burned black like two charred yolks.

I slipped under the blanket and waited for the NoDoz to do its job. Against a pillow wedged sandbag-tight behind me, my head felt full and heavy and exposed like an open root canal, throbbing inside my palms.

My eyes smarted from the chill of the brisk evening air as, patch by patch, I scanned the road ahead for barbed wire or barricades. But the road was unscarred; no army trucks had ripped the dirt open with their giant wheels. At the far end of the horizon, past the checkpoint booths, I saw an anarchy of untamed, foreign signs and arrows, some pointing toward Quebec, others toward Ontario—all places I had never been.

The sun cast an unsteady red across the sky. I couldn't tell how many hours we had passed, hunched in the bunkered metal enclosure of Bobbie's Chevy, watching a uniformed man tap specks of cinder from his cigarette like red warning lights flashed into the dusk of winter. Bobbie had received her driver's license a mere week before, and already we were making full use of it. We had been driving since her parents left for their Florida vacation this morning, and were actually hundreds of miles from Virginia and from my mother. A maple-leaf flag painted on a mailbox, an imaginary line across the dark stretch of highway. These became frightening things suddenly. I peered over the dashboard across the unfortified boundary, and, just like my mother had she been with me instead of in a hospital bed in Virginia, I could see only danger looming in the land, over there.

Keep calm. Everything will be all right. Hadn't Canada offered shelter and refuge for those who sought release from war? Wasn't Canada safety itself, a neutral space unimplicated by the American embargo of Vietnam—the nearest place where telephone connections to Vietnam allowed me to take a wild chance and locate my grandfather?

"All we have to do is cross the border and you'll be able to call Baba Quan. Just like that," Bobbie said. There, on a piece of paper, was my grandfather's telephone number in Ba Xuyen, which I had found penciled in my mother's address book in her bedside table. And as a backup plan, because I had heard that direct connections to private households might not be possible, I also had the phone numbers for Saigon's and Ba Xuyen's central post offices. As the procedure was described in Little Saigon's newspapers, the post office would become the official intermediary to make the arrangements to track down my grandfather. I would call back at the designated time, six hours or so after the initial call, and hope my grandfather had been located. We would charge the call to Bobbie's home phone and I would dial all these numbers, which would be preceded by Canada's international calling code, the country code for Vietnam, the city code for Saigon or Ba Xuyen, and then the numbers themselves. That was how I had rehearsed it.

I cozied my head against the headrest. Bobbie favored straight lines over detours, but in her own way she too knew how to adapt. There, in the car, was the sweet, uncorrupted innocence that made me love her.

One breath in, one breath out. Sit still. Things will fall together. I felt a tightening in my chest. The Americans, rumors had it, could forbid us to return if we stuck so much as half a foot outside the perimeters of their country.

My mother's voice churned inside my head, reminding me of the powerful grip her views still had on me. "They'd jump at the chance to send us all back. Nomads, that's what we've all become."

Besides, I knew from my own reading that refugees were a burden to the economy. Hadn't our local paper warned of the consequences when thousands of Indochinese began settling in Virginia in 1975? We were, after all, a ragtag accumulation of unwanted, an awkward reminder of a war the whole country was trying to forget.

Bobbie had parked the car at an outdoor rest stop, the last service center on the American edge of the border. We were waiting for, I couldn't exactly say—for a miracle to heal me of fear. But the vast vacant sky was shrinking fast, closing in on us like the gray metallic roof of an airless bomb shelter sunk deep inside the earth. The sun, dull and splattered like a burnt yolk, was hiding low, snagged behind a mass of clouds so thick and dull that even the lush cedar-green looked a sludgy olive. We sat silently in the car and watched the rusted orange light scuttle from one end of the windshield to the other until Bobbie couldn't stand it any longer. Every half-hour or so she searched the radio station for Fleetwood Mac or the Eagles.

The strategy for victory is always the unexpected strategy. My impulse was to turn the car around and head south. On the other side, at the northern edge of the road, street lamps smeared splotches of light onto a clutter of snow-splattered signs: BorderPetroleum, Frontier Bar, Poulet Frit à la Kentucky. I felt the tug of my mother through my body.

Bobbie lifted her face from the steering wheel, her hands jiggling change in her pockets. "Mai? Let's see what we've got here. Quarters, nickels, dimes, the whole works. I bet we can use every one of them in those soda and candy machines they've got over there. The Canadians hate to hear this, but Canada's no different from the United States." She grinned. Her voice still sounded comforting, but even my best friend was running out of cool, rational advice. What more could she suggest once she had said things like, "They're not going to deport you," "You've got your papers," "You're legal," "They can't not let you back in"? Even her storehouse of inspirational quotes, battle cries she had picked up from her father's Alcoholics Anonymous pamphlets, hadn't been comfort enough for me: Easy Does It but Do It, Act Your Way into Right Thinking, Think Positive. She twisted open a Coke bottle and watched the foam rise.

I touched my green card in my jacket pocket and felt the plastic protective cover between my fingers. Even the feel of an official document did not comfort. Resident alien, I reminded myself, is just as good as citizen for purposes of crossing the Canadian border.

"Any difference you see is bound to be small. Tell yourself you're not leaving home, just going upstairs." She reached over and squeezed my hand.

I backed away from her touch. Right in front of our eyes, three bird droppings splattered the windshield. Through the blue-tinted glass, I could almost see the giant caterpillar treads a convoy of tanks must have made on the road, emitting gusts of red heat my father warned could blister the skin. The stretch ahead looked difficult, an eerie topography of misshapen memories and warped psychological space trapped in my mind that night.

"I'm just not myself tonight," I said. The truth was, I *was* perfectly myself, and, perfectly, I dreaded, like my mother. Only Bobbie didn't know it, or didn't seem to care if she did.

"Think about bringing your grandfather to Virginia. Think about how good you'll feel after the phone call," Bobbie said. She was a bundle of normality. We had a mission to accomplish: cross the border to Canada, phone the post office and have my grandfather located, and tell him my mother was in the hospital with a blood clot in her brain. My grandfather could then be convinced—or, we hoped, would not need much convincing—to come to the United States. The details as to how and when could be worked out later—plenty of refugees were leaving by boat, after all. It would be possible. My mother's father would surely respond to his daughter's trouble. He would assume a new form and step into the ways of fatherhood. Now, more than ever, he was the buffer I needed to help me make it through the continuing gravity of our family's emergency. He could step in and take care of her, and I could leave home for college with the reassurance that she would not be—would not feel—abandoned. While I headed out to college and into my own new life, there he would be—the dusky, sun-brown face, with Ba Xuyen's sense of permanence creased in his flesh.

I could have warned Bobbie about my mother's paranoia, but, then, it had never occurred to me that her terrible sense of the world could circulate inside my skin, especially when we were so far away from the Virginia I had begun to call home.

Even in nature, there is always deception and potential danger, my mother would warn. Even the Mongols, whose Golden Hordes forced open the gates of Peking and overran the vast Manchurian grassland to conquer Western Asia and

Eastern Europe, had been decisively vanquished in Vietnam, with a bit of clever thinking and a little manipulation of reality.

"When the Mongols rode into the country like thunder on horseback, the people knew their army was too strong to oppose head-on. So they devised a plan," my mother used to say as we sat by our backyard bamboo grove in Saigon. "Everyone in the country painted, on each leaf of each tree, the following message with a brush dipped in honey: 'It is the will of Heaven. The invaders must leave.' When the caterpillars and ants ate the honey, they engraved and seared this message onto the leaves, holy tablets wrought from the heart of the land itself. The words looked supernatural, a spontaneous declaration by the forces of nature that terrified the Mongolians. Like ghosts conquered by an even greater spirit, they fled across the border and disappeared into the night."

The moment the first American soldiers set foot on Vietnamese soil, they should have been told the story of how Vietnam had conquered the Mongols, I remembered Baba Quan's hushed refrain. I tried to concentrate. Street lights bouncing off a row of poplars lining the parking lot . . . Could they be punching me secret Morse code, a supernatural response to my call for help? What magical message could the leaves spin? Which caterpillars and ants would be my spirit guides? I looked through the windshield and saw only my mother's imperfect universe and exit signs pointing south.

Once upon a time, I had shuttled through worse than the U.S.-Canadian border, I reminded myself. The trick of intercontinental flight is to do it with the blindness of ignorance, to overcome gravity's resistance and to fool the soul's instinct for self-preservation. That, after all, had been my mother's strategy almost four years ago, when she packed me onto an America-bound plane. "Only for a short trip," she had promised, "until the situation in Saigon gets better." This had been her plan, or at least the plan she told me about: I would stay temporarily with Colonel Michael MacMahon and Aunt Mary, his wife, and I would return to Vietnam and to her when the communist offensive was pushed back.

Despite my mother's multiple good-luck preparations, that, of course, was not how it had turned out. The day she packed me onto a Pan Am flight out of Vietnam alone with Uncle Michael, a few months before the end of the war, she had burned three sticks of incense, added several photographs to the family altar, pasted strips of paper colored a bright, auspicious red on every window and door, and, as if she hadn't summoned enough good luck or done enough to appease our ancestral spirits, invoked yet another icon from her paraphernalia of luck, a plaster Virgin Mary, her "Sainte Vierge" from convent boarding-school days, which she placed on the table by the front door—just in case.

What else could she have done to ensure our return to Vietnam? How could we have known there would be no coming back from America, no tucked wings or perfect landing in Tan Son Nhut Airport?

"You can lose a house, a piece of land, even a country," she had sighed our first night in Virginia after the war, as we lay surrounded by a melancholic array of impermanence. We were in bed, on a flabby mattress my mother had had to reinforce with her makeshift box spring, a piece of plywood she bought and lugged from Hechinger lumber yard. She had given me the good side of the mattress, the side without the fat purplish stains that reminded me of those dead, water-logged worms clogged in our drain after every big tropical rain.

We had been separated for almost six months. While I stayed in the safety of Connecticut, my mother, true to her obligation as a daughter, had stayed behind until she could convince Baba Quan to leave before the last U.S. military plane departed from Saigon. But even then, fate, unpropitious and hard, had intervened.

It's not my fault, it's my mother's, I could tell Bobbie.

I blamed my mother for my flawed eye. My mother often said karma means there's always going to be something you'll have to inherit, and I suppose that was how I found myself seeing the world through such an eye that night. My mother was my karma, her eye my inheritance. Through that eye I could see nothing but danger in the phantom landscape ahead. The border, this Canadian border, I felt, contained the unthinkable, more ominous with its terrifying nakedness than all the helmeted men and barbed wire combined.

Danger lurked everywhere, every day, for my mother. When we first moved into the apartment complex in Falls Church, Virginia, she had insisted I beg the rental manager for another apartment in the building. "How dare he insult us, making us pay for an apartment no one would want?" she fumed and stabbed the air, once, twice, three times, with her three pitchfork fingers aimed in the direction of the rental office. I averted my eyes from her glare and prayed that whatever plot she was harboring would dissipate. "You tell him we refuse to live in a place that's been hexed with a curse," she screamed and pointed a stern chin at the giant antenna on the building across from our apartment. In the gleaming darkness, the big metallic rod threw a menacing shadow across our window. Aimed straight into our living room, its long wiry spike became a deathly sword that threatened to slash our fortune and health in two.

And so, because our life itself was on the line as far as she was concerned, my mother insisted I apply my halting English to a good cause. "Tell him to give us another apartment, or else tell him to chop down that antenna," she ordered, animal panic in her voice.

I had longed, as we stood staring at the words "Rental Office" suspended over the doorway, for a sudden spurt of courage to defy, but thirteen well-bred years of Confucian ethics had taught me the fine points of family etiquette and coached me into near-automatic obedience. "Tell him we can put several mirrors up to deflect the curse in his direction if he doesn't do something quick," my mother commanded, nudging me inside with her shoulder.

"Please, Ma. He'll think I'm crazy. Nobody believes in curses and countercurses here."

"You tell him, 'My mother said to do it.' He'll know you're just translating. Children," she sniffed.

The manager peered uneasily from beneath a baseball cap, red with "Orioles" stitched in yellow, with curiosity, fascination, and suspicion in his eyes. "Well? C'mon. I haven't got all day." A pair of veins ran along the sides of his prizefighter's neck like electrical wires. "What's Madame Nhu here saying?" he smirked, popping his knuckles and winking at a woman in tight black jeans sitting by his side. The woman chuckled and looked us up and down with her bright-blue eyes.

I concentrated on his face and on my New World tricks. "How do you do," I said in the clearest, most metronomic English I knew. His rubber soles glared from the table, two giant sneakers like two smeared and muddy halves of a yin-yang circle. "My mother saw a green snake coming out of the drain yesterday and again this morning. There's no way she can set foot in that bathroom again. She has a *phobia* about snakes," I added, making sure to emphasize the word "phobia." Psychology is the new American religion, Uncle Michael had once said.

"She almost fainted. And ever since, she's been afraid to go into the bathroom. Can we switch to another apartment? There's an empty one on the same floor facing the other side of the building," I squeaked.

"What's that? Come again?"

"A snake, Cliff, that's what she said, isn't that what you said? And now the poor mother can't pee. How'd it get there in the first place?" The woman shuddered. "I don't blame you. I wouldn't want to pee knowing a snake is watching me," she said, turning to my mother. "Don't worry, Cliff here'll get you another apartment." She gave a quick leave-it-to-me look that promised victory.

"This one even had a long forked tongue and rubbery scales and a long body that twisted back and forth," I said for added effect.

"It gives me the creeps just thinking about it. Poor things. Why not, Cliff? What do you say? It's the same thing, same two-bedroom, same floor, same price." She was now on our side. She leaned over and pinched the manager's cheeks, running her hand over his two-day stubble.

"Well . . ."

My mother sensed uncertainty in the manager's voice and wanted me to finish him off with a threat of our own. "He's insulting the whole family," she coached me. The "whole family" meant not only the two of us and my dead father, but our ancestors going back several generations as well. "Tell him we have to be out today or we'll retaliate with our own hex," my mother ordered.

"My mother says she's sure you can help us, because you're the manager," I translated.

The manager leaned back and sucked on his cigarette, fiddling with the radio knob, pretending to be deep in big, important thoughts. He stacked several quarters on his elbow and flipped them toward the ceiling. "It's all in the wrist," he said with a wink, snapping them up in one swift swoop of the hand.

"Okay. Sure, why not. Whatever Mamasan wants, Mamasan gets," he finally said after a long silent pause, stroking the thick blond hair pushing through his shirt, and squinting at me through threads of yellow smoke expelled from his nose.

"Remember this lesson: you have to stand up to the Americans if you want anything in this country," my mother whispered rapidly, hugging me. Before we moved our things into the new apartment, she had first inspected every room, then burned three sticks of incense in a can on the windowsill to remove all traces of danger.

The antenna's counterpart, in my mother's mind, must have been the colossal black statue of several South Vietnamese soldiers cemented directly opposite the National Assembly in Saigon. On the attack, their brutal guns had pointed straight into the building, the heart and brain of the legislature of the South Vietnamese government itself. "What kind of a way is that to fight a war?" my mother often complained. "Who needs enemies when your own guns are pointed at your head?" And when I shrugged off her peculiar understanding of cause and effect, she would, like a holy woman imparting wisdom, poke me with her finger and insist I hear her advice. "A curse can only be checked by another curse. Did a thousand American bombs succeed in counteracting a curse as big as that ugly statue?"

The new country must have doubled her sense of impending doom, because my mother began to see danger everywhere, danger screaming out of the earth and the sky and even the birds—three hoots of an owl made her skin pucker with fright. Yet she remained miraculously unconcerned about crime or kidnappers or busy cross streets. "Two men with guns came into the 7-Eleven yesterday afternoon and held it up," I had once told her. I could have been in there buying Slurpees and Hershey bars on my way home from school. "Good thing I wasn't in there at the time," I added. "Don't go there," she barked. "They charge too much for detergent, almost double the supermarket price, then act insulted—can you believe that?—when you haggle them down."

A defective traffic light, an inadequately marked crosswalk, or a school bus without snow tires in the winter—my mother ignored my embarrassment and left every neighborhood petition unsigned. What troubled her was something much larger, much more mysterious. She believed in the infinite, untouchable forces that made up the hidden universe: hexes and curses, destiny and karma. That was why she thought she had to be with me, or at least near me, all the time, to deflect their powers, since I was too ignorant to detect danger myself. Only it should really have been the other way around, when you get right down to it. I should have been the one to fear for my mother's safety, for her fragile sanity. At any moment, it was as if she could close her eyes and summon, from the murky darkness of her mind, a world only she could see.

I fingered the map of Canada neatly tucked in Bobbie's glove compartment. In the black stretch of land where we sat, with Bobbie's car swallowed like a prey in the belly of the beast, the border in front of us had become an antenna, and the antenna a cursed statue, a monument of war that brimmed under a loose lid I couldn't keep clamped.

"If you close your eyes and let me step on the pedal, you won't know we're crossing a border," Bobbie exhorted, as we sat staring at the invisible line that stretched beyond us.

Rows of bushes along the road, darkened by impending dusk, were clenching inward like fists. The sky was turning violet-dark, and a migration of cars with red taillights flew past us like flocks of cardinals. Somehow it already felt too late to make the crossing. A bullet of sweat slid down my spine's edge. I was no longer capable of making the distinction between what my father called "one wrong move," which was to be avoided at all costs, and the simple human need to act, once it was relatively clear, at least, that no wrong move would be committed.

My father saw omens not in antennas or other inanimate objects but in the action and inaction, maneuverings and mismaneuverings of political life. It was "one wrong move" which had irrevocably changed our lives. "One wrong move," according to him, and "the entire course of a country changed."

He was referring to what he considered the one wrong move, the one great misinterpretation of Vietnamese symbolism the Americans made after World War II, which did in fact change the course of both countries. In 1945, as my father often recounted, an American plane had flown in salute, and a group of U.S. Army officers stood on a reviewing stand to listen to "The Star-Spangled Banner," while Ho Chi Minh himself—his beard, my father described, silver and majestic like a thunderbolt in a dark night—asserted Vietnamese independence from the French by reading from the American Declaration of Independence. That, my father insisted, that should have been the one signal, the only signal the Americans should have needed to make the obvious and right response. The right response would have made the difference between peace and war, life and death, he said. "Uncle Ho, after all, was a great admirer of the American Declaration of Independence and of the United States," my father explained, shoving an angry right fist into his left palm as he told me about Ho Chi Minh's secret anti-Japanese, pro-American activities in Indochina during World War II and his subsequent letters to Truman—all unanswered—pleading for American recognition of an independent postwar Vietnam. "Under American influence, Ho Chi Minh could have become more of a nationalist and less of a communist," my father had said with conviction, although this was and remained a point of considerable debate. "Who could have thought that a country that fought for its independence from Great Britain would side with the French empire?" he asked. The irreversible "one wrong move" my father lamented was the American decision to side with a postwar colonially minded France against a vehemently anticolonial Vietnam.

And so "one wrong move" became something of an incantation in our house, the equivalent of "think before you leap," only much more so, because my father had infused it with all the apocalyptic forces of history. To commit "one wrong move" was to invite catastrophe, to go against an irresistible movement, to be on the wrong side of a metaphor. To be guilty of "one wrong move" was to be caught in the web of history, the way my family and other Southerners found themselves, in the Southern half of the country, reinforced by the United States in a war against the Northern half, led by Ho Chi Minh and supported by the Soviets and the Chinese.

In the United States, there was no such thing as "one wrong move," of course. With Bobbie, unsound judgments were not a real possibility. In her view, we could gun the engine and send the Chevy into full speed, through the rush and updraft of electric guitars and drums blaring from the stereo system, and straight across that border into Canada.

Admittedly, with Bobbie, borders tended to seem easier to cross, the future itself raucous with possibilities. My first winter in Virginia, while my mother and Mrs. Bay huddled in our apartment in front of the wide-open oven activated to a full 450 degrees to approximate the tropics, Bobbie took me to the park, where we both stood with our faces up and watched the snow fall. Afterward, we walked the full length of Sleepy Hollow Road to the movie theater, where I saw my first American movie. On Saturdays, we prowled every inch of the fancy Tyson's Corner mall. Everything imaginable was for sale, every product a brand. Electric chainsaws and automatic garage-door openers, sleek microcassette players and fully equipped stereo systems, Bobbie knew them all by their names and discussed them with me as if I too had grown up with such gadgets, such wizardry.

It was Bobbie who opened up America for me, steadied its quick inscrutable heartbeat for my sake. For the most part, Bobbie blended in and blended me in with her. But not always. One wrong move, one moment off guard, and I could feel the world slip from my sight, slowly liquefying into the same dreams and shifting shadows I had learned to expect, even accommodate, in the secret of night. We were once in a music store, one among a wealth of stores in the mall. As Bobbie's fingers played an experimental tune on the Steinway, her finger, her index finger—her right-hand trigger finger, to be precise—was turning into a blanched, pulpy stump of gauze and bandages that moved spastically like the severed remnant of a lizard's tail. Stitch by stitch, the superficial cloak of calm holding me together was unraveling. There it was, the raw, pulpy stub of flesh, a bare bone-colored white.

I had grown up with him. He had taught me how to catch fire crickets in the grass. I had watched him play soccer in the humid one-hundred-degree weather of the tropics. "What else could we have done?" his parents had asked. He had been the best volleyball player in our group, and I had looked up to him like the older brother I never had. On his eighteenth birthday, his parents had believed it necessary to commit the act that would decisively save their only child. Cutting off the index fingers of boys to avoid the draft was not an act the government looked upon favorably, and so it had to remain a secret. But all of us knew what had happened. It was 1968, and Vietnam was becoming a land of fingerless eighteen-year-old boys.

I looked at Bobbie. She had fallen asleep, her mouth against the window, steaming it in a perspiration of misty gray film. Outside, the streets looked pewter-black. Imprints of trees pressed themselves against the windshield, black silhouettes that hung like bleak skeletons. I sat still and watched their wintered flesh, bony arms of black bark, jump with the blue moonlight. A slow pressure rolled through me as I sat

ramrod-straight, motionless against the car door. Any movement, however slight, could crack the Chevy wide open like
an uncooked eggshell. I was miles away from the possibility
of victory tonight. The Canadian frontier, prodigious and
uncrossable, looked flat and wide, a horizontal plateau so
utterly open there couldn't possibly be a spot anywhere in
that land for a person to hide.

Canada was impossible to tackle tonight. We would have
to turn around and head back to Virginia. I would have to
find another way to contact my grandfather. What good
would I be to my mother, I tried to comfort myself, if I were
to go to Canada only to be turned away when we tried to
return to the United States? I was, after all, without the protection of American citizenship. In another age, perhaps in
my most wishful and magnanimous daydream, Bobbie's
Chevy could become an elephant, and I a sword-wielding
Trung sister, the greatest warrior of all Vietnamese warriors,
fearlessly defying danger and death to lead a charging army
against a brigade of Chinese invaders. But Vietnam had been
neither a pioneering nor an empire-building country. Ours,
I had learned in school, had been primarily a history of de-
fending, not crossing boundaries.

"Connecticut is not the safest place in America," my mother had insisted stubbornly. Since she left Vietnam on April 30, 1975, she had spent four months in Fort Chaffee, an Arkansas army camp used as a refugee-resettlement center, and we were trying to decide on a place to live. It did not matter that I was already settled in Connecticut with Uncle Michael and Aunt Mary. The paraphernalia of trust that coaxed my mother to Northern Virginia consisted of a Catholic church willing to sponsor us, but, most important of all, Virginia beckoned because it was a mere thirty minutes away from Washington, D.C., capital of the United States and of the Free World. "In war," she said, "the capital of any country is like the king in a game of chess. It's what you protect first and foremost, because it's the most precious. The same way you intuitively bring your arms to shield your face. The way a mother lion embraces its cubs in the folds of its own body."

She did not notice that we had left the age of guerrilla warfare. That, in a nuclear age, Washington, D.C., and its vicinity would probably be the first target of an intercontinental ballistic missile launched by the Soviet Union was not a possibility she had truly considered.

And so it was that on our first night in Virginia, six months or so after I had entered the United States, my mother whispered, "This is now the safest place in the world." From our bed, with my mother by my side, I could see the moon etched against our windowpane, fat and full of milk, clinging with great expectations to the sanctuary of the lavender-blue sky. It hardly mattered that all around us ghosts of a different war lingered, the Battle of Fredericksburg, the Battle of Bull Run, Confederate victories secured by Robert E. Lee's Army of Northern Virginia.

There was nothing to be afraid of. My mother and I were looking at a country in love with itself, beckoning us to feel the same. We'd crossed the rough edges of the war into this lustrous new territory that faced the heart of the nation's capital. We were on a flabby mattress, in an empty but uncursed apartment, waiting for tomorrow to arrive.

"You can lose a country. But no one, no war can take away your education," my mother reassured me as we lay together in bed. "You will have the best education in America," she whispered.

Years later, that was the hook I had used to trick my mother into my idea of college, American-style. Every serious student in America embarked on a four-year quest, to be taught by a master teacher at a college far away from home, I had explained. It was the equivalent of a martial artist leaving her village to study kung fu at the Shaolin Temple, I would say, or even Siddhartha Gautama going away to seek enlightenment under the bo tree. It was as prestigious as a local scholar being admitted to the mandarin rank at the emperor's court. And although she did not do it with grace, she believed me. Bit by bit, I tricked her into believing the reason I wanted to leave was to attend college, not to flee from a phantom world that could no longer offer comfort or sanctuary.

I discovered soon after my arrival in Falls Church that everything, even the simple business of shopping the American way, unsettled my mother's nerves. From the outside, it had been an ordinary building that held no promises or threats beyond four walls anchored to a concrete parking lot. But inside, the A & P brimmed with unexpected abundance. Built-in metal stands overflowed with giant oranges and grapefruits meticulously arranged into a pyramid. Columns of canned vegetables and fruits stood among multiple shelves as people well rehearsed to the demands of modern shopping meandered through the fluorescent aisles. I remembered the sharp chilled air against my face, the way the hydraulic door made a sucking sound as it closed behind.

My first week in Connecticut with Uncle Michael and Aunt Mary, I thought Aunt Mary was a genius shopper. She appeared to have the sixth sense of a bat and could identify, record, and register every item on sale. She was skilled in the art of coupon shopping—in the American version of Vietnamese haggling, the civil and acceptable mode of getting the customers to think they had gotten a good deal.

The day after I arrived in Farmington, Aunt Mary navigated the cart—and me—through aisles, numbered and categorized, crammed with jars and cardboard boxes, and plucked from them the precise product to match the coupons she carried. I had been astonished that day that the wide range of choices did not disrupt her plan. We had a schedule, I discovered, which Aunt Mary mapped out on a yellow pad, and which we followed, checking off item after item. She called it the science of shopping, the ability to resist the temptations of dazzling packaging. By the time we were through, our cart would be filled to the rim with cans of Coke, the kinds with flip-up caps that made can openers obsolete, in family-size cartons. We had chicken and meat sealed in tight, odorless packages, priced and weighed. We had fruits so beautifully polished and waxed they looked artificial. And for me, we had mangoes and papayas that were still hard and green but which Aunt Mary had handed to me like rare jewels from a now extinct land.

But my mother did not appreciate the exacting orderliness of the A & P. She could not give in to the precision of previously weighed and packaged food, the bloodlessness of beef slabs in translucent wrappers, the absence of carcasses and pigs' heads. In Saigon, we had only outdoor markets. "Sky markets," they were called, vast, prosperous expanses in the middle of the city where barrels of live crabs and yellow carps and booths of ducks and geese would be stacked side by side with cardboard stands of expensive silk fabric from Hong Kong. It was always noisy there—a voluptuous mix of animal and human sounds that the air itself had assimilated and held. The sharp acrid smell of gutters choked by the monsoon rain. The unambiguous odor of dried horse dung that lingered in the atmosphere, partially camouflaged by the fat, heavy scent of guavas and bananas.

My mother knew the vendors and even the shoppers by name and would take me from stall to stall to expose me to her skills. They were all addicted to each other's oddities. My mother would feign indifference and they would inevitably call out to her. She would heed their call and they would immediately retreat into sudden apathy. They knew my mother's slick bargaining skills, and she, in turn, knew how to navigate with grace through their extravagant prices and rehearsed huffiness. Theirs had been a mating dance, a match of wills.

Toward the center of the market, a man with a spotted boa constrictor coiled around his neck stood and watched day after day over an unruly hodgepodge of hand-dyed cotton shirts, handkerchiefs, and swatches of white muslin; funerals were big business in Vietnam. To the side, in giant paper bags slit with round openings, were canaries and hummingbirds which my mother bought, one hundred at a time, and freed, one by one, into our garden; it was a good deed designed to generate positive karma for the family. My mother, like the country itself, was obsessed with karma. In fact, the Vietnamese word for "please," as in "could you please," means literally "to make good karma." "Could you please pass the butter" becomes "Please make good karma and pass me the butter." My mother would cup each bird in her hand and set it on my head. It was her way of immersing me in a wellspring of karmic charm, and in that swift moment of delight when the bird's wings spread over my head as it contemplated flight, I believed life itself was utterly beautiful and blessed.

Every morning, we drifted from stack to stack, vendor to vendor. There were no road maps to follow—tables full of black market Prell and Colgate were pocketed among vegetable stands one day and jars of medicinal herbs the next. The market was randomly organized, and only the mighty and experienced like my mother could navigate its patternless paths.

But with a sense of neither drama nor calamity, my mother's ability to navigate and decipher simply became undone in our new life. She preferred the improvisation of haggling to the conventional certainty of discount coupons, the primordial messiness and fishmongers' stink of the open-air market to the aroma-free order of individually wrapped fillets.

Now, a mere three and a half years or so after her last call to the sky market, the dreadful truth was simply this: we were going through life in reverse, and I was the one who would help my mother through the hard scrutiny of ordinary suburban life. I would have to forgo the luxury of adolescent experiments and temper tantrums, so that I could scoop my mother out of harm's way and give her sanctuary. Now, when we stepped into the exterior world, I was the one who told my mother what was acceptable or unacceptable behavior.

All children of immigrant parents have experienced these moments. When it first occurs, when the parent first reveals the behavior of a child, is a defining moment. Of course, all children eventually watch their parents' astonishing return to the vulnerability of childhood, but for us the process begins much earlier than expected.

"We don't have to pay the moment we decide to buy the pork. We can put as much as we want in the cart and pay only once, at the checkout counter." It took a few moments' hesitation for my mother to succumb to the peculiarity of my explanation.

And even though I hesitated to take on the responsibility, I had no other choice. It was not a simple process, the manner in which my mother relinquished motherhood. The shift in status occurred not just in the world but in the safety of our home as well, and it became most obvious when we entered the realm of language. I was like Kiki, my pet bird in Saigon, tongue untwisted and sloughed of its rough and thick exterior. According to my mother, feeding the bird crushed red peppers had caused it to shed its tongue in successive layers and allowed it to speak the language of humans.

Every morning during that month of February 1975, while my mother paced the streets of Saigon and witnessed the country's preparation for imminent defeat, I followed Aunt Mary around the house, collecting words like a beggar gathering rain with an earthen pan. She opened her mouth, and out came a constellation of gorgeous sounds. Each word she uttered was a round stone, with the smoothness of something that had been rubbed and polished by the waves of a warm summer beach. She could swim straight through her syllables. On days when we studied together, I almost convinced myself that we would continue that way forever, playing with the movement of sound itself. I would listen as she tried to inspire me into replicating the "th" sound with the seductive powers of her voice. "Slip the tip of your tongue between your front teeth and pull it back real quick," she would coax and coax. Together, she and I sketched the English language, its curious cadence and rhythm, into the receptive Farmington landscape. Only with Aunt Mary and Uncle Michael could I give myself an inheritance my parents never gave me: the gift of language. The story of English was nothing less than the poetry of sound and motion. To this day, Aunt Mary's voice remains my standard for perfection.

My superior English meant that, unlike my mother and Mrs. Bay, I knew the difference between "cough" and "enough," bough" and "through," "trough" and "thorough," "dough" and "fought." Once I made it past the fourth or fifth week in Connecticut, the new language Uncle Michael and Aunt Mary were teaching me began gathering momentum, like tumbleweed in a storm. This was my realization: we have only to let one thing go—the language we think in, or the composition of our dream, the grass roots clinging underneath its rocks—and all at once everything goes. It had astonished me, the ease with which continents shift and planets change course, the casual way in which the earth goes about shedding the laborious folds of its memories. Suddenly, out of that difficult space between here and there, English revealed itself to me with the ease of thread unspooled. I began to understand the levity and weight of its sentences. First base, second base, home run. New terminologies were not difficult to master, and gradually the possibility of perfection began edging its way into my life. How did those numerous Chinatowns and Little Italys sustain the will to maintain a distance, the desire to inhabit the edge and margin of American life? A mere eight weeks into Farmington, and the American Dream was exerting a sly but seductive pull.

By the time I left Farmington to be with my mother, I had already created for myself a different, more sacred tongue. Khe Sanh, the Tet Offensive, the Ho Chi Minh Trail—a history as imperfect as my once obviously imperfect English—these were things that had rushed me into the American melting pot. And when I saw my mother again, I was no longer the same person she used to know. Inside my new tongue, my real tongue, was an astonishing new power. For my mother and her Vietnamese neighbors, I became the keeper of the word, the only one with access to the light-world. Like Adam, I had the God-given right to name all the fowls of the air and all the beasts of the field.

The right to name, I quickly discovered, also meant the right to stand guard over language and the right to claim unadulterated authority. Here was a language with an ocean's quiet mystery, and it would be up to me to render its vastness comprehensible to the newcomers around me. My language skill, my ability to decipher the nuances of American life, was what held us firmly in place, night after night, in our Falls Church living room. The ease with which I could fabricate wholly new plot lines from TV made the temptation to invent especially difficult to resist.

And since my mother couldn't understand half of what anyone was saying, television watching, for me, was translating and more. This, roughly, was how things went in our living room:

The Bionic Woman had just finished rescuing a young girl, approximately my age, from drowning in a lake where she'd gone swimming against her mother's wishes. Once out of harm's way, Jaime made the girl promise she'd be more careful next time and listen to her mother.

Translation: the Bionic Woman rescued the girl from drowning in the lake, but commended her for her magnificent deeds, since the girl had heroically jumped into the water to rescue a prized police dog.

"Where's the dog?" my mother would ask. "I don't see him."

"He's not there anymore, they took him to the vet right away. Remember?" I sighed deeply.

"Oh," my mother said. "It's strange. Strong girl, Bionic Woman."

The dog that I convinced her existed on the television screen was no more confusing than the many small reversals in logic and the new identities we experienced her first few months in America.

"I can take you in this aisle," a store clerk offered as she unlocked a new register to accommodate the long line of customers. She gestured us to "come over here" with an up-turned index finger, a disdainful hook we Vietnamese use to summon dogs and other domestic creatures. My mother did not understand the ambiguity of American hand gestures. In Vietnam, we said "Come here" to humans differently, with our palm up and all four fingers waved in unison—the way people over here waved goodbye. A typical Vietnamese signal beckoning someone to "come here" would prompt, in the United States, a "goodbye," a response completely opposite from the one desired.

"Even the store clerks look down on us," my mother grumbled as we walked home. This was a truth I was only beginning to realize: it was not the enormous or momentous event, but the gradual suggestion of irrevocable and protracted change that threw us off balance and made us know in no uncertain terms that we would not be returning to the familiarity of our former lives.

It was, in many ways, a lesson in what was required to sustain a new identity: it all had to do with being able to adopt a different posture, to reach deep enough into the folds of the earth to relocate one's roots and bend one's body in a new direction, pretending at the same time that the world was the same now as it had been the day before. I strove for the ability to realign my eyes, to shift with a shifting world and convince both myself and the rest of the world into thinking that, if the earth moved and I moved along with it, that motion, however agitated, would be undetectable. The process, which was as surprising as a river reversing course and flowing upstream, was easier said than done.

All of Little Saigon maneuvered to pull the experiment off. The obsession with optical illusion was something I might have learned from my mother's friends. It became something of a community endeavor, the compulsion to deceive. Mrs. Bay, whose name translated literally into "Mrs. Seven," since she was the seventh child in her family, gave herself a new birthday the day she applied for her Social Security card, for no other reason than that she no longer wanted to be associated with the Year of the Rat. Her husband, who had died years before, had been born in the Year of the Cat. Spurred by the ease with which all of us could produce new identities, Mrs. Bay made herself two years younger and became, in one easy revolutionary twist, a tiger toying with a domesticated pet. "When I see him again in the next life, I will be the boss," she said, laughing. "That crazy old cat will expect to see a rat, but he'll see a tiger instead." In their new shadow warfare, Mrs. Bay would resurrect old battles she had once fought against her husband and rewrite the endings.

Like all of us who made up the refugee community, Little Saigon too was preoccupied with the possibility of astrological and historical revisions. It was as if the refugee portion of Falls Church decided that it would simply stretch its limbs, lean into the wind, and heave itself in a new, untried direction. Little Saigon was the still-tender, broken-off part of the old, old world, and over here, so far away from the old country, our ghosts could roam unattached to the old personalities we once inhabited. There was an odd element of righteousness in this transformation. Out of the ruins came a clatter of new personalities. A bar girl who once worked at Saigon's Queen Bee, a nightclub frequented by American soldiers, acquired a past as a virtuous Confucian teacher from a small village in a distant province. Here, in the vehemently anti-Vietcong refugee community, draft dodgers and ordinary foot soldiers could become decorated veterans of battlefields as famous as Kontum and Pleiku and Xuan Loc. It was the Vietnamese version of the American Dream; a new spin, the Vietnam spin, to the old immigrant faith in the future. Not only could we become anything we wanted to be in America, we could change what we had once been in Vietnam. Rebirthing the past, we called it, claiming what had once been a power reserved only for gods and other immortal beings.

The absence of documentation was not surprising. Even those with identification papers burned them before any authority could see. There was, after all, something awesome about a truly uncluttered beginning, the complete absence of identity, of history.

"Tell the Americans you couldn't have brought anything with you," Mrs. Bay advised her friends. "Who could have thought to bring birth certificates and photo identifications?" One after another, we were all taking leave of our old lives and sharing our liars' wisdom.

"Tell the teachers your daughter was a fifth-grader in Saigon, even if she was only in third grade—steal a few extra years for your daughter, why not. Better yet, tell them your son was in the eighth grade, even if he was really in the tenth. That way, when he surpasses his eighth-grade classmates with his tenth-grade skills, they will think he is especially gifted," Mrs. Bay told them.

There was other advice as well. From my mother I discovered the importance of maintaining a silence.

"Keep what you see behind your eyes, and save what you think under your tongue. Let your thoughts glow from within. Hide your true self," my mother warned, her arms like iron scaffolding clasping me tight. " 'Sage,' " she said, "is a Sanskrit term for 'silent one.' " My mother had already begun to see me, even as early as our first year in Virginia, as somebody volatile and unreliable, an outsider with inside information—someone whose tongue had to be perpetually checked and contained.

But there were real reasons why not hiding our true selves would have been unthinkable, why shape-shifting had been so important even by ordinary standards. America had rendered us invisible and at the same time awfully conspicuous. We would have to relinquish not just the little truths—the year of our birth, where we once worked and went to school—but also the bigger picture as well.

"We're guests in this country. And good guests don't upset their hosts," I had been told. I was not ignorant of history. We would have to go through the motions and float harmlessly as permanent guests, with no more impact on our surroundings than the mild, leisurely pace of an ordinary day. We would have to make ourselves innocuous and present to the outside world a mild, freeze-dried version of history.

After all, there was a difference, especially in 1975, between being a mere foreigner and a Vietnamese. Foreigner was quaint, but Vietnamese was trouble. Once, not long ago, Vietnam was just a country. But in America, Vietnam meant war, antipathies. I didn't want to parade an unpleasant American experience in America.

Even without papers and identifications, all of us in Little Saigon had left too long a trail of history to erase. Ours, after all, was an inescapable history that continued to be dissected and remodeled by a slew of commentators and experts months after April 1975. Against a clenched and complicated landscape, the picture continued to be played and replayed, glowering from the curved glass pane of the television set, a silent rage that careened through the buzzing darkness of our new lives.

In the rectangle of a room where the television stood, months after the actual collapse of South Vietnam, my mother and I watched the slow-motion disintegration of our country through the ice-white lens of an American camera. Lolloping streaks of fire crisscrossed bruised, purple skies, and from a balcony a white bedsheet tied to the end of a pole—the universal symbol of surrender—swayed gently in the breeze, a shadowy presence as strange and surreal as a funeral dress. Even through the glass screen of the television set, we were not immune from the infection that accompanied the imminence of doom. The sad, savage end was in sight, played and replayed slowly, with the pace and rhythm of a second hand, brooding notch by notch across the stark face of the impassive screen.

A South Vietnamese colonel, someone reported, had shot himself in front of the war memorial my mother believed to be a bad omen. Minutes before the South's surrender, the colonel, dressed in full uniform and decked in medals, had walked up the steps leading to the black statue, faced the National Assembly, saluted, and shot himself. I could almost hear the dusky, purple skies of Saigon, bloated as usual with the animal cries of bats and stray cats gorging on garbage and the indefatigable roar of motorcycle engines defying the curfew, and then suddenly the quick rat-tat-tat of the colonel's pistol, quick and clean, like the sound of a monk's clapping palms.

History was being catalogued here, the missed opportunities, blunders, and outright mistakes. Interesting stories were emerging, the commentators noted—America's elaborate determination, for instance, to keep all plans for the final evacuation a secret from the local population.

Weeks before the final American departure, while plans were being worked and reworked, it had apparently been clear that the giant tamarind tree in the parking lot of the United States Embassy would have to be cut down to make room for the final evacuation. To fell the tree would have provoked a national panic—the tamarind tree had become a symbol of American protection, its branches, looming implacably from the embassy compounds, a reassuring reminder of American commitment to South Vietnam. The tree must have struck the ambassador as infinitely connected to history, and he had denied urgent requests that it be chopped down. There would be no panic while he was in charge. Something could still happen at the last minute—emergency aid from the United States, perhaps. But the marines under his command must have known better. They noted the width of the tamarind's torso, the way its branches spread haphazardly across the length of the parking lot. Outside the embassy compounds, Saigon was still struggling to fill its lungs with air. But inside, in the darkness of night, the men surreptitiously sawed through part of the massive trunk, and when the ambassador finally allowed it, all they had to do was topple it, simply and quietly, and with nothing but the weight and force of their bodies.

Already the story was being repeated as standard history. My mother continued to gaze at me to provide her with a plausible translation. "Are they saying anything important?" she whispered. Her undramatic transformation from mother to child could still be a surprise, even though I was beginning to believe that that aspect of her had always been there, like a stackable chair permanently folded inside her body. I reached over and stroked my mother's shoulders. We were in a new, immovable world, fortified by its proximity to Washington, D.C. From now on, our future lay in the capital of the Free World, our new home, where promises, real and hypothesized, would be made as extravagantly as they could be broken.

Bedrooms are dangerous places. Insomniacs cultivate their clandestine selves there; mothers unload their burdens and hoard intricate sheddings; and interlopers like me go to un-earth other people's secrets. My mother's bedroom was dark, emptied of her. A goosenecked lamp scowled from the cor-ner, leaking a meek twenty watts' worth of light into the room. My mother found the dark reassuring. She enjoyed this, the sunset, the vacant streets, dusk seeping through the blinds, bleeding long narrow sheets of gray against the pockmarked floors. I threw myself on her bed and felt the seemingly infinite silence, the expanse of sadness that was peculiarly hers, dissolve inside my body. I had gone into her bedroom with the best of intentions, looking for two new sets of clothes to take to the hospital. "The red and pink pajamas at the bottom of the third drawer of my bedroom chest, counting from the bottom up," she had instructed.

My mother had a routine, a special brand of night lan-guage I had learned to expect. In my bedroom, huddled next to hers, I waited as she made her way across the creaky floors into the unlit bathroom. The sound of water flowing through the pipes settled like a hazy film over the stillness of five minutes past midnight. A few minutes passed, and she retraced her steps toward the door, sidled softly onto the bed, and—click—turned on the bedside lamp.

Once or twice, when I happened upon her in the middle of the night, I'd caught her off guard, half asleep, with her papers spilling from her arms. My mother could be a fugitive even in her own home. She had an instinctive distrust for everyone, which was why I assumed she always went down the stairway and through the cement corridor to throw her papers into the trash compactor in the early morning, before the trash men came.

It wasn't her fault that she'd forgotten her bedroom was a catacomb of recesses in which secrets could be hidden and later found. Here I was, among stray objects she called hers—an old swivel-neck fan, a threadbare towel, a pair of brown slippers. If I were the kind of person who believed in the spirit world, I would describe the feeling as that of someone who had come upon the presence of an enormous ghost, a strange lingering presence that induced a quickening of the pulse. I ran my fingers across the pages, common notepad paper from the local dime store, crowded with columns of black ink. There was my mother's handwriting. I could trace its movements, the deep strokes, the fine, deft lines. Its muscular letters, erect and vertical, marched across the creased pages in a formal, authoritative Vietnamese I could still read and understand but could not, at this point, write myself. I took a deep gulp of air and watched myself contemplate the possibility of touching, actually touching, this untouchable part of my mother's nighttime life.

Mai doesn't believe in the magic that's locked in my ears. She doesn't know that the story of my ears is the same as the story of my mother's life in the rice-growing province of Ba Xuyen. Of course I wasn't born yet, because the story of my ears begins on my mother's wedding day, the day her parents married her to Baba Quan.

In the splashy sunny morning after the monsoon season, in the province of Ba Xuyen in the Mekong Delta, my mother, Tuyet, fourteen years old at the time, filled two big buckets of water from the river and hitched them onto two ends of a pole, hauled the pole onto her right shoulder, and began the long trek back to the house, ready for the bustling activities of that day.

It was the morning of her wedding day. In the span of one hour my mother had to do her chores, she had to have been as limber as a carp to move swiftly across the fields without spilling a drop of water. She hurried home and scrubbed the front steps to the little house. This was the spot where she and her parents would stand to greet the groom later that day.

Bright wedding-red flowers in full bloom stood cloistered on the steps. It was the beginning of a new day, and there were great hopes for my mother's new life. Nearby, water buffaloes in the field wallowed in muddy ditches flooded by fresh rainwater, tadpoles in the lotus pond in the back learned how to croak, banana trees pummeled into hunchbacks by the torrential rain gingerly straightened their spines, and bougainvilleas in budding purple and blinding pink began wiggling their way back up the walls.

Never had it been cold enough in Ba Xuyen for my mother to see snow—flowers from a white heaven, as the villagers called it— for which she was named. Other girls in her village were named after indigenous flowers or called simply by the order of their birth, but her father thought she was rare and special and would do unexpected things, so he named her after snow, "Tuyet." Her name had been inspired by a winter picture of a bucolic French country scene. It wasn't a name any French aristocrat would name his daughter, nor was it a beautiful name for an Annamite peasant girl. But my grandfather doted on her, gave her a distinctive name, and threw a big traditional one-month anniversary celebration in her honor. Well-wishers from the village came in crowds. Her mother displayed her proudly in a small cradle for everyone to see, her reddish and wrinkled face painted with circles of cinnabar, a magic drug to deter evil spirits from jealousy. Perhaps because of her unusual name, my mother was different even at that age, more active, more fierce, the villagers said, even than most baby boys. A fighting fish, they used to call her.

"It can get so cold that their breath does acrobatics in the air just to keep warm. It can get so cold that dragons have to blow fire into the sun so hard their scales drop off. It can get so cold that their monsoon dares not appear, and my Tuyet would have to be dispatched in its stead," my grandfather would boast about his daughter's name.

She was his precious little girl, but even precious little girls had to be married off. And so my mother's wedding day had been more or less predetermined, probably on the very day she was born. The morning of her wedding began uneventfully. Her parents had arranged the family altar hours before. The three incense sticks stuck in a bowl of rice were burning steadily to their bones. The porcelain cups of chrysanthemum tea rested solemnly on the silk brocade. And sweets prepared weeks in advance—candied coconuts sliced into paper-thin strips, ginger diced into thick cubes and coated with rock sugar, tamarinds dipped in syrup to give them a succulent sour taste that tickled the tongue—were proudly displayed on the bamboo table. My mother gave the dirt path a last-minute sweep. Their chickens and ducks and pigs had been herded without protest into the wire pens. The groom's dowry, two soaped-down pink pigs, hunched together in a corner while the family's pigs stared territorial warnings at them.

At noon, when the sun was big and round and directly overhead, my mother watched the procession toward her house of men with trays draped in red cloth and gold tassels. The groom, Baba Quan, held in his hands a platter of betel nut and betel leaves and lime paste—the traditional wedding arrangement that signified everlasting fidelity and love. Along the wedding route, girls with their baby brothers and sisters straddled against their hips watched the ritual from their front steps. Even the earth, replenished by months of monsoon water, rumbled festively under the renewed activities of tadpoles and bougainvilleas. And so the wedding ceremony began and ended with my mother and father performing the requisite three bows before the altar.

That night, in the black stupor of her husband's house, in a village three full days and nights away by horse-drawn carriage, my mother lay lifeless and rigid, against a bed of bleached white cotton, whiter and purer than *tuyet*—snow—itself. The following morning, fresh blood, three drops, and redder than the red mixture released from a betel-nut roll, dotted the pristine landscape of white. The morning after that, in full fanfare, to my mother's astonishment and fear, she found herself seated in a freshly painted carriage being driven along the winding dirt path back to her family house.

Although she didn't know it then, red had become a life fluid for my mother and her family. My mother was returning to her village, fortunately, as an accidental victor in a very old war. Old men and women lined the dirt street and cheered as her wagon passed by. In their hands, strips of white cloth large as bedsheets waved like miniature flags hoisted by a conquered land. An open cart with a red roasted pig led the way, its two plump ears proudly intact, triangular and solid like pyramids pointing at the sky—thanks to the red virginal blood of the wedding night. Along the route, people cried "Tuyet is home," "Tuyet is home," and "The pig has two ears,"

"The pig has two ears." The moment my grandparents saw the pig's uncut ears, they quickly dropped to their knees and knelt gratefully before the family altar.

They had not warned my mother beforehand of the possible doom that might befall the family had she not been able to produce the three drops of blood on her wedding night. Fear and anxiety, they had heard, may cause all the blood, even in a virginal body, to gather in the brain, in which case there might not be any left for the wedding night.

They remembered only too well what had happened many years ago to another village girl. She was "all white and no red," as people said, like a rotten egg with too much white and not enough yolk. Her husband's family had thrown her on an old wagon, the kind used to cart animals and dead wood. Next to her, hanging from a pole pierced through its body, was a giant roasted pig, both its ears shamefully shorn into two little stumps.

When the wagon passed their houses, the villagers had thrown rocks at the wagon and spat in the girl's direction. Several village elders chased after the cart and cursed her karma with hexes they claimed would last generation after generation.

That night, villagers torched the family's barn and drove all their farm animals and livestock into the fields. Flames leapt into the air, lapping up everything with their fiery tongues. With sledgehammers and scythes, the villagers slashed every animal in sight, and the flesh that hung from the carcasses bled pools of red into the soil. The next morning, the body of the bride was found by an old stream, her blood turning the water the bright color of her wedding-red dress. Even the village notables, the keepers of village order and morality, had had to denounce the incident as lawless and excessive.

All the animals were killed, except the pigs. The pigs were spared, so that their ears could be slashed as a warning to bad daughters who ventured beyond the traditional circle of virtue. The next day, a band of pigs without ears could be seen running like lost souls wailing mournful wails that could be heard several villages away.

For reparation, the groom's family naturally got back everything—every box of tea, every roll of fabric, every mother-of-pearl pin—they had previously presented as dowry.

My mother did not know any of this that day when she left the village with her new husband. She only knew, upon her return, when my grandmother told her, that she had escaped a disaster greater than the fiercest of monsoons—the red wedding-night stains had declared triumphantly the modest fact of her purity. There were many shades of red, my mother was told, the angry red of bursting vessels, the blushing red of a modest young girl, the prosperous red of lucky paper, the wedding red of a traditional wedding dress, the bloody, explosive red of war, and of course the proud red of virginal blood. My mother, her mother whispered, had avoided acquaintance with the deathly versions.

What did my mother's wedding day have to do with my ears? One year after the triumphant celebration held in my mother's honor, she gave birth to a baby girl, me. My mother was not like other girls in Ba Xuyen. Born in the scalding heat of the equator, she had, after all, been named after snow. And so she was by nature rebellious. And I became the perfect expression of her rebellion.

The moment I was born, I was already blessed with long, Buddha-shaped ears, so long that the rest of my face had to grow into them. "Push, push," my mother's midwife had yelled, her hands reaching inside to pull, pull, pull me by the head into the world. But as the midwife later told me, it was my ears, my long, long ears, that the midwife had touched, and it was by the ears that I was first tugged from my mother's womb. It was also with my magical ears that I could immediately hear gasps and sighs of the startled neighbors who had gathered to watch the event of my birth. My ears, everyone must have noticed, were almost two times as big as my little newborn face. How many other people in this world can remember the sounds of their birth?

My ears, according to my mother, were ears reborn and made permanently whole to compensate for the stumps of pig ears that had been inflicted generationally on the girls of our village. Inside my ears were the rage and revenge of every girl from every generation before whose return with a shameful and earless pig had destroyed her family's lives—lives my mother had now gloriously resurrected. For every custom the village notables considered harmless and natural under the name of tradition, a pair of supernatural ears would be born to counteract such a belief, my mother whispered. Through my ears, my mother proclaimed, I would have the power not only to heal my mother's fear but also to repair generation after generation of past wrongs by healing the faces of karma itself.

My ears, in fact, were an event so rare, so momentous, that the villagers, some holding strings of beads, others banging on drums, immediately hired fortune-tellers and astrologers, who reached deep into their starry vault to chart my life. That was why I was named Thanh, for the clarity and brilliance that my ears would bring to the family—and, as the villagers hastily added, to the entire village as well.

My ears continued to grow longer and longer every day, until one day they looked like Siddhartha Gautama's ears on the day he attained enlightenment. The villagers called them heavenly ears. Notables came by to show my mother pictures of the Buddha. They compared my ears to his, long and slender and spanning from temples to chin. Acupuncturists told my mother about passages in ancient Chinese textbooks that described the ear as a miracle organ, a curled-up fetus that contained every anatomical point in its membranes. In the ear, they said, lay all the healing powers of the world. A needle inserted in a specific point on the fetal-shaped ear would invoke energy flows in a corresponding point located in another part of the human

body, bringing back to balance the visceral organs causing the physical disorder in the first place.

There is power in these ears, the power to redeem and the power
to avenge. And so my mother believed. I trust whatever I pick up
with my ears. They have become my very own radar. With them,
I can prevent bloodshed and protect our family's honor. Through
my ears, my mother was able to reclaim the consummation ceremony
as her own, to ensure that her fate would never be determined by the
length of something as humiliating as a pig's ears ever again.

Mai would not believe the story about my ears even if I were to
tell her directly. She still talks to me as if I make no sense. Not so
loud, Mom, she whispers. Everything that smells of life before, my
daughter thinks she can scour clean. She has disengaged and unre-
membered so swiftly something as big as a life, disassembling it from
her mind as if it had never been.

She believes she has to go away to learn. She tells me that it's
the American way. College is the American equivalent of the Shaolin
Temple and the bo tree and the emperor's court and other, similar
nonsense. But really it's the Vietnamese way, my Vietnamese way,
that's made me go along with her story, that's made me feel sorry
for this child of mine, so lost between two worlds that she can't find
her way back into the veins and the arteries of her mother's love.
We come from a culture of subtlety. She wants me to let her walk
blamelessly out of one life and into another. And that was my gift
to her, to allow her the satisfaction of thinking I'm unaware. Because
I know the real reason she wants to leave. It's my face, the face of
her mother, her very own face, from which she wants to flee.

How can I teach her that the worthwhile enterprise is the enterprise of learning to live with our scars? She hates imperfection, she
doesn't like to look at anything blemished. She looks at her mother's
black tropical cottons and sees Vietcong pajamas. She looks at her
mother's face and sees scars, takes it for a sign of damage, not a

badge of survival. Tender flesh the color of pearls makes her cringe.

Her own mother, the one she sees as obsolete and defective, is a woman who's gone through more wars than she'll ever know, who's maneuvered through more cultures than I hope she'll ever have to negotiate, who's memorized book after book of Baudelaire and Molière and Verlaine. This woman is a woman she views with suspicion, and for what reason? Because her mother, who has had to learn Chinese and French, and master them better than a Pekingese and a Parisian, speaks English with an accent? Because her mother has a face that's been sawed and planed and chiseled and varnished under layers of finish that's not finished enough for her?

Only from her American teachers can she acquire knowledge, she believes; only from their fountain can she drink the holy water. Not from her mother, who has been an exile many times over, starting with the day I was plucked from the nuns of the Providence School at fifteen to immigrate to her father's house in a village one hundred kilometers away, a house full of strangers and strange rules I had to learn in order to be the best daughter-in-law her grandmother had ever seen.

Who better to teach her to listen for things that have yet to occur than her own mother, who predicted before any political pundit the demise of the French colonial empire in Indochina, at a then little-known place called Dien Bien Phu? I know an omen when I see one, and when the French yelled "Dien Bien Phu, Dien Bien Phu," as if they were yelling "Tiennent Bien Fous, tiennent bien fous"—Hang on, you dopes; hang on, you dopes—I knew it was a subconscious realization that the ineluctable end for them was soon to come.

I remember the way things were between us. How she used to listen, those nights when her father had gone off to make a name for himself as the intellectual whose radical ideas would lead Vietnam into the modern age. We would sit alone on the bench overlooking a mango grove. Her cheeks were soft and tender like ripe coconut flesh pressed against my breasts. Her eyes wide and solicitous and framed by jet-black lashes I made thick and long by trimming the ends every few months. With her arms looped around my neck, she felt so fragile and small. I wanted to shield her from evil and provide for her every need. I was a mother in love with my child, and the urge to hang on to her forever was a hunger no one but a mother could understand.

She loved my stories then. The story of the kingdom of Champa, the story of an entire country's karma.

No one can escape the laws of karma. Nor can a country divest itself of the karmic consequences of its own actions. That's why I wasn't totally surprised by what's happened to us as a country. For every action there is a reaction, for every deed of destruction there is a consequence. It's something as exact and implacable as the laws of physics. No Vietnamese has dared forget the destruction of Champa. None of us can ignore the total demolition of Indrapura and the thousands and thousands of Chams by our ancestors when we expanded southward. My mother, may she rest in peace, once took me to the beautiful ruins the Chams had built in their glory days. She did it not to scare me, but to teach me the facts of life. And as I sit here in the middle of the night and look at us now, a people and a country utterly abandoned, utterly destroyed, it is not bewildered tears I weep, not at all. We all knew what we did to the Chams was an omen of things to come, of karma wrought and karma returned.

Karma is the antithesis of Manifest Destiny, the kind of Manifest Destiny they teach my daughter in her history book about the great American West. Ours is not a nation of pioneers. I truly don't understand the American preoccupation with cowboys who win and Indians who lose. It must be the American sense of invincibility, like a child's sense that nothing she does can possibly have real consequences. Our southward expansion we study with sorrow and shame, not with a sense of conquest and pride. Karma is based less on rights and entitlements than on moral duty and obligation, less on celebration of victories than on repentance and atonement.

But my Vietnamese-born daughter would never accept this way of thinking. The world to her is a new frontier, clean, pristine, ready to be molded and shaped by any pair of skillful and pioneering hands. "You are what your parents say you are. You are what your ancestors were a hundred years ago." These are things she rebels against. She wrinkles up her nose and makes a face when I try to give her the real gems of life. She thinks I am a mystifier out to confuse her world, to make her see double where there are only simple mathematical answers. But to release her into a world whose secret workings she refuses to recognize is something a mother can never do. Because what danger is more dangerous than danger unacknowledged—and in my daughter's case danger scornfully considered, danger taunted, then dismissed?

When Mai was seven years old, on the anniversary of a Vietnamese victory against yet another Chinese invasion, I showed her a picture of the majestic river where our forces defeated the enemy and turned their warships belly-up like panic-stricken turtles trapped in the sand.

"The Chinese once deployed a giant fleet of armored junks on this river," I said. "Our people drove iron-tipped spikes into the riverbed and lured the enemy convoy up the river at high tide, when the stakes were invisible. When the Chinese vessels, big and heavy like overbloated whales, were all upstream, we waited until the tide ebbed before we retreated. Our boats were small and nimble, and we moved easily through the water. The more we retreated, the more they pursued, the more entrapped they became, impaled and immobilized, a perfect target for our troops."

This was a lesson on what not to do. Watch out for iron stakes beneath a beautiful, calm surface, I explained. She laughed and clapped, delighted that her mother was giving her one more jewel to hold and rub in her palm. And I of course held her in my arms like a craftswoman awed by the beauty and intricacy of an object she had somehow herself created.

The same advice my daughter now rejects as bad fortune-cookie advice. She stares, her head tilted, her eyes narrowed, pretending to decipher the hidden wisdom that her eyes tell me she doesn't believe. How has it come to this? How have I failed to retrieve my own daughter from the stranger she has become?

During our old, haunted nights by the mango grove, we had our routines, games of emperor and peasant I hoped my daughter would learn to appreciate and play.

"Once upon a time," I would begin, "when the Chinese governor, a chess champion, proposed a chess match between himself and our emperor to test our national learning, the emperor, who was not a chess player, knew he had to come up with a plan to save face, his and the nation's. After an exhaustive search through every hamlet and village, the emperor's soldiers discovered a peasant who was a brilliant player. The peasant told the emperor to agree to the match, on the condition that it begin at noon. The peasant then donned military uniform and became one of the emperor's guards, standing behind him with a giant parasol to protect him from the dead-noon heat, which could be as fierce, as sharp as a column of red ants on bare skin. This parasol had been pierced beforehand with a tiny hole through which only one minuscule ray of sunlight could pass. By tilting the parasol and moving it in such a way as to illuminate the precise piece the emperor should move, the peasant was able to shepherd the emperor's play and guide him toward victory, saving the country from yet another Chinese invasion."

All my daughter's life, I have played the part of this peasant, pointing my magic finger so my daughter will know which route to follow, shining my light on her bishops, her knights, her pawns, preempting attacks from the other side's invisible soldiers, teaching her how to protect her king and her queen. But my daughter no longer watches or listens to me. Because I am no longer the guide she looks to for her voyage across the chess board, I must teach her everything she needs to know to make that trip someday on her own.

And most of all, I must give her the ears with which I was born, a set of ears so miraculous that they contain all the other senses combined. Ears that can not only hear inaudible sound waves, but see, like a falcon, the most minute flea from far above; that can feel even the smallest change in atmospheric equilibrium; that can unmask the rhythmless rhythm of danger and betrayal and strip open the stenchless guiles of a two-faced face; ears so keen they can sense through the thickest fogs, smell the faintest scent; taste the flavor of poison on another's breath; distinguish the pungent zest of a grain of salt from the honey-sweetness of a grain of sugar without either grain's touching the tongue. Those are precisely the kinds of ears my mother gave me.

My awesome ears, that's what I want to pass down to my daughter.

My grandfather Baba Quan was not a big man, and although he could look delicate and slender like an impeccable specimen of driftwood, it would be more accurate to compare him to bamboo. His beauty was not ostentatious. He was not large or bulky and did not exhibit the arrogance of muscular strength. His beauty was of a different sort, raw and elegant. He was precisely built, with a self-assured and easy grace that accommodated rather than opposed. As a child I could lie in his arms, and they held me like a sturdy hammock on a windy day.

When I was a little girl of eight or nine, on those rare occasions when my grandfather visited, he would tell me about the Confucian covenant that kept us forever connected to our ancestors. Although my mother was a Catholic—she had become a Catholic in a French boarding school—she would sit in the shade by the mango grove and listen as my grandfather spoke about the Confucian custom of ancestor worship.

"The soul becomes sad if it is left unattended by its descendants," Baba Quan explained. "The farther we wander from the earth and water of the burial ground, the weaker our ties to our ancestors become, and the separation is not good for the soul. It drains the heart of blood and leaves a profound hollowness in the center of our veins."

Sitting next to my mother's hospital bed, I was rubbing a creamy lotion called Rose Milk on her swollen ankles. I thought about my grandfather's warning. I was making arrangements to leave the family village, it seemed, and a part of me hoped that my ancestors' souls, all goodness that had preceded me, would cross the Virginia border as well. How strange would it be to feel the spirit of my dead grandmother unfasten, watch its extinguishing from the heart, and acknowledge its absence in the hollowness of my veins? No less strange, perhaps, than to feel the absence of one's father halfway across the world, far from the untended ancestral grounds.

My mother let out a heavy sigh. "In Vietnam, the saying used to be 'Parents point, children sit.' In this country, it's become 'Children point, parents sit.' It's about time I get used to the American way, no?" she mumbled with feigned exhaustion. Although the laceration on her head was still a purple bulge of flesh and she was still attached to an anarchy of tubes, my mother was feeling better. I could tell because she was returning to her usual stoic whispers, her resigned, seemingly indifferent comments that meant the opposite of what they seemed. And I in turn cleared my throat and cast my eyes downward, away from hers. We were engaged in a shadow play that had acquired a life of its own—a reluctant elegance—her stoicism and my guilt.

"The great brand-new," my mother sneered, regurgitating back to me my first impression of America, which she had memorized. "Why should it matter now, this old, century-old, way of life, here in the great brand-new?" My mother, like other bona fide Vietnamese, still thought and saw life in terms of centuries, millennia. I watched her expel each word from her mouth, the syllables hanging like cartwheels of breath crowding the dry hospital air.

Again she sighed and reached out with her good right arm and embraced me. Not to reassure me—quite the contrary. It was to reassure *herself* that her fingers crept, cautious as a spider, around my neck. She was looking for the ivory Buddha. My mother had bought it at a village market from an old Cambodian monk whose chants had infused it with a protective spell. It was a potent charm, and its powers, he had warned, had to be fastidiously guarded. I was to hide it in my mouth, under my tongue, every time I came into contact with something filthy, like a garbage dump, a toilet, or even a crowded Saigon bus. My mother claimed to live in this new country with me and me alone, but her real allegiance, I believed, was to a world of her own, untuned to my way of thinking but perfectly logical to hers.

"You never know how life turns out. People change, families split up. You'll be eighteen next year," she said grudgingly. "They're adults when they turn eighteen in this country." She smiled her crooked smile at Mrs. Bay.

"Different way of thinking, that's all," she said, bracing herself against the pillows. "Good way, *better* way of thinking," she conceded, then took it back with an upward roll of her eyes. This was her new strategy for our battles in America, deftly turning our differences into a war of East and West. It was a tactic as smooth and sleek as hot wax on tender skin.

And so, with this mixed blessing, I left Bobbie by my mother's hospital bedside and headed to the train station with Mrs. Bay. I was going for my interview with the "holy school," as my mother referred to Mount Holyoke College.

Bobbie said my mother must have thought it was a Catholic school like the one she attended, but I suspected she had meant to be sarcastic.

We stood together on the train platform, in silence. By the way she held her body, Mrs. Bay was telling me my timing was bad. I wanted to tell her: I have deadlines, sequences that have to be followed: applications in September, SATs in October, letters of recommendation in December, on-campus interviews now, in February. Every encounter with the world was already confrontation enough without the extra burden of blame and guilt. But my mother, naturally, had already infected Mrs. Bay. The favored mode of interaction was accusation in the form of petulance and silence.

In my mother's absence, Mrs. Bay acted as her surrogate. Every few minutes, she would pause to look me over, to see if there were hard lines that needed rearrangement. But I'd done everything I was supposed to do. I had had my hair cut to maintain the Dorothy Hamill wedge style. I was wearing what both Mrs. Bay and my mother insisted was my most fashionable outfit—a hand-embroidered shirt splashed with wild curlicues and orchids, and bell-bottom jeans.

"Embroidery was very popular," she told me. "Especially with American GIs. I used to take a couple of GIs to the real, authentic embroidery houses, behind tiny alleys they would never have found on their own, and teach them how to haggle until they knew how to get two for the price of one." She laughed, chins shaking on her ample face. Mrs. Bay had gained weight since arriving in America. She favored frosted cupcakes and Hostess Twinkies and even plain Cool Whip rather than fresh fruits and sugared tamarinds more agreeable to the Vietnamese palate. Rolls of fat hung abundantly from her chin like ripe baby bananas. Because there is no word in Vietnamese for "diet," the English word itself had to be directly transported and appropriated as part of the local Vietnamese vocabulary. Before Mrs. Bay invented this English word, most of her friends assumed it was American-specific, and that as a result they would be genetically immune from amassing weight. Next to her diminutive friends, she was truly a giant. "What shame could there be in that?" she would chuckle and ask my mother.

The train was half an hour late. Mrs. Bay unpacked a carton of Dunkin doughnuts and guided a cinnamon munchkin into her mouth. "Doughnut." It was one of the few English words she could manage competently, without accent. She too coped in her own way, devouring America the only way she knew. Cinnamon sugar and Chantilly cream sustained her. She had sprung an additional sixty pounds, fifteen for each of the four years lived in the United States. She jabbered in rapid Vietnamese. "Good outfit for an interview," she said, running her fingers over the stretch of lillies on my shirt. Embroidered clothes were a sign of power and nobility in Vietnam, and embroidery was a highly valued skill. "Dragons and peacocks and bamboo trees were best-sellers with the GIs." Not with American teenagers, I wanted to say but didn't. I knew she meant to please and protect.

At the Mekong Grocery in Little Saigon, it was Mrs. Bay's job to fry the dough and coat confectioner's sugar on her store-made rolls. She saw solace in the measured order of the grocery, in the unambiguous demands of a recipe, the predictability of yeast, sugar, and flour. But she also had a knack for bestowing solace herself, and it was mostly because of her that the grocery became, over time, a popular gathering place for many American GIs. It was always a special sight to behold: a round bulk of flesh bent in concentration over the store's counter, her chin flat against her chest, her right hand working the floured mixture into an obedience of buttery smoothness. She took pleasure in feeling the butter, sticks of it, dissolve under the force of the spatula and mingle with yolks, flour, and sugar. She could stir anxiety away this way, in a dimly lit kitchen in the grocery store, while Bill and other regulars—American soldiers—hovered nearby and waited to tell her their stories.

She was keeper of the Old World, and to them she represented the hidden part of their lives, which they could not show to others, most of all to other Americans. In some ways, like us, they were custodians of a loss everyone knew about but refused to acknowledge. These American men who frequented the store had been too altered by Vietnam, its hidden minefields and burial grounds, to submit to the normality of life north of the equator. Intercontinental migration had not suited them well. They too had been trained to decipher in strangers' eyes the silent fact that they had failed to produce a victory. Vietnam had been their life, and now it must become nothing.

But inside the four cement walls of the Mekong Grocery, there were no collapsed expectations, and there they could lift their faces unobtrusively among us South Vietnamese. In a period of less than four years, from a three-block perimeter that squinted uncertainly into Wilson Boulevard, we had fabricated a familiarity for our own comfort, which had strangely also become a source of consolation and familiarity for the former GIs: the silk fabric and the tortoiseshell accessories in the glass cases; the frozen pulps of jackfruits and durians; the burlap sacks of dried arnica and lemon-grass stalks; the apothecary jars of eucalyptus oil, rice wine, and medicinal fluid steeped in hundred-year-old herbs; even the vats of nuoc mam, salted fish compressed for four months to a year into a pungent, fermented liquid used as a dipping sauce mixed with lime, minced garlic, hot peppers, and a dash of sugar.

Mrs. Bay tended meticulously to these American men. They found in her prodigious presence a peculiar, motherly tenderness. "No, Bill," she would say in broken English, "like I told you last time, see, when you cook pho, you need a little bit of anise and cinnamon stick and a lot of beef bones." With them, she always had a willing audience and a lot of appreciative laughs.

Vietnam-the-war represented a consuming complication of allegiances. Which side were we on?

Mrs. Bay had come to this unerring conclusion: as long as America hated its own soldiers, we would never be welcome in this country. Those who had been in Vietnam, the vets and us, were forever set apart from everyone else, who hadn't.

Our fate, she believed, was linked cross-eyed with the fate of the GIs themselves. She nurtured a tender spot in her breast for them, these GIs who came waiting for her to ask them questions, which she was actually quite willing to ask. Bill would come in routinely. He liked the scent of caramelized pork and fermented fish sauce. He could sweat his monsters with her. And I would watch the faint profile of his body from the back room as he talked about enormous things. His hands made blossoming motions as he imitated, in quickening movements, the shape of a great arc—a fiery blaze, I imagined, that had been released into the darkness of night.

I too had grown quite fond of my mother's best friend. Mrs. Bay's gregarious nature was the perfect counterpart to my mother's reserve. As we waited on the platform, I pressed my thumb in the palm of her hand, massaging a swell of tender tissue. It was still early morning, the sky hadn't yet beaked its way out of the clouds, and in the murk and fog of the early-morning breeze, Mrs. Bay looked blurry, like the future itself. She cupped the raw winter air in her hands and blew hot breath into her palms. In her big white overcoat that flapped in the wind, she seemed slightly unreal, whiter than the winter-bare birch, almost as white as the mourning white of a funeral garment.

Both Mrs. Bay and my mother had seemed unreal since the first day they arrived together in this country—upside down like an animal dropped headfirst through a trapdoor. In many ways, they continued to live in a geography of thoughts defined by the map of a country that no longer existed in terms I could understand.

Once upon a time, when we were together in Vietnam, my mother, of course, had been utterly understandable. I could see her in the corners of the back room in our Saigon house, beyond the beaded drapes that divided the living area from our place of worship. A melodic chant could be heard; a wisp of smoke from the altar slipped between the strands of bead and carried the perfumed scent of incense into the rest of our house. I was six. And one day soon, I too would learn the routine of worshipping before the family shrine, the candlesticks, the teacups, the rice bowls—the solemn process of recalling our ancestors.

Later in the morning, before lunch, my mother would join my father in his study. They conversed in French. *"Oui";* *"Regarde-la"; "Si tu veux,"* they said. By the way my father tilted his head in quiet concentration, I could guess that the ebb and flow of her convent-school French was something exquisite. My father was a philosophy professor. He never published his papers without submitting them first to the flawless logic of my mother's mind.

In the late afternoon, when it was slightly cooler and a shade would be cast by the trees that lined Saigon's boulevards, the three of us would go for a drive in my father's Citroën. The front grille and the chrome hub caps gleamed, because he polished them every evening with a soft chamois cloth. Our shadows clung to the shine of the metal doors. I sat in my mother's lap, her hand cupped around my waist, and if they were too busy with their own conversation to notice, I could stick my head out the window and feel the breeze rush into my face. When we turned into the smaller side streets, my father would slow down the car so I could observe the food stalls and the roadside stands.

Along the sidewalks, women walked with heavy baskets of produce hooked on bamboo poles laid across their shoulders. Children carried pails of water filled from spigots on street corners. Chickens and ducks, tied upside down into bunches of twelve, dangled from the handlebars and backseats of motorcycles. Cyclos, three-wheeled cycles pedaled by drivers for hire, carried as many as three passengers weighed down by bundles of scrap wood and straw mats. Old, beat-up buses filled with people from the outer provinces, some sitting on actual seats, others hanging from the back rails and the front steps, and the rest perched on the rooftops, along with loads of sugar cane and rice, headed toward the market. The wind ushered us from behind, and the multitudes parted for our car.

"There's the sticky-rice vendor." My mother knew, from the vendors' songs, the coded cadence of their voices, the distinctively nuanced tap-tap-tap of their wooden sticks, what it was they were hawking. There was no getting around the difficult architectural makeup of their selling language. It was a mystery to me but not to her.

By the time we made our way through the alleys and streets, we had brown paper bags filled with pomegranates and betel nuts, papayas and mangosteens. Sometimes, my father had a deadline and my mother was needed to read his text. Then we opted for a prepared meal of pho, white noodles in a beef broth with a faint touch of cinnamon and anise, cilantro and parsley floating on top. The sidewalks were filled with stools, wooden perches no higher than ten inches, and all around us, woks, saucepans, and clay pots simmered on portable charcoal stoves. Occasionally, the vendors stoked the fire and rearranged the coals, which glowed in the hiss of the orange flames.

Sometimes on the weekend, we headed out of Saigon. Because of skirmishes in the countryside, my father picked destinations that were at most a two-hour drive from the capital. Our Citroën usually headed toward Vung Tau, a beach resort the French called Cap Saint-Jacques, so we could see what my father called "the country." On the stretch of highway between Bien Hoa, a half-hour drive from Saigon, and Vung Tau, at the entrance to a military cemetery, a tall, life-sized statue of a soldier stood solemnly, his broad metal shoulders slightly slumped, his face a stark and melancholy black. It always beckoned us. It was a famous statue. The soldier honored was a soldier of the Republic of Vietnam Armed Forces, of course, and stories about it abounded. My father told me that the statue could lift itself out of the ground and walk at night. It was known that on hot summer days the soldier had asked passersby for water. On certain occasions when the North Vietnamese or the Vietcong had launched their nighttime attacks, some houses had been warned in advance by him. A severely wounded South Vietnamese soldier, a survivor of a battlefield massacre, had come to the statue one evening and seen hot tears in its eyes.

At all hours of the day and night, cars came to a halt in front of the statue so people could observe a few moments of silence. We had never driven to Vung Tau without stopping. With my father on one side and my mother on the other, I paid our respects. I placed a pot of flowers next to his giant muddied boots, and a bundle of joss sticks on either side of him. I could almost hear the soldier's steady, thick-booted steps against the sun-baked cement. As we returned to the car, I often wondered if the sigh I heard came from my parents or from the black statue itself.

For those like my parents, who were both born in the Mekong Delta, "the country" always meant the lushest, most tender, most compelling part of Vietnam, the part that revealed a slice of green rice fields. Even though we were far from the delta, the occasional rice fields that could be glimpsed from the Saigon–Bien Hoa highway continued to beckon and tempt. My parents caught each moment and held it in their eyes: the flooded fields, a girl lugging water in large bamboo tubes lashed to a body-and-shoulder yoke, women slashing stalks of rice, old men kneeling by a roadside shrine. For them, that was the country's soul, their childhood itself.

One autumn night, our first in Virginia, when autumn was still unexpected to me, my mother and I were watching *I Dream of Jeannie* together in our living room. The sun had just gone down, and our apartment was cast in a pale-pastel light. Jeannie was making snow fall, in a neat geometric pattern that covered only Major Nelson's house in Cocoa Beach, Florida, in the middle of July—to the astonishment, of course, of Dr. Bellows, the perpetually perplexed NASA psychiatrist. As my mother and I watched, I began to notice the growing collection of strange details accumulating in our new lives, the curiously cold air, an autumn cold I hadn't yet known, which could insinuate itself right through our pores to settle just below the skin. I was wearing a bulky wool sweater, but my mother was still in her tropical garb. In a threadbare cotton blouse, she piled another blanket onto her body and edged closer to my part of the couch, forcing her sockless feet under my flannel pants for warmth. It was an undramatic moment, meaningless to her, perhaps, but completely significant to me. I could have offered her reality: a sweater, socks. It would have been as simple as that. But somehow, at that moment, my mother, imperfect and unable to adjust, died in my mind.

The train was pulling in. Mrs. Bay scooped me in her arms. "Call your mother when you arrive. Uncle Michael will pick you up, no?" she asked. I waited for last-minute axioms. She and my mother had lobbed enough Old World proverbs for me to know they had one for every occasion. "You know how mothers are. You're all she's got left in this new country. With all that she's been through, you don't want her to worry, do you?"

The monotonous sound of the train was an invitation to float, the engine emitting smooth, continuous snorts and sneezes. I clamped myself against the fake-leather seat and absorbed the echo of my mother's sorrow in my body. If my grandfather were here, he would be able to make things right. His presence alone would be assuaging to her. I knew the inconsolable shame and sadness that she had been carrying in her since the day Saigon fell, when she had had to leave him behind, "pacing in the shadows of the unlucky statue with guns that pointed unluckily at the congressional building," as she described it. That was where they were supposed to have met each other. Could they have mistaken the time and place? Could he have changed his mind and remained in Ba Xuyen? Had he been hurt, shot by a renegade bullet? My mother had spun multiple versions of what could have happened to her father, and what could have been, and each version was always as terrible and as consuming as the next.

Suddenly I imagined myself kneeling. Our Father, who art in Heaven . . . I was bowing low, making quickly, very quickly, the sign of the cross. My mother was in bed, held together by a fragile scaffolding of bones. On her head, a zipper of black surgical threads struggled to keep a still-raw wound in place. I did not believe, but just in case, what risk could there be in a little childhood prayer?

The train lurching forward and the tracks and landscape moving back gave me the feeling of being caught in a vortex of mystical forces, in a ferocious continental drift—one mass splitting in two, going in opposite directions—traveling at the speed of light. Except for the fecund heat of the tropics and the tall coconut palms, the railroad route from Virginia up north toward Uncle Michael's Connecticut could have been the same route connecting Bien Hoa to Saigon. Street urchins could have been sailing their white paper boats along the roadside gullies; bare-chested men in cotton shorts could have been on their roofs, nailing down sheets of metal rusted and warped by the sun and rain.

Through the window, I could see Baltimore and Philadelphia and Newark and the makeshift shacks along the tracks, huddled together like old tin hooches discolored by tropical mildews and black diesel fumes on the outskirts of

Saigon. The sameness in the landscape gave the peculiar impression that the train, in spite of its movement and speed, was also standing still, and for a moment I felt disoriented, unable to tell whether the train's motion was real or imagined, whether we were gaining ground or simply kicking in place.

Uncle Michael had been a colonel stationed a full six years in Vietnam. When I first saw him, a few months after the Tet New Year in 1968, he had been strapped to a stretcher, curled like a newborn, viscous and pink and covered from head to toe in placenta. I could tell he had been freshly hurt: the scooped-out flesh on his face was red, not brown; his breath was hot but not overly sour; and the blood in his nose had not yet congealed, so, unlike the other patients, he had no visible rim of red along his nostrils. I was seven years old and an occasional student volunteer, a novice still unaccustomed to the odor of formaldehyde and rotting flesh and saturated waste, and I had had nothing more than a healing balm of cold compress and a plastic cup of water to offer him. That day when I met Uncle Michael, our volunteer group had visited the American Third Field Hospital, where wounded American soldiers were customarily hospitalized.

He had been on a routine Tet patrol on the outskirts of Saigon when his tank was hit with several grenades fired from a Vietcong launcher. That Tet, although the Americans and the Republic of Vietnam Armed Forces had received intelligence reports that Vietcong attacks could be expected, all of us continued to prepare for celebration. There were rumors that troops on Tet leave had been recalled to their units. From our window, I could see a circle of soldiers with M-16 rifles slung across their shoulders and Colt .45 automatics strapped to their waists. It was not a terrifying sight. Peddlers hawked spicy, sugared tamarind and sweetmeats, and children exploded red cartridges of fireworks hung like strips of lucky paper from cherry-blossom branches. My mother continued to sweep our front steps. Gold chrysanthemums spilled from ceramic pots; lilacs and cherry blossoms flicked clusters of light into our garden. Our brick courtyard shimmered with colors.

Based on the lunar calendar, which begins with the year 2637 B.C., Tet, which usually falls in late January or early February on the Western calendar, is the most celebrated and most cherished holiday in Vietnam. My father had gone to the bank and taken out new money that gleamed with a fresh, crisp gloss. He slipped each folded bill into the palm-sized rectangle of a lucky red envelope and waited for the first day of Tet to pass them all out to me and other children. At midnight on the eve of Tet, in accordance with custom, my father made his symbolic survey around our property. As he traveled the perimeter of our house, he mulled over the details of the past year. All past offenses our household had committed would be acknowledged, and he would ask that they be pardoned. He promised that the next year would be marked by a greater goodness. He promised to be a better version of himself. When he returned, he would be the first person to cross our portal, and so would influence our fortune for the rest of the year. Newly blessed, he would bring righteousness back to our home.

All of Vietnam, in fact, had been shedding the burdens of the past year. Debts had been paid off, dust swept away. Grudges had been forgotten, and wrongs righted. War would cease, at least for the duration of Tet. A new karma would be ushered in with the new year. New clothes had been ordered and ironed. My mother bought a silk ao dai, a flowing dress that is fitted tightly around the waist, where it splits into two panels, a front and back, which flow to cover a pair of black satin trousers. I too had a new ao dai for the first day of Tet that year, a rose-colored one with a faint watered pattern of silk moiré. To scare off evil spirits, we relied on firecrackers, on the explosive fury of sound and light against a starfield of flowering purple-and-black smoke. From my window, I could see a raw streak of red hissing its way against the moonless night. Behind it an apricot afterglow trailed like an exquisite taillight across the sky.

The Vietcong had chosen the first day of Tet to attack Saigon. But for the first half-hour or so, all of us had mistaken the scattering of gunfire and machine gun as the earnest rumble of Tet firecrackers. It was the Year of the Monkey. Granted, monkeys are unpredictable, and so the Year of the Monkey would be rife with surprises. But in our mind, it was inconceivable that the sanctity of Tet could be broken. We had placed our trust in the Tet cease-fire, which the Vietcong had publicly requested. No one could have predicted a breach of that truce.

Secured behind our locked gate, my parents and I watched as the city succumbed to the raw blistering red of rocket fire. Rumor had it that the Vietcong were hostile to all private property, and so my mother promptly removed her wedding band and hid it, along with her other jewelry, inside the trunk of my elephant-shaped hamper. Artillery aimed at Tan Son Nhut Airport and military targets throughout the city threw blossoms of smoke that clung to the sky and kept us trapped in the slow but livid shadows of war. For almost two weeks, Saigon was a hothouse that bred a combustion of burning chemicals and fuel. My mother resorted to our emergency reserve of rice and beans, noodles and freeze-dried meat. On occasions when the fighting subsided and the enemy retreated to a different part of the city, my mother ventured briefly to our neighborhood market. With me by his side, my father continued writing in his study. We listened to gunshots exploding nearby, a thumping staccato of tat-tat-tat that caught and held in the restlessness of my father's study. With his steadfast hand cupped around my shoulders, my father assured me there was nothing to fear. I was in the force field of his enormous arms, surrendering to his embrace as he read the news to my mother and me from *The Stars and Stripes*, *Paris-Match*, *Hoa Binh*. Morning after morning, the same grainy picture of black-pajamaed Vietcong with Russian AK-47s crouched in the U.S. Embassy courtyard made the front pages of all the major newspapers. Although the sneak attack had indeed been a surprise, the offensive, most experts agreed, was a complete military failure for the communists, who had predicted, wrongly, that their presence alone would motivate a spontaneous uprising in Saigon. But even in the outposts where the Vietcong had temporarily gained control, villagers had in fact rallied to support the South. The situation was resolving itself militarily. But it would not matter, according to my father. Nor would it matter that almost three thousand civilians had been executed by Vietcong death squads and dumped in mass graves in the imperial city of Hue. What mattered, my father told me and later proclaimed to the press, was the sight of an enemy supposedly on the verge of defeat, raging through the embassy grounds, the very symbol of the U.S. presence in Vietnam. And he was right, of course. That one fact had courted at the very least ambiguity if not outright fear in all of Saigon and apparently Washington, D.C., as well. The battle for the embassy was quickly dubbed the Battle of Bunker's Bunker, after Ellsworth Bunker, then the American ambassador. The papers quoted my father, who had been among the first to declare it the beginning of the end of the American presence in Vietnam.

My father had been a member of the Third Force, the opposition movement that presented itself as the middle ground, the alternative to both the Vietcong and the government. People must have looked at him and thought, here was a man who could not, as men were encouraged to, make up his mind and act with certainty. But it was an accusation he never found disconcerting. He relished complexities most of all, because extremes of any kind made him cringe. "Do I contradict myself? Very well, I contradict myself," he'd say with a shrug, quoting, he claimed, Walt Whitman.

And that was why Uncle Michael and my father became friends the moment I introduced them. The first time I saw Uncle Michael, he was strapped to a bed, with a drainage tube up his nose and a thermometer in his mouth. He gave me a funny cockeyed wink that I tried to reciprocate but couldn't, prompting him to show off by blinking both eyes in rapid succession. We became friends over the course of his month-long recovery. Sitting by his bedside, I felt nothing but pure and raw pride when he told me how he outdid the meanest Montagnard from the Pleiku hills. I had heard about the Montagnards from my father. "Stone-age tribes of savages," they were called—mountain people seduced by the CIA and equipped with American carbines and mortars. They were feared the way one feared wild beasts and jungles and other unpredictable, untamable things. It didn't surprise me that Uncle Michael was the only outsider, Vietnamese or American, the Montagnards had ever allowed into their fortified camps at the height of a tribal mutiny that had kept the highlands paralyzed for months.

"They wanted to see how much I could endure," he told me. "Part of the hazing ceremony involved drinking buffalo urine and eating tiger's testicles and smoking the bitterest Cambodian red marijuana the chief had to offer." As I listened to his exploits, I imagined him in his crisp army-green uniform, a hero winking his way through unadulterated hostility with self-evident charm and authority. By the time he left the tribe after a three-month stay, he had single-handedly convinced the entire tribe to lay down their arms and end their rebellion—all by relinquishing his pistol and bayonet as proof of his good intentions and steely equilibrium. That was how I liked to picture him, in his polished-brass belt buckles and spit-shined boots, entering the bamboo-spiked gate to the Montagnards' camp as casually as if he were crossing the threshold of his own house.

I knew my parents would want to meet him. Uncle Michael's fluency in French and Vietnamese was a rarity among Americans, and my parents liked to broaden their horizons. In fact, when I spoke about Uncle Michael, it was my father who suggested I invite him to our house. Uncle Michael was no average American, my father recognized right away, the very first day I brought him home after his discharge from the hospital. After all, how many other foreigners knew to appreciate intuitively the durian, the perfumed pulpy flesh deep inside the thick, thorny exterior that could be pried open only with hammer and chisel? Whereas nonnatives likened the durian's smell to "baby's vomit" and worse, Uncle Michael considered the fruit a rare but delicious delicacy.

From the beginning, Uncle Michael and my father's friendship was a complete surprise to their other friends.

Some people thought it strange that a Vietnamese who couldn't choose sides would side so easily with an American army man. But between them, it was not difficult to believe that love and ordinary kindness formed the basis of human relations, and that war was an illusion. No matter which side they were on, their shadows, as my father described it, would be cast in the same direction.

In their own way, they were both iconoclasts with a common weakness: a deep-rooted disdain for brutish, clear-cut answers. However, their devotion was ultimately not to the fervor of slogans or politics, but to ordinary friendship. They had no pretenses that ideas are capable of holding a singular truth. Perhaps it was the way Uncle Michael took to the durian that impressed my father. Perhaps it was the way he intuitively understood the orderlessness of Saigon's traffic, the streets that had neither lanes nor traffic lights, crosswalks nor stop signs—or at least nothing that anybody ever obeyed—which confounded and terrified almost all foreigners. Whereas other pedestrians stammered their way across the boulevards and around traffic circles, Uncle Michael could wait for that precise split-second pause in the vertiginous rush of motorcycles and cars and then immerse himself in the flow of things; he understood that a decisive stride through ongoing turbulence was necessary to get to the other side.

Uncle Michael was the kind of man who believed he owned as far as he could see. A graduate of West Point, he had certain inherited notions of American benevolence which his own experience as a World War II soldier had reinforced. Possibilities, that was what America represented to him. That was his modest wish for Vietnam.

Upon his release from the hospital, Uncle Michael had

been reassigned to a staff position in Saigon. He visited us almost every evening. More than anything, I loved listening to their political talks, my father and Uncle Michael's. Outside, monks were burning themselves, engulfed in flames more orange than saffron robes. Outside, rioting mobs and helmeted soldiers clustered behind metal shields were whacking the hyperkinetic Saigon air with swinging black pugil sticks. But inside, in the familiar sanctity of my father's air-conditioned study, where the two men stashed themselves for days, I curled up and listened to rumbles and predictions, reckless and apocalyptic, but always reassuring because it was their loved voices that I would hear. From the private little cave I made under my father's table, I considered the vagaries of their pronouncements. From my father: You're turning us into a giant billboard for Shell and Coca-Cola. . . . You Americans are not equipped for a war in Vietnam. . . . You're going about it the wrong way; Westmoreland's WHAM operations, acronym or not, are never going to win any hearts and minds. . . . And from Uncle Michael were multiple versions of these persistent questions: Aren't the Vietcong communist stooges, and what about those dominoes? What about those dominoes?

Their discussions, though flushed with certainty, did not clarify. No instant answers or Euclidean truths—no obviously noble intentions, no undeniably evil designs. American tyranny; American goodwill. Who could tell the difference any longer?

Over their daily cups of café au lait Vietnamese-style, coffee my mother boiled then mixed with condensed milk for them to sip all night as they mulled the war, thread by thread, like a Persian rug they had been commissioned to weave, they would have their tête-à-tête, their punches and counterpunches. And I would listen to their chorus of English and French, which could continue uninterrupted, through thunder and lightning and power blackouts, sometimes even into the early morning. On rainy nights, my father would retrieve his favorite from the cupboard—snake liqueur he called Vietnamese vodka. The strong, pungent flavor, he claimed, came from the fermented viper steeped in alcohol and sealed, body and all, in the bottle. In a language lost to everyone outside the circumference of my father's study, my father and Uncle Michael would explain as I listened and guarded, like a sentry on duty, their inconsistent and contradictory hoards of knowledge. Once in a while, my father would recite the poetry of Baudelaire he had learned from my mother, stretching the flawless syllables over his lips.

My mother, Uncle Michael, and I were the only three people my father wanted with him on his fiftieth birthday. We were on a boat on the Saigon River, with the Majestic Hotel standing to our left; a gray, ponderous vessel with a headlight like an electric eye shimmering to our right; and a swollen moon shining full-beam, the searchlight of Heaven itself, as my mother called it, looking down upon us from above. Soldiers hunched over their lookout posts and equipped with binoculars occasionally gazed in our direction, and even though we could hear the ominous rounds of mortar and rocket fire a distance away and the dull rotating blades of a helicopter just above, we were still charmed by the air of celebration we had learned to fabricate: food made from scratch, three different cakes, plain white ceramic plates, ordinary good cheer. You could almost forget you were in Vietnam. My father could hook a worm here, cast a pole into the river, and show me the ways of baiting with patience and silence. The silvery water quivered beneath our feet, and I watched as patches of light from a complex of houses along the river's edge floated a feeble glow into the darkness.

"Bonne anniversaire," my mother had wished. She wore a silk ao dai. When she sat down, she lifted the back panel and wrapped it in her lap. I could see beauty and grace in her every gesture. We had champagne glasses, which we made sure would produce the clear, lucid "ping" of crystal with each toast. Mine had been filled with orange Shasta that Uncle Michael bought from the American PX. I could see our faces against the dark waters of the river. My father's was particularly happy. He was a man whose birthday was being celebrated by his wife, his daughter, and his best friend.

Later that night, Uncle Michael presented my father with a birthday present, a dozen boxes of sea swallows' nests of the highest grade, saliva spun into a gelatin of white filaments, drying rapidly in the sea salt and wind, and used by the birds to build nests hidden among crevices along jagged cliffs off the coast of Nha Trang. Swallows' nests were highly prized delicacies. Those who gathered these nests used bamboo ladders and long poles lit by candles, for the nests could only be found along the higher portions of the cliffs, and never in caves that faced south and were thus lit by the sun's rays. It would be a meticulous and painstaking task for my mother, but she would turn my father's present into glorious food. She would soak the nests in sugared water, removing with tweezers the feathers that floated to the surface. The softened filaments would be boiled in stock, flavored, and made into a steaming soup. Most Americans would not even know about swallows' nests, much less venture into the rush and agitation of a Saigon sky market to look for them, my father said with admiration.

Soon after my father's fiftieth birthday, Uncle Michael

ended his duty in Saigon and returned to the United States. Something collapsed inside me as I watched my parents prepare for his departure. For his fifteen-hour trans-Pacific trip, my mother packed a thermos of swallows' nest soup and a container of glutinous rice, a care package I carried on my lap when my parents and I drove Uncle Michael to the airport. It had never occurred to me that he would ever leave Vietnam, or us. My parents and I watched him cross Tan Son Nhut's departure gate. He gave me a thumbs-up as I winked him a sad goodbye.

And then everything changed for my mother and me. Our house, and Saigon itself, entered a slow, deep freeze, a glaciered hush that took over and defined our lives with surprising finality. A few months after Uncle Michael's departure, my father died an unexpected death in his sleep. "His breath sucked clean from his lungs and straight into an angel's," Uncle Michael wrote in a letter to my mother and me. Uncle Michael claimed my father had appeared to him at the moment of death, an outline like a flash of white laser at the foot of his bed in Connecticut, bidding him goodbye. Parallel planes, lives that continued beyond the polish of tombstones, these were matters entirely plausible to Uncle Michael. We consoled ourselves with the fact that my father had been blessed, a man who had been bestowed the luxury of dying nonviolently in the middle of a war.

On the fifteenth day of the lunar month, with my grandfather Baba Quan by her side, my mother gave my father several new suits of gilded paper, an elaborate three-story mahogany house, and stacks of shirts and gowns made of silvery paper, which she burned on a pyre of sandalwood. Three thousand years before Christ, when Chinese emperors had decreed that the living be buried along with the royal dead, an idea, backed by Confucius, was conceived to use paper figures as offerings instead. I could feel my father's breath soft against my face like a wisp of dandelion, and the smell of expensive wood roasting in the sodden, humid air.

My grandfather had made the long trip from Ba Xuyen to be with us and to pay his final respects to my father's spirit. He was a Confucian and believed in the worship of spirits and the sanctity of the ancestral land. I didn't want to be the needy, unconsolable child, but as my grandfather held me in his arms, I could not help wishing that Uncle Michael were with us as well. He could have made the trip back to Saigon—and never left again. And I could easily imagine being surrounded by my father, my mother, my grandfather, and Uncle Michael as all of us celebrated a more festive event—Tet, or the Midautumn Moon Festival, or somebody's birthday. But I watched as my grandfather put together an elaborate arrangement of betel nuts, used for every solemn occasion—weddings, funerals, and other cere-monies. My father's picture stared at us from the family shrine.

"Bow to your father," my grandfather said to me. "He's still here. There is luminous motion between us and our ancestors, and this history can never be taken away from you," he reassured.

"See how I prepare the betel nuts for your father," Baba Quan said as he drew me close to him. I had watched the ritual and heard the story many times before, but this time my grandfather's favorite betel-nut story felt especially com-forting.

I watched him gather in his callused palm a few slices of betel nuts that had been husked, boiled, and sun-dried. My grandfather rolled the nuts in a betel leaf, which he smeared with a pellet of lime, and concocted a betel-nut mixture which, when chewed, created a hot, steaming burn in the center of his chest. The part I loved most came next: the ample flow of brick-red fluid squeezed from the betel-nut mixture that immediately stained his teeth, made him light-headed, and caused him to blush without shame.

"The betel-nut story begins with two men in love with the same woman. When the woman marries the older brother, younger brother is heartbroken. He leaves home, unaware that his spirit, which has to watch over his ancestors' graves and can only live in the village land, cannot make the trip with him. He wanders until he reaches a river and collapses with exhaustion by the river's edge. His body, barren of his soul, becomes cold, and his heart, which is equally barren, turns into a dry limestone by the waters of the river, among a bed of jagged pebbles.

"When older brother leaves his village home to look for his brother, he too begins to lose his soul and collapses at the same spot by the river's edge. But his heart is filled with warmth for his wife, and when he dies, he turns not into a limestone but a tall, roof-rimming areca tree that bears thick clusters of green betel nuts.

"In the meantime, the woman also leaves home to look for her husband. She too doesn't realize she has left her soul behind, arrives at the same riverbank, and collapses. Her heart, however, is a female heart in a strict Confucian world, and upon her death, she becomes not a tall upright tree but a twisted betel vine that has to wrap itself around the betel tree for support and nurturance.

"Over time, villagers nearby begin to notice that even in prolonged periods of infertility and drought, the areca tree and the betel vine are always sturdy, even when all other vegetation dies. Word about the story spreads from village to village, until the king too learns about it.

" 'There is luminous motion that binds family together for eternity. The blood of family can never be diluted. Mixed in a bowl, it will come together in a thick bright mixture,' the king declares.

"The king wraps a betel nut into the betel leaf, which he oils with ground-lime paste from the limestone, and chews this new concoction. A bright-red liquid, redder than blood pumped from the human heart, flows from this mixture. The incident is passed on so that, over time, the betel nut becomes a symbol of eternal regeneration and devotion. And when old people like your grandfather chew it, we pray for our family blessings and for our ancestral souls. We think of our loved ones and of the inextricable connections that keep them tied forever to our souls. There is no death," my grandfather whispered. "There's your father, right here among us."

"Is it really you?" I wanted to ask. Wisps of smoke floated from a pyre of spirit money. I touched the hard, shiny round-ness of the betel nut and felt the warm flow of red contained behind the inedible green exterior. I tried to cling to my father still, to his smile, his singular powers of concentration, the unerring patience he always had with me. Around us, people were oblivious, feasting on spring rolls, sticky rice, and my father's favorite, grilled-shrimp paste wrapped around sticks of sugar cane. My father would always be well fed, and his spirit would soar. I could adopt my grandfather's view. It could be gorgeous, death, a sacred and benevolent begin-ning beyond the bend of this earth.

Around us, red flames lapped the air, devouring heaps of ghost money, silvery papers painted in denominations of one and five thousand my mother fed into the avid fire. We were sending money to him. His needs would be tended to in the other world.

"It's all right," my father told me evenly. Although my eyes smarted from the flame, I could see the delicate exfoliations of cinder at the fire's edge, carrying our offerings skyward to feed my father's soul. "Everything will be all right," he repeated.

Soon after my father's death, one city after another, and another, starting at Phuoc Long Province, succumbed to Vietcong attacks. Square by square, images projected from our television set jumped with scatterings of gunfire. From the frozen surface of the television screen, I could see the country churn and swell with refugees, marching their hopeless march southward. At night, our windows shook to the distant thump of artillery, sending slivers of glass into the air. The night-light by my bed flickered each time the buckled floors shifted, and even the moon quivered, slipping a slow, lanquid slip from its socket in the sky. From Saigon, we could see a capillary of red, a poppy, tea-colored tinge brewed along the sky's edge a few kilometers away.

Uncle Michael and Aunt Mary's house was a white saltbox set a proper distance from the road, with pines, hemlocks, and other evergreens to give the lawn a cool winter shade. In the front yard, at center stage, still stood the big gray boulder, once the elephant back on which I rode in my garment of rhinoceros hide, charging toward victory against the Chinese invaders.

On this cool, raw day, everything, the earth, the sky, even the air, seemed to have acquired a maximum lightness, bleached and starched in preparation for a snowfall the meteorologists had been predicting for days. Illumined in an expanse of white, the house appeared visually, microscopically acute, superreal. I scanned the corner near the exterior basement wall where I had found a hornet's nest years ago. In the backyard, twisted around a tree trunk were the tattered remnants of a badminton net Uncle Michael had hung for me. With so many clues left behind, this was to be sure the same house I once entered with fear and anticipation, that first day when Uncle Michael introduced me to Aunt Mary.

"Be on your best behavior when you meet her," my mother had instructed as she packed me onto the plane.

In my bedroom upstairs—the MacMahons' guest room, which had been mine since the night of my arrival four years before—I found, on the small desk, in a folder, newspaper clippings about Vietnam that Aunt Mary had been collecting. Aunt Mary sent them to me periodically, articles about boat people and Vietnam vets and Little Saigons, in downtown Hartford and elsewhere. I usually saved them until the evening, when I could find in the soft-edged hush and gleaming darkness of the night the sanctuary necessary to venture into something as uncertain as Vietnam.

I gathered myself against the old colonial bed and leafed through the folder. All the articles had been carefully cut and stapled to blank pages, some highlighted with a yellow marker, others with red exclamation marks in the margin. I made a note of each story, because an itemized acknowledgment would please Aunt Mary. From the lower right-hand corner of a *Hartford Courant* page, a Vietnamese boy smiled contemplatively as he was inducted into the school's National Honor Society. On the next page was a grim article about tension in a neighborhood. It began unspectacularly, with standard descriptions of homeowners and shopkeepers. Then, following the introductory paragraph, in clear inexorable print, neutral as the news itself, was a story about how a Vietnamese family had been suspected of eating an old neighbor's dog. The orphan pup had been the old man's only companion.

What was I supposed to say to this? It wasn't Aunt Mary's fault. My dilemma was that, seeing both sides to everything, I belonged to neither. I had become the intermediary, but, unlike my father, it was the clear-cut, not the complex, that I longed for.

For dinner, Aunt Mary made pot roast, steamed asparagus, wild rice, and, for dessert, apple pie. Uncle Michael, his hair still close-cropped after all these years, put on the solemn airs of a chef, cleared his throat, sharpened the carving knife, and flicked his thumb across the blade before digging into the thick roast. In his burlap apron, he looked the part of a rugged hunter, strong-limbed, sturdy, eager.

The large eat-in kitchen was painted an inconspicuous beige, its walls covered with mementos from Vietnam—a conical straw hat from Danang, large lacquer-and-eggshell paintings, placards with names of places I knew only as battlefields. An Loc, Kontum, Khe Sanh. I imagined they told stories of bloody secrets that could be glimpsed only beneath the shine of the brass frames. On one wall was a small picture of my father, standing with his hands in his pockets, in front of a gushing Dalat waterfall. His body was pitched slightly forward, in the posture of a front-runner.

"How's your mother doing?" Aunt Mary asked. "Last time Michael talked to the nurses, they said they were letting her go."

"In a week," I said. What had the nurses told him? I

peeked to my left and saw his face, even and unperturbed. "She'll be in a rehab center for intensive therapy for two or three weeks, depending on her progress, and then she'll have visiting nurses to help her at home," I said.

"Michael knows one man who went through four years over there, house-to-house fighting in Hue, without any major incident at all, and then—boom—one month after coming home, he slipped in the snow and hit his head against his own driveway and died," Aunt Mary said. "Your mother's fortunate that she's recovering so well from that stroke. These must be hard times for her." She smiled her sympathy smile. "I'm sure these must be very hard times for your mother," Aunt Mary repeated.

"She'll be fine, though," I insisted. I could see her body under my eyes, slack and languid one minute, twisted in knots the next, ready at any unpredictable moment to go in and out of yet another delirious dream. I cradled my temples flat against my palms and felt big green veins throb quick little drumbeats against my skin.

"Are you okay?" Aunt Mary asked.

I nodded and gave a quick, reassuring smile. I was not one who favored opening everything up for surgical dissection. Some things cannot be shared, like the way I was seeing her husband that very moment, next to dying flesh and unbathed bodies swaddled in cotton and gauze. Uncle Michael on a metal bed, cocooned in a fold of army blanket under mosquito netting, drawing ragged breaths. His hands over his head, he was pulling the steel headrest, his breath making a low-pitched moaning sound. I could feel the howling echo of the hospital walls, its hot searing pulses battering against my skull. One wrong move, a reckless moment off guard, and there, right there under my eyes, was the unbidden life, the subverted life I lived. The malevolent world of red that kept Uncle Michael permanently fastened to me was right here, in the stunning chemical red of Mercurochrome, the bright arterial red of an unclotted wound, and the luminous red of tangled nerves that kept us stitched for eternity to the things of the past. He would forever inhabit this ragged outer edge with me.

I took a quick look. Aunt Mary's brows were knitted into a thin, cautious line. She was watching me. I suspected she was trying to imagine my mother, and me, and maybe even Uncle Michael, the topography of his life from 1968 to 1974, which she couldn't possibly know, the part he had away from her when he was with us over there. Here was her husband, an American who returned from Vietnam with a love for the durian, a strange fruit that supposedly smelled like old garbage. My mother and I had once sent a crate of durians to him in Connecticut, but, according to Uncle Michael, the post office had called to say rotten food had been received and had had to be discarded.

Here was the American replica of my father, his death and life absorbed quietly in a Farmington house. Their combined history flowed through Uncle Michael's veins. I looked at him, the way he still stroked his wrist and played with the thick, complicated hairs sticking out from his shirtsleeves. And I had the feeling that, if I were to blink and reorient my eyes just a bit, I would be watching him from a bench in Saigon with my father. I would see street children—the "dust of life," as they were called—cling to his uniform, some begging for money, others pulling on the curly, raucous hair that glittered like froth under the bright tropical light. "GI, you number one," they would yell if he complied with their requests for Hershey's chocolate, and "you number ten" if he refused. He was now a retired colonel in Farmington, with six unprootable years in Vietnam—now a soldier without a war—and I an immigrant from Saigon. Vietnam remained like an implant in both our brains.

I chewed slowly, opening wide, relaxing my stiff jaw with each bite. Uncle Michael forked up a bit of meat from his plate. I could feel a tiny tear dislodge itself from my eye and descend invisibly within me. Tonight, more than any other night, I could see in myself the ability, honed since America, to apply makeup, to conceal and disguise.

After dinner, we cleared the table. Aunt Mary rinsed the plates, then scrubbed any last bit of food still left on the forks and knives before throwing them in the dishwasher. I collapsed in the den, on the gold carpet marked by occasional spots of raveled threads in areas busy with comings and goings. The den was the MacMahon family room, and it seemed almost impossible to think it had not been here forever. I took in the quiet seamlessness, the sense of inevitability that inhered in the house, feeling its breath rush in quickening pulses through our common history. There was a continuous accumulation of sweet history in this house, trophies on the mantelpiece, a haphazard collection of seashells picked from a number of casual trips to the Niantic beaches.

Draped over the couch was a big tartan blanket, with the MacMahon clan's very own pattern and design, red-and-green plaid interspersed with black stripes. Light from the old lamp, its gray parchment shade painted with rolling green Scottish fields, gave the room a hazy, placid feel.

Our apartment was so different. My mother wanted it maintained as a mere way station, rootlessly sparse since the day of our arrival. She had no claim to American space, no desire to stake her future in this land.

She had even taken American disposability a step backward with her special kind of twist. Plastic spoons and knives, picnic plates and Ziploc bags, tin foil and Styrofoam cups, these were all modern-day inventions my mother had decided to reinvent, the refugee way.

Why should something be discarded just because it's designed to be disposable? In our kitchen, my mother handwashed plastic forks and knives. She saved used clingwraps and aluminum foil, folding and stacking them in our cupboards and drawers. There was nothing to hold on to there. Nothing could stick in such a place. Even the one painting we had in our living room, a painting of a Vietnamese rural scene, a recent present from Uncle Michael, hung on the wall like an antiquated map, its black lacquer finish refracting everything the world had to give but absorbing none of it. After all, absence itself would spare us from the roots of new history.

Here, in Uncle Michael's Farmington, Connecticut, landscape, an old bagpipe could always be found leaning against the wall. I imagined him pulling mournful drones out of the ancient double-reed pipe. This was a stable sanctuary, I thought, in which to keep things people treasure and preserve and pass down to future generations.

In the familiar blue nightgown and flannel robe, Aunt Mary, propped against a cushion, sat next to me. I stretched out on the floor and snuggled by Aunt Mary's side, pulled into the generous circumference of her force field. I felt new and small, as if I had just nuzzled my way out from the depths of the womb into a cusp of solace. My bare face rubbed against the soft fuzz of her robe. To our left, the sliding glass door absorbed our profiles. I could see our own faces frozen in the icy black glass as if we had, since the beginning of time, occupied the very depths of its interior.

Like those of a trained Braille reader, my fingers groped the carpet's surface. I slid my baby finger an inch or so into the slit between the carpet and the wall molding and pried a still-shining 1975 penny from its hiding place. I had placed the penny there one week after my arrival in the house— when the men had come to install a new carpet for the family room. Nineteen seventy-five, that terrible year, was still as present, and still as inevitable, as ever.

The Pan Am flight out of Tan Son Nhut Airport, Uncle Michael had told me, would follow the usual charted course, the course for tourists, the course for businesspeople. It would head first for Manila, then Guam, then Honolulu, on to Dallas, then finally Hartford, where we would drive to our house in Farmington. I was already his family. "Our" house, he had said, plural, not "my," singular.

Manila, Guam, Honolulu. I hadn't understood he was really telling me how lucky we were to be able to leave by the simplest, shortest, and safest air route available. I would never have imagined that, only a few months later, the way out of Vietnam would be the uncharted one by sea.

The plane moved slowly along the runway, then stopped. Saigon had been hit by rockets several days before, but I could almost believe the war was in another country. Even in the sanitized air of the plane, I smelled the raw, saturated heat of the afternoon, ripe like the overpowering ripeness of a banana or a mango clogged and swollen in its own rotting juice. Weathered buildings, even the tall air-traffic-control tower, cowered under their own shadows. But it never occurred to me that things were irremediably wrong or unfixable.

I did not know the political reality of the country then. I was thirteen when my mother told me there would be no debacle. I did not know that a communist victory was practically inevitable and preordained as early as 1973, when South Vietnam had had to sign the Paris Peace Accords under considerable American pressure. Nor did I know that the cease-fire had meant that, whereas the United States exchanged its prisoners of war with the North and withdrew its armed forces from South Vietnam—"peace with honor," the Americans had called it—North Vietnamese and Vietcong troops did not have to withdraw but could remain permanently in the South, a prelude, it appeared, to the debacle of April 30, 1975. My father called the remaining communist strongholds "leopard spots," pockets of enemy scattered in the heart of the South itself.

But in February 1975, mine was still an unimpaired world in which my mother's words were the complete truth. There were no surprises in that world, at least surprises that resulted from precautions not taken. My mother, after all, had drawn me to her breast and whispered her assurances in my ear. I was coming back in a few weeks, a month or two at the most, and she would bake me éclairs studded with chocolate chunks, and cream puffs drenched in strawberry syrup, and when the durian season was in full-bloom, she would feed me its soft, supple flesh by the spoonful. During my absence, she would feed the birds for me, especially my black merlin, Kiki, that she had taught to talk. Saigon had always gone through sudden changes of mood, and this was simply one of those changes.

Everyone on that Pan Am flight—except me, of course —must have understood the big meaning of things choking the Saigon air that afternoon. Thinking back on that February day, I can sense the urgency, the sense of danger that must have gripped Uncle Michael. I see things now I hadn't been able to see then: the screeching sunheat, the fried cockroaches embalmed on the black tarmac, the anticipatory hush in the plane that drowned out all voices, the red apricot glow of rocket fire still glued to the far end of the sky. . . .

People sat like scarecrows in their assigned seats, their eyes in deep space, safely shielded behind the daily headlines: "Congress Votes Against Emergency Aid to South Vietnam." "Thieu Calls U.S. Vote a Betrayal." Somehow it was understood you were not supposed to move, as if the stillness of sounds that couldn't truly count as real sounds—real sounds like firefights and rocket blasts—had to remain undisturbed, a heaving sigh, a buzzing hum in the inner ear, the sluggish folding of a newspaper. I sat next to Uncle Michael and kept quiet, sealed inside the sorrowing stillness of the plane.

An Indian woman in a watery silk sari withdrew into her seat and let out a sharp sigh, as if the air had suddenly become unbreathable. Across the aisle, an American couple, the woman wearing a pink embroidered ao dai and a strand of pearls, hoisted their luggage quietly into the overhead compartment. No one had the appearance of a tourist. But despite the signs of ordinary people fleeing, still, nothing so obvious as the upcoming collapse of a country could have entered my mind that day.

From the rectangular window I saw the shade of my own face—an unflattering smudge of gray—looking back at me. A few meters beyond, a group of soldiers heaved sandbags against a chain-link fence wrapped in coils and coils of concertina barbed wire. In the hot yellow fog of the runway, they moved like dinosaurs, prehistoric and graceless under the weight of steel pot helmets and ammunition pouches.

Even the earth itself had disappeared, and only the bleached, anemic reflection of the heat against the macadam runway, an ether of hot gases, remained visible from my window seat.

In the pressurized cabin, the flight attendants moved back and forth, floating in and out of the cockpit as weightlessly as astronauts. I could see the extended wing flaps, feel the throaty roar of the engine through my sandals as the plane lumbered and geared into power, slowly lifting itself from the field. A galaxy of electronic devices, phosphorescent squares and flashing red lights, put out tiny beeps as the captain announced our takeoff.

When the plane finally launched into the empty sky, I watched myself hang on to the last bit of ground below. From high up in the sky, one or two minutes into flight, what I could see of the country was already an altered land, no more than the soft imprint and shape of a thing that had once been but was no longer. The urge to touch it again, even the monochrome expanse of powdery gray, stayed with me throughout the scattering of turbulence and calm. Keep calm. Everything will be all right. Don't look and it won't hurt. I am not afraid. I clenched my teeth and closed my eyes as the plane headed straight into very uncertain, very uncharted territory indeed.

The fear of separation I suddenly understood that day to be a fear as primordial as the fear of death. Once felt, it stays forever trapped, like a child's muffled cry, inside one's chest.

Two months after we left Saigon, although it had seemed like light-years afterward, I saw my future unfold on television, from the family room in Farmington. All eyes across the world must also have been on the television set that April of 1975. We had all been transfixed by the sight of it, and although some of us, like Uncle Michael and me, had tried to avert our eyes, we all ended up staring at it, as if we were passersby caught among the accumulated wreckage, the blunders and pileup by the roadside. It was on TV, a luminous color origami cut from the dark of night, that I witnessed my own untranslatable world unfold to Americans half a globe away.

Among the irregular tin-roofed houses, in an epic battle for Xuan Loc, inside the only column of space left to fight, South Vietnamese troops had put up a valiant battle as their world spun away like a dead star. Life, it seemed, would persist for a while at least, even in the face of all odds. Cluster bombs left a trail of feathered smoke in the sky, while aerial helicopters wove in and out of the clouds like desperate dragonflies. Armored tanks, steel-treaded, thundered through the capital city. The country would have no choice but to stand still and take the bullets. Saigon, I almost smelled, was soaked in an inexhaustible odor of burnt chemicals, reminiscent of the dizzying outrush of heat and dust and smoke I had witnessed during the Tet New Year seven years before.

Of course, I had been watching all this, along with Uncle Michael and Aunt Mary, and like the rest of America, in the safety of our living room. I saw how Farmington, Connecticut, and just about every city in the United States had wanted the tragedy to end. It was as if all of America were holding its breath, waiting for a diseased body, ravaged and fatigued, and now all too demanding, to let go. Death must be nudged, hurried, if only it could be.

Tibetan legend, my mother had once said, describes dreams as recollections by the human soul of its nightly wanderings. Attached to the belly button, the key knot and one true threshold through which life itself was once imparted, is an invisible silver thread that ties the soul to the body. Without this retractable umbilical cord, the soul would be utterly lost in the chaos of its dreams. In the MacMahons' family room, as Aunt Mary fed me blueberry Pop-Tarts, I listened to the rasp of sounds coming from the early-morning news and watched myself slip from the silver cord into the ancient frontier of dreams.

In this imaginary world, a helicopter skittered on the edge of the U.S. Embassy, breathless under the weight of several Vietnamese hanging from the closing doors. In the background, against a swelling updraft of turbulence, the chopper's raucous blades splintered the air, sending metallic flashes that rotated like a typhoon across the sky. Below, concertina wires flared their silvered thorns. And, pressed against the embassy walls, people waved letters and identification cards, hoping to prove a strong enough American connection for the marines to allow them inside the guarded compounds.

Operation Frequent Wind, they called it. The message for the helicopter evacuation from Saigon every American had been told to watch for: a coded weather report on the radio, "It is 105 degrees and rising," followed by Bing Crosby's dreamy rendition of "White Christmas," repeated every fifteen minutes.

Operation Frequent Wind, Operation Frequent Wind, the TV commentators reported. I liked the sound of it in my mouth. It was a sound strange enough for a Tibetan dream.

Then, suddenly, in a voice of mingled sorrow and surprise, a network newscaster announced, "It all began with the best of intentions." Behind him, on top of the U.S. Embassy, American marines pointed their bayonets and rifles like sharks' teeth against their astonished old allies, in fear, the newscaster explained, of an American massacre by a frightened local population desperate enough to try anything, anything at all, to keep the Americans from leaving, from abandoning.

In the background, Saigon collapsed into itself, an afterimage of a city suddenly no longer where it had always been.

Almost four years later, in Farmington's Cineplex, cushioned on velour seats, Uncle Michael and I were watching three small-town Pennsylvania boys leave an ordinary steel-mining existence to fight in Vietnam. A succession of hypnotic scenes played on the giant movie screen—dreary American steel mills, tropical jungles, prisoners of war in bamboo cages immersed in a brown, churning river, dark, smoky back rooms in low-slung, unprosperous Saigon buildings where disillusioned GIs newly addicted to war came to play Russian roulette and gape unflinchingly at the grotesque underbelly of life.

We watched their numbing game. Click, click, click, a sigh of relief, and the revolver could be passed on to the next person, and the next; click click, click, and then an explosion, a spurt of blood. For the seduced and addicted, the compulsion had to be answered, the game played over and over, this time, at night, in backroom gambling parlors in the fissured alleys of Saigon.

Halfway through the movie, Uncle Michael bent down and whispered, "I was in Vietnam for six years and I've never seen or heard of anyone doing this before, at least on this massive a scale." In one hallucinatory scene after another, against a disturbing background of incomprehensible grunts which supposedly constituted spoken Vietnamese, the roulettelike spin of a gun as arbitrary and senseless as Vietnam would dictate the life and death of American innocence. Vietnam was becoming a huge allegorical black hole into which all things primeval could be sucked.

After the movie, Uncle Michael and I sat together on a bench, under a beam of blue light that illuminated the vaulted passageway leading toward the theater. I could see the slight tremble in his chin, his eyes irritated by the dry winter heat.

And almost before I realized what I was saying, I asked, "Did you actually shoot people?" It was probably inappropriate, dumb, or even rude, but it was the persistent question on my mind.

He could have said, "No, of course not," and I would have believed him. Instead, he replied, "Why, . . . well, yes, naturally, those kinds of things happen in a situation like that." He lowered his voice. "I was no longer nineteen then. It was not my first war, and pulling the trigger becomes harder, not easier, the older you get." He stroked the pleats of his corduroy pants in quick successions. "But, still, you go off with all the ammunition you need to do what you need to do."

I looked at his face. I looked at our common past. "Where were you mostly?" I continued, taking advantage of this propitious moment to ask. The movie was our momentum; I understood the importance of seizing the moment, because I too maintained barriers that were rarely unguarded.

"Everywhere. We were sent everywhere."

"Everywhere where?"

"Well, everywhere-everywhere that you can imagine. We were part of an elite fighting unit. My Company D was stationed in Can Tho, and all twenty A-teams were trained to move on all terrains in all conditions. You could describe us as . . . versatile. But I suppose you could say that my team was stationed mostly in the southern part, in the delta."

"You were in the delta?"

"Mm-hm. There were beautiful rice fields everywhere in the delta. I would stand under a coconut tree and stare at the shadowed waters, emerald and turquoise, that skimmed the tips of the rice plants. It was like staring at a magic mirror. And then, for a moment, you could actually believe that everything stays that beautiful all the time. I guess you didn't want to believe that there was something awfully terrible down there, underneath all that beauty, that could blow you up in one instant."

Uncle Michael paused. Around us, a group of teenagers giggled and struggled with their cardboard trays of hot dogs, hamburgers, and milk shakes.

The delta, I thought; how exotic and colorful, and how familiar.

"And the rainstorms. When the land is that flat and vast and the sky that unobstructed, you can see the budding beginnings of a rainstorm as it first gathers in the tropics, and later, as it is pulled in from the horizon's edge. You can see it take shape, the delicate laser beams that accumulate and press against the clouds before the sky becomes a purple sheet of electricity. The delta, I think, is truly the most gorgeous spot on earth," Uncle Michael sighed.

In Vietnam, I had never been more than a hundred miles from Saigon, and rice fields and unobstructed skies did not figure in my memories. The delta, though, had a special pull for me. It was where my mother was born. It was the place Baba Quan would not leave. And it was the place where the spirits of my ancestors remained, a supple burial ground for all those ancestral souls sustained by the collected years and the sanctuary of history.

"I suppose you notice the fury and the beauty of rainstorms and the greenness of the rice fields when you're there because you always have to be watchful. You watch out for the terrible things, but then you surprise yourself because you begin to notice the beauty. You're always noticing, because, even when you're not on a mission, your fingertips and the pores in your skin are still taking everything in. You never miss a beat. Your nerve endings bristle at the slightest movement. Because it's always there."

"You mean the Vietcong?"

"Well, you could call it the Vietcong, but it's really 'it' itself. 'It' is always there. The Vietcong, maybe, but it's more than the Vietcong. It's the situation. The disease you could get if you weren't vigilant. You'd leave your camp for night duty and you'd come back with a case of head lice and dysentery. 'It' could be the fine sand that drifted with the breeze and clogged your nostrils and made you choke. Or 'it' could be the booby traps, the ready-to-explode grenade with its pin removed, weighed down and hidden by a land mine placed on top. Defusing the top mine would trigger the booby-trap grenade underneath into active mode, and 'it' would explode exactly when you thought 'it' had been defused.

"At other times, 'it' was the way you'd have to get all armored up for the march through a rice paddy. You'd tuck your pants in your jungle boots, lace them tight, and button yourself up. Sometimes you'd have flak jackets and ponchos, and still, halfway through the march, you'd feel it—the soft, persistent suction of a leech pressed on your bare skin. And you'd think to yourself, how can I get to it?

"And 'it' suddenly becomes a riddle, because you don't

even know you have a layer of skin, or at least the skin you think is there doesn't register as something that's yours, because all you can feel is the dead weight on your body. The M-16, the .45 Colt, the ammunition, the backpack of water canisters and chow. They're all on your body, and pretty soon you have no skin, no flesh, only dead weight on your back, and that one sucking leech that you just can't get to."

The unvarying monotone with which he used to inform me of the names of the paraphernalia he carried was a surprise to me. Uncle Michael knew a Vietnam that I did not.

"And other times," he continued, "the 'it' is the shock that comes over you when you realize a terrible mistake has been made and can't be undone. One evening, around dusk, we were marching toward a village known to be an iffy one, partially controlled by the Vietcong and partially controlled by the government, and I thought I heard some strange noises. Now, there was nothing necessarily strange about strange noises in a jungle, but this noise somehow seemed different, for no particular reason, except that it was the kind of noise that gave you a sensation like little shivers threaded on a string along your spine. The noise was coming from a thick bramble of bushes, and at this point we were all on guard.

"As we got closer to the noise, we realized it was the moan of someone already gone, on the verge of dying, or maybe even already dead. It was an eerie sound, really, the sound of death trapped inside the body of a little boy around six years old. And you couldn't help staring at it, at the sound that is purely and anatomically induced by this tiny little biological body as it prepares to let death take over permanently. It was a little bit grotesque and a little bit miraculous, but at the same time astonishingly stark and uncompromising. And we

just stood there and watched—the stream of blood that continued to leak from a hole in the brain, the muscular reflex
that made the eyes drift to the sides, the flutter of the eyelids,
the bubbling in the nostrils, the toes curling inward. . . ."

I slipped my hand around his wrist. Cautiously, he continued: "I suppose we were transfixed by this, the aliveness
of activities taking place even as the little boy was dying. And
as we stood there, 'it' happened, the thing that every soldier
prays won't.

"Just as we were about to move on, we heard this quick
shuffling sound. The boy's body suddenly moved, and his
right arm lifted itself right off the ground into the air, and
it looked as if it could have thrown a grenade at us. Right
then and there, a flash of machine gun blasted from the tips
of our fingers, with an effortlessness that seemed almost like
magic. And before we knew what had happened, the boy had
died a second death, his body shredded open by the terrible
convulsions of gunfire from our rifles.

"Only after the sizzle of gray smoke disappeared, only
then, did we see the shadow of a little kitten which must
have hidden all along, like a tiny fist, by the boy's side. It
stared us down with its enormous black eyes before it scampered away on four little bloody paws. And before I could
breathe a sigh of relief that the boy had already been mortally
wounded before we opened fire, we heard another sound. A
horrible wailing sound raging from the edge of a rutted path.
'Your mother is coming, your mother is coming,' a woman
was screaming, a scream so chilling it passed through the
length of my body before she was even close to us.

"I felt sick in my stomach, as if God had made some
awesome mistake and had actually been caught in the act.
Because I couldn't move and I couldn't speak. We just stood

and watched in silence as the woman walked—actually walked—with a sense of quiet, exaggerated dignity, toward us and the body. She said his name once, 'Thong,' as she picked up a piece of his bloody shirt. And she just stared at us, and you could see the hatred and the sadness in her eyes. She looked at us again, then removed her cone-shaped straw hat and covered parts of him with it. And she left. She just left. And we stood and watched this boy, partially covered by a hat, whose mother now believed he had been indiscriminately murdered by us, a group of grown men highly trained to act only with the utmost amount of precision.

"And the irony, I suppose, is that we had been silently but wrongfully accused of doing something that didn't happen but could very well have. And although all of us knew what really happened on the outskirts of that village, it's always there, this soundless vacuum that makes a lonely space in your heart, right here," he whispered, pointing to the center of his chest. "It's always there, this enormous feeling that swallows itself over and over and can't be contained, because, even though you know it hadn't happened that day, you also carry that gnawing, lingering suspicion that it could very well have. And of course you occasionally wonder whether it had in fact happened, because of the howling, ravenous conviction forever carried by a stranger in a nameless village that it did."

"Where is this village?" I asked. Uncle Michael was still here, but in a slightly separate life, outside the embrace of our common sphere.

"It's a village that doesn't exist on any map. The locals had a name for it, but no one on the outside did. And when it got to the point where it was beyond reclamation, I don't think anybody even bothered to formally record its existence.

It's just a hamlet, really," he explained. "It's a small speck of wilderness in An Xuyen," he added in a quick whisper.

"An Xuyen . . . Isn't that right next to Ba Xuyen? Baba Quan is from Ba Xuyen," I said.

"Hmmm?"

"My grandfather is from Ba Xuyen, and I think that's right next to your village in An Xuyen, isn't it?"

He nodded. "Yes, right. They were quite close to one another, those two villages. But the delta is not that big, so I suppose you could say every village is adjacent to the next one."

"Sure, but how about my grandfather? You must have met him. My mother said it was the sort of place where people knew one another. Did you know him?" I slipped my arm over his shoulder.

He was silent for a moment. "I did know your grandfather. After your parents and I became friends, your mother, in fact, asked me to stop by his house if I happened to be in the neighborhood." He chuckled at how suburban that sounded.

"So you knew him pretty well? I mean, you met him more than once."

"Well, I guess, yes . . . sure. Your mother wanted me to keep an eye out for him. It was dangerous, and she worried about his safety. So occasionally I'd visit him and bring him baskets of gifts from your parents," he answered. "He had a special liking for whiskey," he added with a wink.

"What was he like?"

"Your mother doesn't talk much about him, does she?" Uncle Michael said. And it was true. Beyond the basic variations we had pondered about his disappearance, it could not be touched much, the subject of that final day in Saigon.

I touched Uncle Michael's hand. "No, she doesn't," I confessed. "She doesn't talk much about my grandfather at all."

Uncle Michael nodded. "Let me see what I can tell you. He was a farmer. Hardworking. Very strong sense of right and wrong. Devoted to rituals and tradition. He swept the village temple and its courtyard, even though he was not the official temple-keeper. He was reserved but quite amiable once you got to know him a bit."

"But what was it like for him there, in that village? What kind of a life did he have?" I wanted a different kind of information, perhaps less mannerly, more urgent, to match the urgent sadness that lay beneath my mother's reticence.

"He had a typical farmer's life. There are rituals, routine, and days and nights of hard work. I can't tell you what a farmer does all day to keep busy. But I know he was a strong farmer. And a self-sufficient and versatile farmer. And he was a fantastic fisherman. I saw him one day, in the early morning, skimming the foamy waters along the rocky coast on a lethal pair of six-foot bamboo stilts, casting a massive fishing net into the sea. It was a special method that allowed fishermen to avoid the jagged rocks that lay beneath the breaking waves. But it required muscles and unbelievable agility."

Because my grandfather had no permanent, definable shape, except the shape I myself provided with my own memories and imagination, I had no preconceived expectations. He was capable of anything, a majestic grandfatherliness un-miniaturized by the little disappointments of daily life, superb fisherman in a pair of muscled legs and precise stilts, surfing through a swell of waves. He was free to be everything, a grandfather, like all grandparents, who came to their grandchildren with just the right measure of generational distance and none of the exaggerated, ever-present desire for closeness that parents brought to their own children.

"Did the fighting ever get close to him?" I asked.

Uncle Michael's answers meandered with the sluggishness of someone who was being ushered on a very reluctant detour. "There was quite a bit of war in the delta, so, sometimes, sure. But your grandfather was quite a survivor himself, you know. He had all the remarkable instincts of a farmer. He knew what to do."

"Uh-huh."

There was a pause. Uncle Michael looked at me silently. And finally I said, "Like what? What did he know to do?" Uncle Michael was prone to a certain degree of sweetness, at least with me, and could be coaxed into compliance.

He put an apologetic hand on the back of my neck. "Well, there's one story I'll always remember. I suppose you could say it's a story about how I owe my life to your grandfather.

"My unit was walking on a winding dirt path along the outermost edge of your grandfather's village. And of course I knew it was the village where your mother had grown up, not just because I had been there on other occasions but because I recognized her descriptions. The big rock by the river's edge, wedged between two giant coconut trees. The rows of spindly pedestrian overpasses that hovered thirty meters or so above a web of canals, like a Venice in the tropics. The villagers called them 'monkey bridges,' because the bridge was a thin pole of bamboo no wider than a grown man's foot, roped together by vines and mangrove roots. A railing was tied to one side, so you could at least hold on to it as you made your way across like a monkey. Only the least fainthearted, the most agile would think about using this unsturdy suspension they call a bridge. Your father, by the way, also told me that was where he first saw your mother, 'an apparition in white pantaloons,' as he put it, floating with remarkable lightness across the bridge.

"In any event, as we were walking through the outskirts of the village, heading toward the village common, I knew we would have to pass through this vast, wild area dense with undergrowth and surrounded by hills and ravines. We used to have an outpost there, so the terrain was not completely foreign to me. But, still, the area was extremely isolated and, because of the hills, seemed to be perpetually covered in a dense fog.

"And there we were, a column of five, marching single-file along this thick, vine-covered trail, and we already had our grenades out, with the pins straightened and ready to do what some of us had begun to call the 'two-step.' Step number one, trust your instinct and go with the goose bumps and shivers on your skin. If you sense danger, act as if you can see danger itself. Step number two, restrain your impulse and force yourself to reevaluate your fear, because the army doesn't want men who are easily spooked, but accomplished soldiers who can prove their equilibrium by mastering the fear, in a two-step, split-second decision.

"Cautiously we took our two steps, one foot in front of the other, parting the fog as we went along. I knew the land climbed slightly upward in the direction of a pagoda some-where in front of us. And as I looked slightly to my left, I sensed the swiftness of a somewhat distant silhouette stepping out of the fog, like an animal stepping out of a picture book, and then, before I could even contemplate doing step number one, trust your instincts, BOOM, it happened. Two guys at the head of the column lugging the thirty-pound mine detectors with their sensing plates and headphones plugged in their ears had stepped straight on a mine. And now our trail was suddenly no longer foggy but blood-bright, as if someone had illuminated our path with a giant floodlight.

"And at this point, all of us froze, because we all knew the awful reality we were in. The area must be heavily mined, with explosives packed in an encasement of plastic and thus invisible to our metal detectors. We were doing step number one, trust our instincts, which told us there was terrible earth ahead. But we couldn't do step number two, restrain our impulse and reevaluate our fear, because step number two is designed only to preempt premature action, and there was absolutely no avenue of action that was available to us at the moment. Step number two makes the most sense if step number three—retaliation—is a practical option.

"And so all we had was this terrifying one step, fear, fear, fear. I had all the modern equipment in which we had been trained to put our trust: a compass, binoculars, maps, all of which were supposed to show us the way. And they were utterly useless at that moment, because ahead of us we knew the way had been marked by little ripples of explosives buried in every crevice of the land. And as we stood motionless, I began to imagine the shape of death, the hum of the wilderness, the black bats with wings, and I began to feel all of us dissolve into the world of our greatest fears.

"And suddenly, like a scene out of a movie, a shadowy figure in human form drifting on a gray wisp of mist floated from a cliff top toward us. Although we could see it, an odd weightlessness rising from the fog, we could not pinpoint its location. It appeared to be part of the land itself, nowhere and everywhere, and couldn't be brought into precise focus. And then we heard a whisper, 'Mako, Mako,' which seemed to come from all directions. The guys were tense, and I was tense, but there was nothing to do, because it appeared to be not here or there, almost from another world, not that any of us truly believed in other worlds, but ghosts and spirits seem very possible when you are faced with shadows and voices that shimmer in the mist. The whisper emerged from the air, as if it were disembodied from any physical being, lingering, just lingering, like vapor and steam.

"But then I knew right away that it was a familiar voice, calling a familiar version of my name. And so right away I gave the group our safety signal, two quick slaps against the butt of my M-16. It was your grandfather's voice. That was what he called me, always 'Mako, Mako.' I blinked and stretched the muscles in my eyes, trying to bring the figure into focus. Your grandfather seemed to be levitating above us, blending into the gray glow of the explosion's aftermath, whispering 'Mako' as he made his way, I finally realized, across a monkey bridge, gesturing for us to stop and stay where we were with a wide-open palm.

"There was only one way out, he told us. My Vietnamese was still pretty good then. He would help us, he said. He had seen and heard certain things, and he knew the formation of the underground board and the grid of coordinates where the mines had been hidden. He had seen a lot from the old pagoda on the cliff, where villagers came once a year to honor the souls of those who had died without descendants. They used to come more often, but because of its location, the pagoda was no longer frequented, and except for him, the area was pretty much deserted. He kept talking to us from the monkey bridge, waiting, he said, for the fog to clear.

"Like a chess board, he said. The earth underneath the ground carried the secret logic of a chess board, in which explosives had been secreted like chess pieces in designated squares. He had seen the etchings of it one evening after performing a ritual of weed-pulling from the tombs behind the abandoned pagoda. He had had a full bird's-eye view of the chess-board grids and the explosive chess pieces, a calligraphy approximating the shape of the Chinese ideogram for 'death.'

"And, believe it or not, your grandfather's tale imparted great comfort to us, the soothing certainty in his voice, his assurance that he knew not only the shape of the ideogram but also its beginning points. He had seen the men pick as the beginning coordinates a bamboo tree with a distinctive base three footsteps up from the mouth of a gully, with a set of slashes carved toward the bottom of its trunk.

"And this was what he did. As the fog lifted and he was sure he could find his way, he crossed the monkey bridge and went straight to the slashed bamboo tree. From there, he told us, he would imagine the entire chess board laid across the land. He would identify all the points and markers where the mines had been buried, the path of danger. And once he had the coordinates of danger, the space on either side should be safe. The men had rehearsed the coordinates so they could later defuse the explosives if necessary.

"As we waited, holding our breath, your grandfather began counting with his feet, estimating the distance between the first marker and the second marker, which he said was a tall betel-nut palm diagonally situated from the bamboo tree. This tree was the second marker, because it was the only one in the grove that shot straight up, then swerved leftward into an angle. He knew it was so, he assured us, because he had heard the men count with their footsteps and describe the designated markers among themselves.

"Once he could imagine the entire plan all laid out in front of him, he took the steps. He actually took the steps, marked the safety of the path he was taking with a trail of colored pebbles, and, unbelievably, miraculously, made it across that entire mine-riddled expanse. We, like little children, meekly followed the route he had marked to make it to the other side.

"The next day, we sent a unit specially equipped to sweep open the land. And there it was: from our helicopter above, I could see the strange formation of underground trenches filled with Toe Poppers and Bouncing Betties, land mines that jumped in the air and exploded, and, worst of all, bamboo stakes and spears infected with buffalo feces, undetectable electronically, that had been hidden by a plastic cover camouflaged under layers of dirt and leaves. Only someone with immense mental precision and concentration, not to mention immense memory capacity, could have conjured up a mental image of the heavily mined path and walked a few steps off the dangerous design toward safety. Your grandfather received a special medal from the province chief for that act. And when word got to the American military command, he was given a U.S. citation as well."

After a pause, Uncle Michael shot me a satisfied look. "Now are you happy?" he seemed to say. And I was.

We resettled ourselves on the bench, Uncle Michael straightening his legs with a long catlike stretch. "It sounds almost like a storybook story. You know, like it's almost too good to be true," I said.

"Sometimes there are astonishingly good endings even in real life."

"Does my mother know that my grandfather helped your unit?"

"Oh sure, she came back to the delta for the ceremony in his honor. It was a big event. You must have been around nine then. Your father didn't want you to go, and for good reason. The outposts were just too dangerous then," Uncle Michael sighed.

I was not completely ignorant of my mother's emotional makeup. I knew she still carried the landscape of the delta in her flesh, the sound of water buffaloes wallowing in muddy fields and tadpoles jumping in freshwater ponds. And I knew that she also carried the memory of my grandfather in her heart.

"Do you think it's possible to bring my grandfather to the United States?" This extraordinary feat, for which he was awarded a medal for bravery—two medals, in fact—could only be looked upon favorably by the United States.

"Hmm?" Snapping his head as he quickly turned to stare in my direction, Uncle Michael seemed surprised by the question.

"Do you think we can bring my grandfather to the United States?" I repeated. "After all, he had been willing to come, and he probably would have been here with us now if something hadn't happened at the last minute."

"I suppose he might be in Ba Xuyen still, but we don't know for sure where he is. He might have moved. But in any event, there is no airlift now, and it is not so easy to get out." Uncle Michael turned me toward him with a swiftness and directness that surprised me, and looked me straight in the eye. "It's not 1975 anymore, sweetheart, and leaving is a very dangerous endeavor. For ten boat people who make it ashore, a hundred more drown at sea."

"The U.S. Army can help him, can't they? He helped the army," I persisted. "You can tell the army the story you told me. Plus there must be some record of it somewhere, don't you think?" Uncle Michael could not possibly understand the situation. He had not been there when my mother had moaned her call for help and asked for her father.

Uncle Michael shook his head. "Even if that were the case, the army can't do anything, if at all, until he actually makes it out of Vietnam. We just can't get to him, and I don't want to raise false hopes for your mother. From what I can decipher from the papers, the preparation for escape alone is quite complicated. Bribes have to be paid, often in gold bullion. A boat has to be purchased, from someone willing to sell it to potential boat people. The hazardous inland route has to be mapped. Supplies enough for surviving at least thirty days have to be accumulated and transported. How or if he would manage to make the escape is completely beyond our power."

There, almost within my reach, though, was the afterimage of my grandfather's heroic deed. That must count for something. This could be the unexpected opening through which my grandfather could be brought to the United States.

"And then, for those who end up in refugee camps in Thailand or Malaysia, the waiting process can take years, even with the army's intervention. Papers would have to be produced; some tangible proof of either military or political connection with the United States would have to be demonstrated. All of this takes time. It has to go through the right channels. Do you think someone like your grandfather would be willing to wait his life away in a tent city surrounded by barbed-wire fences?"

Naturally a question posed that way could only be answered with a stiff shake of the head and an undistilled "no."

"In Vietnam, he at least retains his dignity, as an elderly

man who understands the rituals of the earth and the devotions that a pagoda requires. In the United States, someone his age would simply be lost," Uncle Michael continued, as if I needed further convincing. If he had been someone with a need for expressing the absolute naked truth, he could have added, "Look at what has happened to your mother. Do you want the same thing to happen to your grandfather?"

And although he hadn't said anything of the sort, the truth of what had been deliberately left unsaid nearly broke my heart in two.

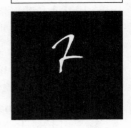

If the dreaded college interview was to be a battle, and the interviewer my opponent, this would be the battlefield strategy my parents taught me. I would follow the luminous motion of history, with all its implications and possibilities of victory. I would enter the realm that had delivered Vietnam into a history of brilliant battlefield maneuvers that I could imitate to win over the interviewer.

And so, in the frigid hush that followed an extravagant snowfall in Farmington, I sat in the MacMahons' family room in the glow of dawn and imagined the multitudes of stories I had been told about the Trung sisters. I could see my father strumming the guitar, plucking our ancient, mournful history from the hollowness of its wooden frame. We had driven back five Chinese invasions, three Mongol, and two French. In the molten light of our country's history, all of us could abandon our blemished lives and acquire a more exhilarating and victorious existence.

My parents had stories that offered the sweet shield of this history to me. They were given to generous and creative revisions and would fill our world with different, more magnificent details with the retelling of each story. In this world, I was Trung Trac, the first fighter, along with her sister, to elevate guerrilla warfare and hit-and-run tactics into an art of war, the first Vietnamese to lead a rebellion of peasants against the Chinese empire.

They imparted with a wave of the hand a sense of inevitability to the details of their stories. It was something to behold. There, in their gaudy world, was a house filled with servants, a field of flat land on which I and Trung Nhi, my sister, trained in the swift, fluid movements of the martial arts. There, in the year 40 A.D., I became an expert pole-and-swords fighter, and my sister a skilled empty-hand-and-dagger warrior.

The year I turned twenty, my sister and I began to recruit villagers from near and far for our fledgling army. A tiger had been ravaging the countryside and killing the villagers' livestock. Rumor was that this tiger had special powers hidden in the dark-black stripes that ran the length of its rich orange-colored coat. My strategy had been not to fight the tiger but to confound it by painting the metal blades a bright orange which would fling stripes of orange, more magnificent than the tiger's black stripes, into the night air. My swords crossed and uncrossed. With each stroke of the blade, I produced a mythical creature with a pitch-black coat carved from the night, marked by sleek stripes of orange fire from my metal knives: an orange-on-black pattern directly antithetical to the tiger's black-on-orange markings.

The tiger was bewildered by the seemingly invincible beast. I waited for the precise moment when I could see confusion in its eyes, when its leg muscles stretched tentatively upward, ready to leap toward me. Like the trained warrior that I was, I knew not to oppose an adversary head-on. I stepped to one side, and rather than block its powerful paws with my hand, I pulled it forward, deeper in the direction of its own motion. I used its own momentum to throw it off balance, and with one swift slash of my sword sliced its body in two.

The villagers applauded my bravery and proclaimed me their general. I carved our oath to liberate the country into the tiger's skin and used the parchment as a proclamation urging the people to rise up against the invaders. Of the generals my sister and I chose to lead our units, thirty-six were women.

I trained them in the eagle-claw style of fighting, which I had improved by combining its hand movements with the kicking movements of another, predominantly kicking style. We learned the swift, circular dance of the praying mantis. My recruits were taught how to lie in wait, how to stalk, how to position their hands as in prayer before striking the enemy with the back of their wrists. I, of course, taught them the most bewitching of all styles, the drunken-monkey style, a riot of freewheeling movements that seemingly contained no pattern and no discernible rhythm, best designed to confound an opponent. We practiced on all kinds of terrains, during the day, with the sunlight blinding our eyes, and at night, when the black sky, bleached with stars, glowed like a diamond mine.

In essence, we were preparing for the thrust and parry of all-out guerrilla warfare, the poor person's weapon. My army would strike physically and psychically at the enemy. We would turn the country into a narcotized landscape haunted by shadows from above and tunnels from below, creating a night voice that would spook the invaders. We would hide in rice fields, jungles, and swamps, and we would attack when the enemy was off guard. We would camouflage ourselves

and blend in with the grass and the trees, leaving no foot-
prints and exuding no odor; we would appear and reappear
noiselessly in the blackness of nights; and we would unleash
terror in the hearts of the enemies. With such tactics, we
would unsettle the enemy's nerves and turn even an armed
force one hundred times our strength into a terrorized one.

I had developed an ability to see things before they occurred. It was I, in fact, who first predicted that China would
be conquered by the Mongol nomads led by warriors like
Genghis Khan, Hulegu, and Kublai Khan, who went on to
capture an empire that included not just China but Persia
and even Russia—everything except of course Vietnam, a
country that could not be conquered, because the land always
opened up and swallowed its conquerers. With this foresight,
I paid special attention to the Mongols' mode of fighting,
knowing it was already destined to be particularly effective
against the Chinese.

I knew the Mongol nomads would be hunters, so I taught
my army to hunt. Our bows were made from the resilient
wood of the mulberry, and our arrows were reinforced with
tips of steel. I showed them the correct way to take aim, to
release the bowstring, to practice without allowing the forces
of the mind to impede the instinct of motion. When their
arrow could shoot itself, I knew the time was right for us to
attack.

One week before our first move, our generals met in my
tent. We chose our routes, grouped our divisions, and
mapped our opening move. We learned the enemy's weak
points and our strong points. My tactic was to attack,
octopus-style, with multiple and separate columns, each an
independent arm with the ability to cover and complement

the other, as well as the ability to converge rapidly and support the other should danger arise.

Our aim was not to win every battle, but to confound the enemies and make them paranoid after every encounter.

Our first target was a fortress occupied by the Chinese governor located in a valley surrounded by mountains. Although I did not know it then, the strategy I used would in fact provide the blueprint for a strategy used one thousand years later to defeat the French at Dien Bien Phu. I placed a small number of soldiers—our bait to ensnare the enemy—at the center. We would sound a battle cry of drums and conch shells and reeds that I prayed would alert the Chinese governor to our plans and draw him into our web. To inflate their confidence, I was deliberately making them see a weak front. But I had strengths—columns of reserves which I had amassed on the mountains' edges—invisible to enemy eyes. Those of us hidden in trenches dug inside the walls of the mountains would pound those trapped in the valley below with an incessant stream of spears and arrows.

To get to the heart of the governor's fortress, we spent one hundred nights digging an underground network, through which we crawled to emerge like armed ghosts in the night, tightening the noose around the invaders. At the same time, as our troops appeared from the earth below, we also unleashed our invisible reserves hidden above, inside the mountains. With that combination, one division tunneling underground, the other blasting rocks and arrows from the mountain above, we threw the enemy off balance. I had accomplished my first objective, to inject doubt into the enemy.

And because the strong point in our octopus style was mobility and coordination, our strategy was to engage in quick skirmishes and feign defeat, simulate flight. The Chinese governor instructed his troops to pursue and destroy our generals at all costs. We had planned our escape routes beforehand. I ordered our troops to retreat and disappear like burning grass in the dry season. We fanned out in all directions, each column poised to reverse and outflank the enemy at a moment's notice. The governor posted his troops all along the escape routes. We were forcing their troops to disperse in pursuit. Scattered in pursuit, they provided perfect weak points for our counterattack. Our smoke screen had worked—the hunter had suddenly become the hunted.

The governor's army had been massively equipped with the most up-to-date weapons. But I could tell they were soldiers who relied primarily on body mass and muscle strength and seemingly superior weapons. Our army had been trained in the opposite style, the soft style of fighting. Never oppose force with force, because the weaker one would always lose; when faced with a giant force, always step to one side and strike when the opponent is not prepared. And so, when the enemy charged, we immediately yielded and provided no resistance. Encountering only the emptiness of air, their forces immediately lost power. When we pushed against them, they toppled with the full force and weight of a massive trunk. That was how we toppled China, by focusing on our strong points—our fluidity and softness—and exploiting their weak points—their brute force and unyielding hardness.

My sister and I continue to be venerated by our people, who built shrines and declared national holidays in our honor. Both North and South Vietnam had claimed us as their own. When the communists defeated the South, one of their first official acts was to turn Saigon into Ho Chi Minh

City and rename most of the major streets in Saigon. But one street was left intact, the Street of the Trung Sisters.

Aunt Mary, Uncle Michael, and I arrived at Mount Holyoke's admissions office with half an hour to spare. The waiting room, painted an unobtrusive pastel, held several tables of dark, polished wood, a few oversized leather armchairs, and a long bench covered in a tapestry of earthy yellow and British racing green. It was a room designed to calm—streamlined and without clutter—with two harmless paintings of country scenes no one could possibly find offensive.

Here, in the heart of South Hadley, where clapboard houses and white poplars lined an uncluttered landscape, "be yourself," Aunt Mary's advice before we left the house, suddenly acquired an underlayer too complex to comprehend. Aunt Mary couldn't possibly understand that immigration represents unlimited possibilities for rebirth, reinvention, and other fancy euphemisms for half-truths and outright lies.

My mother would agree. "Americans play catch with one knife," she would explain, "but we've mastered the art of juggling many knives." It was a statement she would utter with pride.

In the snow-blown light, as the flakes meandered slowly down the frosty windowpanes, I could almost see my mother's knives shimmer against the glass, slicing the air with flashes of silver sharp enough to confound even the most experienced interviewer.

"Mai Nguyen?" a tallish woman in her early thirties glancing at an index card asked in an uncertain voice. She had tinted blond hair, large glasses, a blue dress cinched at the waist by a wide glossy belt. She quickly scanned the room and zeroed in on me.

"Mai Nguyen," I repeated to myself. In the prevailing hush of the room, it had an especially clumsy ring, an undertone of impermanence. It felt, in fact, like a borrowed name, on loan to satisfy my teachers' insistence on rhyme and order. "Mai Nguyen" was my American name, or at least the American spin on my name. But it sounded unnatural. After all, tradition dictated that "Nguyen," a family name, be granted pride of place, a position at the beginning. "Mai," an individual name, should tag a few respectful steps behind.

"Nice to meet you, Mai . . . or is it May?" She put out her hand for me to shake.

"Mai," I muttered. A fury of air bubbles crowded my lungs. My first thought was: It is not too late, I could still flee. I could simply elect to walk out the door, act on reckless impulse without fear of consequences. Outside, the sun threw broad sheets of light, even and pristine, against the winter-white roads. I took in a gulp of air and smoothed the red wool skirt, pleated and brand-new and bought by Aunt Mary in honor of this very occasion.

She nodded. "Mai you are, okay. I'm Amy Layton. I'll be interviewing you today," she declared. Aunt Mary and Uncle Michael stood up and introduced themselves simply as "Mary and Michael MacMahon."

I shook the woman's hand and made sure it had a nice firm grip. She turned her back and led me down the hall, into a small office with framed diplomas and campus pictures on ivory-colored walls.

"So you come from Vietnam, Mai?" She leaned back against her chair, papers in hand, opening the interview with the one question that always numbed me to the nuances of normal conversation.

One breath in, one breath out. Everything will be all right. The options are not unlimited—a yes or a no is all that's required. For a moment, what I saw in Amy Layton was a strain I'd seen in so many Americans, an undertone of ambivalence behind the cordial, easygoing façade. She could have turned into the school-bus driver who informed me the first day we met that her husband had done door-to-door combat in the streets of Hue in 1968. "My husband lost both his legs over there," the woman had said, and I hadn't known what to say in response.

"Yes. I came in 1975," I said evenly, keeping my gaze level and steady and my posture perpendicular and upright. I would have to spiderwalk right through this. The information, after all, had already been included in my application, in the standard slot requesting seemingly innocuous information like an applicant's place of birth. Once it was revealed, I had thought I should make the most of this personal history. My five-hundred-word essay was about living in a country at war and leaving it on the verge of peace.

"Were you there until 1975?" she asked.

I whispered a noncommittal yes. The Trung sisters' strategy would be to guard our weak points and keep them hidden from sight.

"So you were there the whole time the war was going on?" she persisted in an unreadable voice.

Which war? I wanted to ask. America was just beginning to stare at its bruises. The war about America's loss of innocence? About the American rite of passage and the American experience gone wrong? As a leader of the Third Force, my father had insisted on adopting a Vietnamese perspective by calling the "Vietnam War" the "American War" or the "Second Indochina War." I was surprised by my silent out-rush of frustration. When had I turned into an alternate version of my father?

She cleared her throat. "It must have been very difficult. You've done a remarkable job adjusting," she declared.

I whispered a quick thank you. What did this woman expect as a response? Can we start the interview over? I wanted to plead.

She swung her chair around to flip through her file cabinet. "Did your family leave with you?" She smiled, holding me hostage with her piercing eyes. This must be her idea of exchanging social pleasantries. Instead of preliminaries like "What a nice skirt you've got," or "What a rotten day it is outside," I was getting this kind of searing chitchat before the interview could officially begin.

"I left with a family friend first . . . an American . . . and stayed with him and his wife until my mother could leave."

"Oh, yes," she said, shooting her shoulders forward. "Mr. and Mrs. MacMahon." She looked pleased, grinning as she scanned a stack of papers she'd tagged with paper clips and markings of various colors.

"Where did you live in Vietnam?"

"In Saigon, right in the downtown section." What I wanted to add but didn't was a description of my house: plain limestone painted a custard yellow with a brick court-yard surrounded by a wrought-iron fence on a wide boule-vard lined with French villas and old tamarind trees. I'd concocted a habit of silence where Vietnam was concerned, but suddenly, as I sat there looking at a woman I'd never before seen, I felt an urge to reveal something palpable, some-thing that would make the country crack open so she could

see the tender, vital, and, most important, mundane parts—
the ordinary, restless aims of my neighborhood, one among
many, composed of brick and limestone houses among an
arbitrary clutter of storefronts and makeshift stands; the un-
even, buckled sidewalks on which my friends and I drew
geometric patterns for our early-evening hopscotch games;
the streets that surged with a flotilla of paper boats when it
rained.

I wanted to tell her: It was not all about rocket fires and
body bags. I could lead her through my neighborhood, at
the Midautumn Festival. I could walk her to the bakeries,
where bakers pulled from their oven trays of moon cakes, fat
with stuffings of cashews, lotus and watermelon seed, round
duck-egg yolks, and raisins. I could tell her about the
fifteenth day of the eighth lunar month, when the special
midautumn moon, round and fat, actually looked like a circle
of frozen lace, a stark, silvery whiteness glued against a beautiful cobalt sky.

Although adults too celebrated, it was really a festival for
children. Against the darkening skies, the sidewalks flickered
with a luminous constellation of candles my friends and I
placed inside our lanterns, cellophane papers shaped into
boats and hares, frogs and unicorns. Adults gasped at the
prosperous procession of colors and shapes that answered the
moon's bright light. There was a kind of sweetness in that
world, the world of my neighborhood, less cushioned and
more austere perhaps than what we'd hoped for, but it had
once been a place I would have gladly given in to. But I
couldn't manage even a meek description of the house or the
festival for Amy Layton. The Vietnam delivered to America
had truly passed beyond reclamation. It was no longer mine
to explain.

"Gosh, what a shock it must have been. What was it like over there?"

"It was . . . different," I said after a short pause. The safest route, I realized, lay in adopting no discernible route at all, drunken-monkey style.

"It's very hot there. And humid," I added. "I thought seventy degrees was cold when we first arrived. My mother put up the heat." It was in my interest to sidestep as much as possible. I was not about to confront her preconceived notions head-on. The Trung-sister strategy, the strategy of fluidity and softness, is to master the art of evasion and distraction, to use momentum, not brute force, as leverage.

"Uh-huh . . . Good thing you didn't start out right away in New England. But now both you and New England, I'm sure, are ready for one another." She laughed. "The important thing is how you've pulled everything together here. It's not a bad place to be, I don't think, once you get the hang of it." She smiled, experimentally. "And you seem to have done that quite nicely, I'd say. Let's see. It says here you want to be a doctor, right?"

"Yes . . . yes." It was a litany devised to please my father. The physical sciences, he used to say, are a safe, predictable arena. "Since I was a child," I quickly said, thankful for the new subject matter. Keep her on the subject of your credentials, I told myself.

"Same with me." She smiled, delighted. "I went to Mount Holyoke too, you see. Premed all the way."

I felt a weight lift from my chest. "I went to Mount Holyoke *too*." She was already seeing me as an admitted student.

"My real job's at the health center. I'm just doing this to

pitch in . . . one of my duties as a happy alum." She flashed me a big wide-eyed smile.

"I think your file's in excellent order," she said, holding up my folder. "Your academic performance is excellent."

"I've really enjoyed high school," I stated. "You may also notice that I do some community work with the Lions Club." Being well rounded was also important, Uncle Michael had coached.

Amy nodded convincingly. For a girl born at eight-fifteen in the morning the Year of the Water Buffalo—a most unpropitious astrological combination, according to my mother—I had done quite well. Water buffaloes live in the world of rice fields, a world that demands as much vigilance and devotion as it is prone to shocks and disappointment. In that world, she claimed, one learns to accept the sheer arbitrariness of nature, to relinquish one's life and work to the vagaries of wind and rain—to a realm of anarchy one can neither command nor fully understand. A life of inevitable toil, my mother had predicted for me. "Especially because you were birthed in the morning, when the buffaloes have to toil in the field. Eight in the evening would have been more lucky. The buffaloes would be going back to the pens to eat and sleep," she had sighed.

But I did not have to answer my mother's humbled view of life. What my mother hadn't realized was that I was also born in the middle of August. In America, where anything was possible, that made me a Leo, king of the jungle, not beast of burden.

"Well, I have to say I'm impressed. You speak English very well. You sound just like an American." She shrugged. "I would've never guessed . . . otherwise."

130 · *Lan Cao*

"Thank you," I said, smiling as if the interview had been as easy to negotiate as a fish deboned.

After the interview, she walked me to the waiting room and introduced Aunt Mary and Uncle Michael to a tour guide. "It's been a real pleasure," she kept saying, holding on to my hand as we said goodbye.

The campus grounds, covered in frozen snow and patches of pine-needle green, lolled around old stone buildings with delicate archways and high ceilings. There were steeples and turrets, clock towers and a fortresslike library with gallery interiors and stained-glass windows that gave the college a look as ancient as a castle in an antique print. In the quiet, milky light of this cold day, among these astonishingly beautiful sights, a stately glow seemed to shine on the entire campus. We walked ceremoniously up a slope, toward the fenced-in grave of Mary Lyon, whom the guide described as "the founder of the oldest continuing institution for the higher education of women in the United States." Tradition and history are important for a college founded in 1837, our guide touted.

As if on cue, Aunt Mary praised the pitched roofs and admired the details etched on the apple-colored walls. Dappled light threw lacy imprints into a cobblestoned courtyard. "Beautiful stonework," Aunt Mary gasped as we passed the old college chapel. The guide happily agreed. The building, photogenic but antiquated, stood among clusters of oak and pine. You could sense the passage of time working its way through the foundation. I imagined dead mice and old wires curled recklessly in the walls, rusty pipes among antique fixtures.

The new wing appealed more to my sensibility. Red brick

dormitories and concrete buildings that rose like geometric blocks from a foundation of asphalt and cement. Constructions like those, unhumbled by age and decay, had once been part of my Saigon childhood, colossal structures that climbed the sky, seething with naked power. How strong, I had once thought, these American workmen who could defy gravity and swim in the air with nothing but loops of rope around their waists, operating forklifts that grasped the air in their metallic lobster claws. In their gracefully muscled arms, raw cinder blocks and exposed metal beams could become solid superstructures towering tall and lean over our archipelago of more elderly shops below.

"Let me show you the library," the guide offered. "Then the gymnasium after."

From a distance, a group of students emerged from class, carrying books, laughing. Here, for four years, among these tall pine trees and cloistered halls, they would be allowed the luxury of errors. They would be capable of anything. They were, after all, relinquishing themselves to the world of grand ideas, where anything that was imaginable was utterly believable. My mother was right. Education does confer direction, dignity. "A college for women. The challenge to excel," the school's motto beckoned. They could beat their wings and lift themselves up here. Ten years from now, they could lead wholly different, more disappointing lives, but they would always have this life, this movable world. They could always take this world, the unminiaturized world of their education, with them, wherever they went.

As my mother always said, no one, no war, could ever take that away.

8

The landings held a plump mixture of curry, garlic, and fish sauce odors. As Bobbie and I approached my apartment, I could see a shimmering agitation of smoke leaking outward from the crack under our door. My mother was burning votive candles, which signified that an event of some sort was taking place inside. Although she lived a tight-lipped life outside, in the untamed interiors of our apartment, my mother, at Mrs. Bay's urging, had no trouble fabricating continuity —an ongoing life unruptured by the events of 1975. The past few months had been an arduous succession of changes: almost four months in the hospital, of which a full week had been spent in intensive care, three weeks in a rehabilitation center; and now home.

A feast of hot-pot beef, vegetables, and cellophane noodles and an assortment of pastries and baguettes had been arranged on our dining table. This was my mother's Little Saigon community, a cordial and modest grouping of exiles intent on maintaining the steady rhythm of the old along with some practical twists to usher them into the demands of a new American life. It was their weekly get-together, a new routine Mrs. Bay had devised since my mother's release from the hospital to impose order and form on my mother's life. A knife made hard chopping sounds on a cutting board. In the living room, a cork or two popped, releasing a stinging whistle of pressure into the air. My mother was in a corner, turning paper towels into napkins. One by one, she cut each sheet into four equal parts. She folded one sheet into a square, then another. I edged closer to her, and joined in.

One day, when my mother was first released from the rehabilitation center, I had found the apartment solidly sealed from the outside, the blinds on every window, even the tiny one in the bathroom, pulled all the way down. In the counterfeit darkness of a bright spring afternoon, my mother had laid her body diagonally across her small twin bed, with a blanket securely draped over her, like a corpse wrapped from head to toe. I could see her, one minute on the bed, altogether undone like bits of glass reglued, and the next minute in the center of Saigon, where she was perforce as unremarked and as natural as the law of gravity or a rule of war itself.

How do you feel? How are you today? I asked her every day. A sense of distance and remoteness had attached to her body, and it was at moments like those that I understood the true meaning of absence. My days were threaded with an ongoing fear that translated into a hollow sense of remove as well, remove from everything, except my mother's health. In one of my desperate attempts to reach her, I had felt inclined to steal the confessions I knew were still stored in her drawers. I wanted to break through the membrane that kept us apart and plunge headfirst into a prenatal space where I could reach my mother's true thoughts. But I simply couldn't, not with my mother constantly by my side.

At first she had refused to work on her physical-therapy

program unless I forced her into it, standing watch over her at six-thirty in the morning, as I got ready for school, and again at three in the afternoon. Back on bed, feet flat against mattress with hips and knees bent, raise buttocks, or rock knees from side to side. Stand with feet firmly on the ground, twist body from left to right.

The speech-therapy exercise she had had the most trouble with was reading. I was instructed to make sure her eyes stayed focused, word by word, line by line, going from left to right, and not in a hodgepodge of directions across the page. Because her CVA, cerebral vascular accident, had occurred on the right side of the brain, my mother suffered what the nurses called "left neglect," meaning that her left side could appear as separate and apart from the rest of her body as somebody else's disembodied left side. To counteract this, we had to highlight the left margin with a yellow marker to draw her eyes back toward the left each time they reached the right.

"Don't be concerned if she seems disoriented. It's normal to get time and place mixed up for quite a while," the visiting nurse had assured.

"You are in a dark space. There are rows and rows of chairs. People sit silently, faced forward toward a big screen. Now, where are you, and what is this place called?" the nurse would ask my mother.

On one of her outpatient visits to the neurologist, when her left side was still being meticulously massaged and rehabilitated, my mother had responded to the doctor's questions in either complete confabulatory fashion or almost Zen-like contemplation.

"Mrs. Nguyen, can you move your left hand and clap for me, please?" the doctor had asked.

My mother nodded. Without a slight moment's hesitation, she ventured to produce a steady stream of clapping motions with her good right hand, stopping at the medial plane of the body as if resistance were being provided by a not-too-mobile left hand.

"Are you clapping yet, Mrs. Nguyen?"

"Yes, Doctor," my mother had replied. It appeared that, in this moment of neurological crisis—when cross-wires between the right and the left sides of her brain were not completely functional—my mother had managed to hear the sound of one hand clapping. In the midst of sensory disorder, my mother's left brain—the side neurologically charged with imposing and maintaining order out of a constant, perplexing influx of sensory perceptions—continued to cling to the last imprint of coherence it had stored in its brain cells, the imprint of order. It still believed—mistakenly, of course—that the left hemisphere enjoyed full and unfettered activity.

I was becoming, in the most obvious and unmistakable way, the chess champion directing my mother's pawns with my magic parasol, telling her which piece to move into which square across the board. She did not rebel. I could see resignation, compliance in her bleary eyes as she swallowed the rice gruel I fed her every morning and every night her first month back from the rehabilitation center.

There had once been moments, years ago, in which my mother had been capable of anything. That was when we had Vietnam with us. She carried the outdoors and the indoors with her, and almost all things large and small that occurred in my vicinity could be traced back to her. After my father and I took a stroll, we returned to our house and on the table would be several plates of sandwiches, for instance. My mother must have been the one who had split the baguettes open and stuffed them with *jambon*, leaves of lettuce, and slices of fleshy red tomatoes. Our afternoon treat, freshly made no more than fifteen minutes before our return, always awaited us. That was all my father and I had to know. All we had to do was allow ourselves to be taken to the table. My mother had been the cause of many things, even when we never gave it a second's thought.

And now, as I watched her struggle with an act as slight as picking up a spoon, I could feel the intense desire to reclaim it, to stake four wooden posts around it and insist on its immutable, physical presence—the solid geometry of my mother's life that had always provided me with comfort and sanctuary.

"Please pick it up," I would say to myself as I observed her struggle to convert the brain's intention into actual reality. "Please pick it up." If she could, that, I thought, would be the sweetest blessing of all.

"Do you love me?" she once asked, clutching my finger like a baby as I fed her a bowl of tamarind soup after her physical therapy. The question startled me. Ours was not a family that spoke so directly. Here was yet another sign that she was letting go of motherly authority. One of the privileges of motherhood in our house had always been the power to presume that a certain motherly connection established since the beginning of time would be incapable of either subversion or dissolution.

I nodded. "You know I do. I'll take good care of you, Ma," I tried to reassure.

My mother looked away, then nodded. And I knew what she was thinking: Why did it have to take something like this for you to pay me any attention at all?

She smiled softly and brought my face toward hers, caressing my cheeks, fingering my hair. "Open up, Ma," I said, trying to slip a morsel of fish between her teeth. She looked frail, her finger like a chicken bone inside my hand. Here was my mooring, this woman I called my mother, curled like a sick child in the half-light of her curtained room. No one could love me as much, yet no one could seem as alien. Every night, in the background, I would hear Mrs. Bay unfold packets of herbs purchased from a Chinese herbalist, carefully funneling each packet into a separate jar.

My mother and Mrs. Bay both preferred traditional over Western medicine, which meant they had an unorthodox routine to follow. Before my mother's bedtime, Mrs. Bay would burn the tips of licorice and wormwood twigs and apply them to various points on my mother's body. She would massage my mother's temples and her back, the flat muscle mass that shuddered a slight upward incline toward the shoulders, and then the forehead with tiger balm, pinching specific spots she considered sensitive nerve endings—"to aid the body's circulation," they both proclaimed as I watched from a shadowy corner of my mother's bedroom. They would pay particular attention to my mother's long, Buddha-like ears, to the acupressure points that coincided with the essential coordinates on the human body.

The job of watching over her seemed more daunting now than ever, for I had had to relinquish an array of after-school obligations to devote myself to her care. "The nurses seemed worried that you had so many nightmares," I would occasionally suggest, experimentally.

And my mother would smile. After a brief hesitation, she would say, "I hope I'll never have to go back there again." She would shudder. And, of course, yes, I would agree, yes, yes, and together the two of us would sit in silence as she struggled to move back into the world of the living. There was no way, though, to check for clues, because my mother would inevitably turn bonelessly unreadable and absolutely neutral. "I've had trouble sleeping lately," she would declare. "Too many bad dreams, I believe," she would say as a way of punctuating a conclusion to our conversation.

To my surprise, after her return from rehabilitation, my mother, freed from the recollections of an unconscious past, had simply not uttered a word about my grandfather. I had not expected it, a voracious silence that was capable of sucking oxygen from our common space. It was as if Baba Quan had never existed, a mere phantom one of us made up in our mind, a ghost of a name, no more, no less, she had once called out to in the middle of a foglike dream.

But thanks to Mrs. Bay, a new life was beginning to seal itself around my mother. Lately, I could say with a certain degree of certainty that she was truly recuperating. Her friends had been insisting that she be catapulted into the buzz and updraft of their newly instituted activities, and she was beginning to comply. And so, for the past few weeks, our apartment had become a busy site for evening feasts and weekend hangouts. My mother would be able to claim the graciousness of host, although Mrs. Bay and others would do all the preparatory and clean-up work. It was an act of devotion on their part.

Our apartment was a railroad flat, everything laid out on one very long, very narrow line. But even from the blind end of my bedroom, I could hear Vietnamese opera blare from the cassette player in the living room, a slightly eerie mix of high-pitched screeches sharp enough to scratch the eardrum and deep soulful sighs sung, I imagined, by women in mournful white faces painted with dark half-moon brows.

"We want to keep all her senses fully charged," Mrs. Bay confided to me. "We want to keep her busy and active. So she'll always be in the middle of a plan that needs tinkering." I understood their intent, to keep my mother away from solitude and in a furnace blast of continual activities.

Incense sticks held in an old condensed-milk can burned a constant red glow. On the altar were pictures of my father and my four grandparents, frayed silver along the edges and yellowed like turmeric around the corners. Sometimes, depending on events or circumstances that I did not know, a sixth picture—of a jowly-faced man with a scraggly beard and multiple chins—would suddenly appear, then disappear. My mother said it was the picture of Uncle Khan, my grandfather's landlord, our family's benefactor, a man who had paid for her education and whose debt she was still repaying with offerings of red wine, sticky rice, and paper money.

Because of the large teak frame, Mama Tuyet occupied center stage on the altar. Her lips were painted in a reddish cinnabar tinge, her face was colored a faint rice-powder white, and her eyebrows were what my mother called "distant-mountain brows," sharp-pointed tops above eyes that wept from afar. Whereas women of her day wore their hair neatly combed or tightly twisted in a bun, my grandmother had dazzling white hair, thick untamed strands flying left and right, spirited like a swordswoman chasing dawn and dusk from east to west. My grandfather, Baba Quan, eyes pried open, sunken in deep sockets like those of an astonished Frenchman upon arrival in Vietnam, looked startlingly delicate and diminutive by her side, almost invisible in the clear plastic borderless frame my mother kept leaned against the altar's back panel.

An extravagant collection of activities centered on the family shrine, as the sweet scent of incense hovered placidly above us. Bouquets of yellow baby bananas and frozen durians, imported from Thailand in plastic boxes, crowded the bright red altar.

Tonight, in the living-room area, under a pale neon light, a gathering of Mrs. Bay's friends were setting up the rules of the hui, a community pot of money designed to give those who would otherwise be unqualified for bank loans immediate access to a lump sum of cash. Here was a gloating scheme of ingenuity, an immigrant strategy for economic survival that was taking on great possibilities.

Mrs. Bay had been trying to talk my mother into a joint venture. They could be entrepreneurs supplying freshly baked goods for Vietnamese grocery stores in the area. Only earnest, solid food that had dough as its base truly interested her. Bread, doughnuts, cakes. Everything they needed was already in the cupboard: flour, sugar, shortening, yeast, and other ordinary ingredients. Best of all, she could imagine making a profit out of her love of baked goods. The hui would provide them with the necessary financing.

This was how the hui would work, according to Mrs. Bay. "Let's suppose we have ten members," she declared. "Each will put in one hundred dollars, so there will be one thousand dollars in the pot." She glowed with enthusiasm as she explained the rules to me. "The administrator of the hui gets to draw first. I'm the administrator, so I will draw one thousand dollars the very first month. Just like that," she boasted. "Who needs bank credit?" She was already disappearing into an ardent and prosperous future.

"The next month, everyone except the person who wants to collect from the pot will put in, for example, some amount less than one hundred dollars—eighty-five dollars, perhaps. I will have already drawn from the pot, so I will put in the full one hundred as payback. The total will then be drawn by the second drawer. And it continues, see? The third month, everyone will put in eighty-five dollars again, except the previous two drawers, who will each put in one hundred dollars, which covers part of the interest to be repaid to the eighty-five-dollar contributors. The lump sum can be drawn again by the third member, and it goes on and on until all ten members have gotten a chance to draw from the pot."

Mrs. Bay was eager for me to reveal some degree of awe. She stood before me, sure and wide as bliss itself. The hui worked because it combined commercial calculations with unmitigated trust. Every borrower who dipped into the pot for instant lump-sum cash would be entrusted with repaying the amount in incremental portions—by making monthly one-hundred-dollar contributions to cover principal and interest—until the pot had been fully rotated.

The baking business could work. Mrs. Bay's deep-fried dough balls and French baguettes were gaining a fast and vehement following. There were other plans from other members for community investment as well. Mr. and Mrs. Tam had methodically drawn up a plan for a packaging-and-mailing service which would allow us exiles to send "care packages" to our families in Vietnam—within the limits imposed by the American embargo, naturally. Mr. and Mrs. Hai, who used to work in the ice-cream business in Saigon, had decided that nostalgia could be exploited—with sensitivity, of course. Their ice-cream parlor would specialize in replicating with unwavering precision the decor, arrangement, atmosphere, and taste of the old Givrard and Brodard ice-cream parlors in downtown Saigon, where coconut, pineapple, orange, and other fruit-based ice cream would be served in their natural fruit shells. For businesses that required a bigger start-up cost, there would be other huis—bigger ones, to accommodate more members, who would bring more money to the pot.

Our apartment was generating serious energy, shifting from its usual somnambulism to a flushed and slightly kinetic mode. And I must admit Mrs. Bay was right. My mother was working her way back into the land of the living. This weekly infusion of furious, manic activities and the intravenous rush of real life and real dreams were giving our home a new sense of hope. Now, when I walked into the apartment after a full day's absence, I could be momentarily surprised by the change. I would be able to detect a mild domestic order among its walls, or at least an attempt by the apartment's inhabitants to impose some symmetry among the household objects—a teapot and its set of eight teacups on the living-room table, a stack of paper towels cut into napkin-size squares, a jar of roasted peanuts by the living-room couch to accommodate drop-in guests. In the drawers, spoons facing the same direction nested in a cutlery tray. It was still a parsimonious and unextraordinary space, but there was incipient hope in its walls. Ours was becoming a space that could accommodate visitors.

"Thanh over here and I will become tycoons soon enough," Mrs. Bay laughed, pointing to my mother.

"My ears tell me next year things will change," my mother said jokingly. This was a different mother, a more optimistic mother. She was mingling with her friends and moving through the crowd effortlessly.

Mrs. Bay reached over and gave my mother's ear an affectionate twist. "See how long and wide they are? You don't want ears that curl inward, crowded and miserable like a poor, hungry person. These ears are good, open, and expansive. We'll be assured of a bountiful and virtuous future. With my baking skills and her brains, we'll do fine. We'll have little if any start-up cost, and we all know there is a market for my goods. The grocery is usually sold out of my baguettes within two hours."

My mother could be seduced into the American Dream, into becoming the modern version of our Trung sisters. She was becoming what she had once been, the way I remembered her, chasing after street vendors, rummaging through straw hampers of steamed peanuts and sticky rice, her chatter spilling from the street into my room like a carefree breeze.

"Bob's really happy today," Bobbie whispered.

"Mm-hm. She's enjoying the attention, I think," I answered. "B-o-b" was a nickname we had recently picked for my mother, a shorthand reference to the "bag of bones" she carried in her frail body. It allowed us to discuss her even when we were within her immediate vicinity. Based on our multiple references to "Bob," my mother believed him to be a new friend we had made at school. "Invite him to dinner, if you like," she would occasionally suggest. And we would politely decline. "Bob can be difficult to be around sometimes," I would explain with a straight face.

"When will the fortune-teller arrive, Aunt Thanh?" someone asked my mother. My mother tilted her head and smiled. There is no fixed "I" or "you" in Vietnamese. Our pronouns change depending on whether one is speaking to one's mother, father, maternal or paternal grandparents, aunt, or uncle, and whether the aunt or uncle is from the mother's or father's side. The "aunt" used to address my mother signified great respect. It was reserved to address one's father's older sister, which meant my mother had been placed on an even higher plane than the speaker's father. Although she had been managing and cleaning the vegetable supply seven days a week, ten hours a day, in a Vietnamese grocery store for the past four years, her identity was that of a professor's wife. We had a different country and a different person to return to, and refugee etiquette meant that the store's customers, even doctors and merchants who had made something of themselves in this country, still treated my mother like the elder that she had once been. What mattered, at least in 1979, a mere four years after our arrival, was not so much what one did in America as what one used to do in Vietnam.

"She's on her way," my mother said. "This fortune-teller is reputed to be the best one outside Vietnam." She walked across the scuffed floors toward the cupboard and pulled out several packages of tamarind candy and salted plums. Ours would be an obliging space of raw and unmeasured bounty this evening.

"The absolute best," Mrs. Bay chimed in. "Do you know how well known she is? Powerful men used to listen to her every word," Mrs. Bay explained. I must not have demonstrated sufficient interest, and she was addressing herself to me. "Real-estate developers in Vietnam would never construct a new building without first consulting her. Architects designed in accordance with her instructions. When she told them that a hotel they were building faced a mountain where the spirit of a dragon had dwelled for years, they did what she told them to do. They altered the building's design and created a large round hole near the top so the dragon could fly right through without being blocked."

Bobbie and I looked at one another. This promised to be an evening of fun. There was always comfort in watching my mother enjoy herself, but tonight I could also attach a certain degree of interest to the entire affair. On certain occasions, I could adopt the anthropologist's eye and develop an academic interest in the familiar. I could step back and watch with a degree of detachment the habits and manners of Little Saigon.

Detached, I could see this community as a riot of adolescents, obstreperous, awkward, out of sync with the subscribed norms of American life, and beyond the reach of my authority. I could feel for them, their sad shuffles and anachronistic modes of behavior, the peculiar and timid way they held their bodies and occupied the physical space, the unfailing well-manneredness with which they conducted themselves in public—their foreigners' ragged edges. Here, in one corner, was a grouping of elderly women and men too unattached to the ways of the United States even to be aware of their differences. They had never managed, nor had the desire to manage, the eye-blinking, arm-folding maneuvers needed for a makeover. Here, in a walk-up apartment in a suburban neighborhood thirty minutes from Washington, D.C., they continued to present themselves as reproductions from the tropics.

Every summer, they ventured into the streets with their usual paraphernalia, umbrellas and towels wrapped impertinently around their heads. They would drape the towels over their heads, then flip the two hanging corners diagonally on top before twisting the tips into fat, bulging knots. Once this headgear had been worn by peasants who worked the rice fields, and by old women in black pajamas whom GIs called "VC mamas" on late-night movies. I used to look at them and picture more palatable possibilities—sultans and genies

flying out of bottles and lamps, flamboyant turbans of paisley and silk like the ones in *The Arabian Nights* or *Ali Baba and the Forty Thieves*.

"If you have to be different, you have to be acceptably different," I would think to myself. Stereotypes aren't my enemy, as long as we tinker with them in a way that strikes an American chord. Instead of drabby cotton towels, I could picture parrot-gold umbrellas opening against the midafternoon sun. I could imagine tight kimonos, vulnerable shuffles, and decorative combs. They would still be different, but they would be American-palatable and exotic.

Our apartment was fast becoming an illuminated glow of impulses and noise, a television set itself. There was a new invasion of neighbors from a building several blocks away. They were all members of the highly devout and tightly knit Cao Dai sect, and they walked through our door with a sense of unitary purpose, a fluid column of white cotton garments making its way toward our family shrine.

"The fortune-teller is here," one of the women told my mother. "We picked her up and escorted her here."

I could see by the way she dressed that the fortune-teller was also a member of the Cao Dai, a religious sect composed of eclectic elements from the world's major religions. The Cao Dai faith, founded in the 1920s, holds that the divine and singular truth which exists in Christianity, Islam, Buddhism, Judaism, and other, local, animistic beliefs, has been subverted by human frailty. Only a few mortals have been able to see through the illusion and are therefore included in the list of revered saints for worship: Victor Hugo, Sun Yat-sen, Joan of Arc, Louis Pasteur, and Charlie Chaplin, among a few others. Blessed with the all-knowing Cao Dai eye—

depicted ornately on a mural in the Great Temple in the province of Tay Ninh—these saints are revered as way-showers with supernatural vision.

Mrs. Bay hurried about the living room, lighting row after row of votive candles. My mother was sitting cross-legged on the sofa. Around her, a group of women and men, heads swaddled in beige towels, sat attentively, their chins clamped on their knees, as Bobbie and I lingered along the outer edge of the crowded circle and watched the stranger. In the center, a woman I had never seen before began stroking a deck of cards with bony hands. In slow, precise movements, the stranger composed and recomposed the cards in formation-like rows and columns across the living-room table. Mrs. Bay, thighs clasped close against her body, displayed a shamelessly obsequious air as she watched the mystical deliberations.

Above our heads, the neon light put out a steady hum. On the far wall, a white shirt waiting to dry on a wire hanger dangled in the foggy light, a ghostly object. The stranger began a series of intonations, breathing noisily. As my mother and Mrs. Bay and the rest of the audience shifted their weight forward, inching their upper bodies closer to the center of activities, Bobbie and I too edged closer, whispering to each other. What else could we do? My mother looked up and shushed us with an index finger pressed sternly across her lips.

With a quick twist, the fortune-teller flipped one last card, face-up, and placed it smack in the center of the table. She took a deep breath and peered at the cards, analyzing the hidden configurations behind the queens and kings she had pulled from the deck. My mother and Mrs. Bay followed the insistent index finger that tapped each card, sliding the ace, then the king back and forth, shuffling and reshuffling its position with each move.

After a long pause, in which the fortune-teller solemnly closed her eyes and inhaled the incensed air, held it in her nostrils, and then let it out bit by bit, until it dissolved like a soft fog into the emptiness of our living room, she stared straight toward the ceiling with wide-open, avid eyes. "I predicted four years ago, when we arrived in the United States on that terrible April day that 1979 would be our lucky year. Evil will self-destruct in the end, I said then. And that's what I'm seeing right now in the cards," the fortune-teller proclaimed.

She sipped a steaming cup of chrysanthemum tea and continued. "The communists will destroy each other soon enough, and in no more than two or three years, we will be going back home."

She leaned forward, snaked her upper body over the coffee table, and pecked the king of diamonds with her lips. "It's right here in this card," she declared.

And now I understood the implicit motivation behind today's seemingly harmless ritual. So this was what the evening was about, our hidden pockets, the ragged seams and pleats of our history. Little Saigon was once again resurrecting hope from dead space. While I was in Massachusetts, several armored divisions from China had crossed Vietnam's northern borders. And now, with the fortune-teller's help, my mother and Mrs. Bay had decided to restitch the fabric of history. The border dispute between Beijing and Hanoi could turn into a more serious event with true, significant consequences. Something could coalesce from the dictates of battlefield skirmishes. The Hanoi government could emerge from its battles militarily diminished, and multitudes of possibilities could follow from this singular event alone. The king of diamonds would navigate us through difficult waters.

Clearly, life would continue to be lived as normal, but now we would have a sweet ending awaiting us beyond the rectangle of playing cards.

"We will have a different future now," the fortune-teller said, and laughed, with a dreamlike suggestion that passed as reality.

They stood together watching the rows of spades and hearts. Mrs. Bay worked her fingers along the curve of an ace. "Have you been able to figure out American time? These Americans are always rushing rushing. When they finally have time to stop the rush, they find out their children are putting them in a nursing home. And they become dead ghosts," she sighed.

"This is where the skirmish is taking place," the fortune-teller said, pointing to a smudged area on a map my mother had tacked on the wall. "Yesterday, it was over here," she declared, moving her finger back and forth as if she were tracking troop movements across the Vietnamese map, a slightly bent, half-moon country shaped like a starved sea horse trapped inside the sky. Legend had it that Vietnam was once a wild horse with a long mane and a lustrous body. Too many wars made the horse so sad that it retreated into its present shape, a long twisted peninsula hanging on to the coast of the South China Sea like a starved sea horse waiting for happier days.

This war, though, would be resolved happily. My mother was already calculating how many months it would take the Chinese tanks to destroy Hanoi, her fingers counting one, two, three, four. . . . I gave her hand a quick, cautious squeeze. Couldn't she see how futile these predictions really were? Couldn't she see this was not the opportunity that would return her to the space my grandfather inhabited?

I could almost see what my mother must be seeing as well—the car as it followed the designated route, laboring through the nervous streets. Fear was being hoarded right there, among the crevices and sidewalks of a Saigon street no more than a few hours before the official moment of collapse. It was April 30, 1975. The old Citroën stopped, then continued momentarily. Full of hope, it steered around the corner. There was the tamarind tree. Next to it was the bench my mother used to sit on with her father. The other passengers in the car agreed: they could allow themselves a few more minutes, but that would have to be all; then they would have to go, as if no tragedy of any significance had occurred.

But now, with recent events, this was what she could have instead. She could have a plane that would take her back to Tan Son Nhut Airport. She could begin the process of searching for her father—from our house in Saigon, at their old house in Ba Xuyen. She could return to the place of warmth, where all wounds would be healed.

I realized that no expenditure of logic or interjection of reality would alter my mother's newly minted optimism. Mrs. Bay clicked her glass of plum wine conspiratorially against my mother's. They would soon map out their new, more full-figured future, where they would once again have the sky market and a slower-paced existence south of the equator. I wondered to myself: Did they know that Hanoi had one of the largest armies in the world, behind only the United States, the Soviet Union, and China? Did they know that they would not be able to count on American intervention to provide aid to the ragtag army of South Vietnamese guerrillas poised along Thailand's border, ready to infiltrate the swamps and jungles of the countryside? The visual details of the last days the United States spent in Vietnam seemed to have escaped them. I could still picture the Chinook-46, escorted by a circle of Cobra gunships, making a quick landing to evacuate the last Americans out of Saigon. Through a screen of heat and smog, canisters of tear gas had been dropped on a mob of South Vietnamese huddled along a row of mildewed and irregular houses below. As the helicopter struggled to settle itself in the air, its engine began sucking up clouds of tear gas, momentarily blinding the last eleven marines along with the crew and pilot. It appeared that the United States had flown its last flight out of Vietnam with visibility completely obscured. The description, which I had read in a recent newspaper account, had struck me as infinitely ironic and strange.

In the kitchen, my mother refilled the kettle with water and worked a pair of scissors through an unopened pack of lotus tea. She would have liked the evening to be prolonged. She would have liked people to continue to offer their current-event knowledge and wisdom. Here, in this apartment, the events of the past few months would be delivered into our living room for uncritical absorption and consumption.

Four years after North Vietnamese tanks crashed through the gates of South Vietnam's Independence Palace, the war, it appeared, at least in our living room, could still be won. "Who's to say, in the scheme of things, when the war is really over? A million boat people leaving, hundreds of thousands of prisoners in reeducation camps, one of the biggest rice-growing countries in the world importing rice, the economy in shambles. Who can call that victory?"

America would have a self-interested stake in our endeavor as well, to refight the war and produce a new ending. "Wouldn't they want an unblemished record?" one of the Cao Dai women asked good-naturedly. "Wouldn't they want to say they've never lost a war?"

Americans hate losers, I wanted to say. They don't want to have anything to do with us. They're not trying to win the war, they're trying to forget it.

As the evening wore on, I wanted to tap my mother's shoulder and inform her that television coverage by the privately owned networks of South Vietnamese anticommunist insurgencies did not translate into official government approval of or support for American reentry into the aftereffects and wreckage of war. A band of former South Vietnamese soldiers training in the jungles of Thailand, supported by financial contributions from the Vietnamese exile community—it was a journalistic matter, no more, no less, to report on the sad but interesting facts of an all-but-extinct history struggling with its last remaining gasps of life.

"Even Joan Baez has been converted," someone proclaimed.

"She has finally understood the hard, unsentimental nature of communism," another echoed. Her activities on behalf of the boat people had been reported in the Vietnamese press and she had been granted absolution. Joan Baez, the singer whose searing, melancholic voice had provided the antiwar movement with raw poetic beauty, had been issuing a series of unambiguously bold denunciations of the new Hanoi regime (while Jane Fonda, the papers had duly noted, had not). Against the majestic background of the gleaming Lincoln Memorial, she had held a benefit concert to raise money for the hundreds of thousands of boat people who were fleeing on makeshift boats across the South China Sea. After the concert, a candle-lit constellation of concertgoers, led by Joan Baez and a group of Vietnamese monks and priests, had marched toward the White House and petitioned President Carter to send the Seventh Fleet onto the high seas to rescue yet additional reminders of America's most troubled war.

"How many people, if given a choice, want communism in Vietnam? It seems like the boat people are speaking with their feet to say they'd rather risk it all than remain," one of the Cao Dai women said with a growl of gratification. "They say she has a good voice, this Joan Baez," the woman declared. A wisp of steam from the tea clouded her glasses. "She's brave, isn't she, especially when you compare her behavior with the behavior of Jane Fonda."

"It's like comparing night and day." The fortune-teller nodded agreeably.

Now we were on certifiably firm ground, where a predictable course of feelings running from disdain to rage could be easily summoned and displayed. It was a picture we had seen a million times, Jane Fonda in a North Vietnamese olive-colored pith helmet, draping herself flirtatiously behind a colossal antiaircraft gun somewhere in Hanoi. It was not something that could, or would be allowed to, recede permanently into the margin of history. The conventional refugee wisdom on the subject, or at least the more benign one, was: "Only in America would they let her come back after that visit to Hanoi."

That apparently had been the North Vietnamese sentiment as well. According to Mrs. Bay, Hanoi did not trust Jane Fonda's pedigree as an authentic antiwar activist and had actually suspected her of being a CIA agent. It had seemed inconceivable to them that someone who had sabotaged her country's war efforts had not been arrested or imprisoned. Tolerance for unorthodox political expression was simply not an ideological possibility.

Actually, Mrs. Bay had probably fabricated the story as an illustration of North Vietnamese stupidity. Anything that could shine an unflattering light on the victor would inevitably be appreciated as an occasion for comment.

It was a common refugee obsession to come up with a story that cracked open the undeniable fact of communist victory and allowed us a momentary sense of superiority.

"Repeat the story you told me to the fortune-teller," Mrs. Bay said, nudging a young man in ill-fitting jeans. He was one of the thousands of boat people being resettled by a Presbyterian church in the area. His was a particularly tragic story, with a sad but not altogether extraordinary ending—the death of a mother, a father who might have drowned but whose fate was not known with certainty, and the rape of a sister by pirates on the South China Sea.

The man willingly complied. Exposure of North Vietnamese flaws and eccentricities was never an occasion for restraint.

"On April 30, 1975, when the North Vietnamese swept through our streets, I stood in our front yard and watched them. To tell you the truth, I was curious. They had been like shadows in our lives. I am a Northerner, you see, and a Catholic. When the country was divided into two in 1954, we believed that the Virgin Mary was going south, and so my family and a million other Catholics fled southward. We'd never seen the communists in the flesh before, and here they were blasting through Saigon itself in full divisions of artillery and tanks. 'They are so young-looking,' I remember thinking. And they looked lost. They had never seen a refrigerator or a motorcycle or indoor plumbing, but it was clear they did not want us to know they had been lacking. So when we asked them, 'Do you have these things where you're from?,' they would always reply, 'Oh sure, everyone has them.' And so we decided to ask, 'What about Brigitte Bardot? Do you have Brigitte Bardot also?' And because they must have thought it was a brand of television set or cassette recorder, they quickly answered, 'Sure, we have so many Brigitte Bardots in the North. Every house has a Brigitte Bardot.'

"One of the young cadres had an aunt in Saigon, next door to our house. So, for several weeks, he stayed with her. She told us that she woke up one morning to find him in the kitchen, holding a bra filled with coffee grounds over a tall water glass. He was struggling to hold the bra cup over the glass with one hand, and with the other hand pour boiling water through it as if it were a coffee filter."

Mrs. Bay and the fortune-teller laughed and rolled their eyes with unfastened abandon. And so the focus of the evening shifted to the victors' fumbling ways, their ignorance and deficiencies.

"Have you ever had a reading?" the fortune-teller asked me, seeing that I had withdrawn from the group.

I was normally not prone to astrological contemplations, but what harm could there be in a little bit of astrology? I could see why it might be comforting to believe that the universe was predetermined by the elliptically different orbits of stars. After all, the appeal of astrology lay in the possibility of freedom, a freedom from the futility of daily aspirations and daily fear. It allowed us to believe that, if human enterprises could not alter the course of history, then humans could simply declare themselves free from the brutishness of everyday endeavors. I understood the temptation.

"Can we ask personal questions of the cards as well?" I asked the fortune-teller.

"Historical, personal, the cards make no distinction," the fortune-teller answered with unobscured enthusiasm. Her eyes lit up. "Do you have a question, child?" she asked.

"My question is about my grandfather," I said. "I'd like to know if he is all right in Vietnam, and if he will be able to come to the United States." His was a mystery, like all mysteries, that asked to be solved, that pleaded for resolution.

The woman nodded. I could hear my mother's voice, a low rumble from the kitchen, where she was instructing someone on the imperatives of charcoal roasting.

"You can shuffle the deck now," the woman instructed. "How many people are still alive in your family?"

"My mother, my grandfather, and me," I said. My father's parents had been long dead, and so had my mother's mother, Mama Tuyet.

"All right. Now, after you've shuffled the deck, you can cut it in half, and I'll start dealing the deck and dividing it into three piles. One pile for you, one pile for your mother, and one pile for your grandfather, all right?" She looked me straight in the eyes. I paused. For some undeterminable reason, it seemed as if we were embarking on a common quest, engaged in a conspiracy against the wishes of my mother. "Now turn the top card from each pile over, and let's see what we've got."

I did as she asked. I turned over the top card from each of the three piles. And I could see, right there on the flat surface of the living-room table, the general perimeters of our lives laid clear and bare. I did not understand the particulars, of course, but I saw the true import of our lives, the three solitary piles of cards like three anchors of a pyramid, my mother, my grandfather, and me against the desolate flatness of a pockmarked living-room table.

The fortune-teller scanned the orderly columns, unambivalently stark, but simultaneously lush with hidden possibilities. She took the necessary long and deep breaths, pausing to allow the formation to sink into her skin.

"I'm going to need more information to pinpoint the precise meaning of this configuration. I can't tell which of the three cards you turned over represents you, your mother, or your grandfather. To do that, I'll need dates and time of birth and that sort of detail. But based on what I have here, I can tell you, there is some barrier, some resistance coming from one of these piles here, see?" the fortune-teller said with customary certainty. "So, from the three sources we're dealing with, I can identify that a problem is being presented by one of the sources. The ace of spades on this pile is putting up a fight. There's no resistance coming from the other two piles, the jack of hearts and queen of diamonds. So I can see a problem that's keeping your grandfather away from the other two piles, and it comes from this card here."

I looked at the three variations arranged on the table. I knew something about our family history. I knew all too well my mother's singular sorrow over the one definining moment of her life, when she had failed to remove my grandfather from the dangers of a collapsing country and had had to make the escape herself. I knew she needed to create an untangled path through which she could escape blamelessly from the guilt and shame of abandoning him. I knew of her unconscious dreams—delirious on occasion—for a reunion, and her desire to have my grandfather delivered from the dearths of Vietnam into the relative peace and comfort of Virginia. And I also knew that I too had done almost everything I could to reach across the wrath and fury of political vengeance and trade embargo to make a true human connection. It had been personal inadequacies, not lack of desire, that had kept me from crossing the border to pick up the telephone.

And so, by the process of elimination, this was my conclusion, that the source of the resistance emanated not from my mother or me but from my grandfather alone. His continuing devotion was to the past, not the future, and the luminous motion that he dedicated himself to was the luminous motion of the soul and the transmigration of the ancestral spirit, not the bodily inclinations of the physical person. My grandfather had always straddled the line between the living and the dead, and I could imagine the lessons he had tried to teach me with the story of the betel-nut tree. The constancy of the ancestral land and the village burial ground—modest though they were, these were things that mattered to him. My grandfather would not be easily convinced of the need to cross the ocean's depths for the purpose of starting a more convenient and modern life.

What did this mean for my mother? Would she have to live permanently with the fear that she had failed him? I wanted to reach into my inner reserve and call up the power to heal. Her recent recovery into hope and health meant that a possibility for happiness could exist in her flesh and skin, and this possibility gave me the will and the desire to make sure she would be soothed and consoled.

"What card game are you playing?" I could hear my mother ask as she approached the fortune-teller and me. She was in her noisy, electrically charged mode. But she was still as thin and bony as the nose on her face. "Don't bet too much on the game until Mrs. Bay and I have had a chance to spin money from bread," she joked.

"We're not playing a game. We're doing a little looking into the future at Grandfather," I answered. The fortune-teller nodded in agreement. Rows of inscrutable cards lay unabashedly by her side.

"We think we've figured out the cause of your separation, Aunt Thanh," the woman boasted.

My mother's breath quickened. "You're looking at the cards to uncover my father's future?"

"Yes, your daughter wants to know what's keeping your family apart. And we've narrowed down the source, or at least the source as it can best be represented in the cards."

My mother frowned. Three furrows cut deep across her forehead. "The source as it can best be represented in the cards?" she asked flatly.

"Yes. We know the culprit is the ace of spades. But who or what the ace of spades represents is not something I can tell this precise moment. But with more information, the truth can be revealed. Your father is somewhere out there," the woman assured. "Astrology is about revelation as well as interpretation. We have the revelation, and it was cleanly and clearly revealed. Interpretation is the next step. I'm going to need your help with that."

"Interpretation is the next step?" my mother repeated. She angled her face away from our line of sight. I could detect it right away, the slight but palpable inward retraction of her body and the simultaneous withdrawal, slow but steady, from the immediacy of the present. If there were such a thing as a shadow slipping from its physical attachment to recede into a murky gray, that would be how I would describe my mother's transformation, a boneless and liquefied absence that lay beyond the human touch. I believed I knew the moment. I had experienced it myself on many occasions.

"Yes. Who or what does the ace of spades represent? Do you have any idea, Aunt Thanh?"

My mother shook her head. "The ace of spades," she whispered. "I can't tell you. I truly can't venture a guess," she confessed. "Who is the ace of spades?"

"I understand you had a tragic mishap the last day you left Vietnam. Perhaps a mix-up in the time or the place where you were supposed to meet your father, and that you had to leave without being able to tie the loose ends. If you give me the time of your rendezvous, I can go back and measure it on the astrological chart to see if it was a good or bad time of day. That may help you understand what happened," the fortune-teller offered. "But if you want to see into the future, we can try that also. Give me the year, time, and place of his birth, and perhaps I can analyze the information and make sense of this ace of spades."

My mother sighed. She gave me a tender enough look, but again I could detect the quality of reproach in her eyes.

"Truly, it would be no trouble at all," the woman added. "The resistance is coming from only one source, not two, not three, but only one. It won't take any time at all." She meant to be generous. She had interpreted my mother's hesitation to be demure reluctance to impose, no more, no less.

I sat quietly and listened to their exchange. In the silver light, my mother's silhouette cast a faint sea-horse curve against the dark window-shine. I could almost trace the slight bend of her back, the stillness of her posture as she sat motionless under a single unhooded bulb. After a few seconds' pause, before she decided to assert herself as mother and host and insist she did not want to trouble our guest further, I finally stepped in to rescue us from the awkward uncertainty of a protracted silence.

"I'll bet anything the ace of spades is Grandfather himself, right, Mother?" I declared with well-mannered enthusiasm. The obstreperous ace of spades. My grandfather's inexplicable absence would withstand even the cards' old-fashioned omnipotence. Careful, be very, very careful. My mother was not likely to be logical when it came to Grandfather and his whereabouts. "My grandfather was not the type of person who would leave his home, isn't that right, Ma?" I ventured to ask, cautiously, so as not to wound. My mother's heart could still break whenever my grandfather was mentioned.

My mother nodded eagerly. "Yes," she whispered. "Yes. He was a farmer who loved his land," she repeated. "He must have changed his mind about leaving at the last minute." My mother reached over and flicked a speck of dust from my shirt. It was a phrase we had said ourselves many times.

Later that evening, after the last guests had left, my mother arranged a platter of stir-fried tripe with fresh parsley and licorice basil, lettuce leaves, coriander, cucumber wedges, and chopped chili peppers. It was another of the many offerings to spirits I had seen her make over the years. She set the platter on the altar, on top of a brand-new yellow lace doily. The doily still surprised me. For the past four years, my mother had reused plastic forks and spoons and mixed blue china cups donated by a church with pink saucers from the dime store. Several months ago, the doily would have been an unusual touch. But lately things had been different.

My mother was kneeling in front of the altar, back bent. Her world was tilting beyond my comprehension. I looked at her and wondered what she saw. Our ancestral spirits had filled all space, from the apartment to the upper spheres, with a hazy ether's glow. I was usually as implacable and exact as the sciences my father had taught me, but for one moment, I could not resist the urge to run my hand experimentally through the air, feeling for the medium through which my grandparents' spirits were traveling.

Across the room, on the coffee table, rows of cards shimmered like a lost city at night.

CHAPTER

9

My grandfather's last day, or what I supposed to be his last day, in Saigon lingered like a lantern on a gray, motionless night. I imagined his slow agonies: a frail figure pacing the cement sidewalk below a row of rusty corrugated roofs. On the other side of the street, in a fenced-off park, a stark black monument for soldiers from the Republic of Vietnam Armed Forces crouched in assault, in combat position, their guns pointed directly at the South Vietnamese National Assembly to produce an inadvertently strange and slightly puzzling effect. Somewhere in this park, at some spot near the monument, they were supposed to have met, my mother and her father. As my mother recounted it, the plan had been meticulously designed. Uncle Michael had ensured that they could depart with papers proving the necessary American connection, and crossing guards along the route to the U.S. Embassy had been appropriately rewarded with bribes.

With prayerlike persistence, my grandfather must have paced the park's length. He must have watched his digital watch flick away each precious minute and second. And he must have eventually called it off, when he realized that the designated moment had passed irretrievably into a twilight time that could no longer be classified as day or night.

Had he witnessed the end firsthand, while I saw it on a television set halfway across the world? Had he seen the swiftness with which flocks of choppers flown by South Vietnamese pilots had been ditched from the United States Seventh Fleet into the sea? One after another, like dazed dragonflies, they had made their escape from Vietnam into international airspace, landing on the safety of American flight decks, and one after another, they had been unloaded, millions of dollars in American military hardware, jettisoned into the South China Sea to make room for incoming American evacuation helicopters and South Vietnamese escapees. The picture of a helicopter, courtesy of the American taxpayer, jackknifed headfirst into the ocean while hordes hovered above, waiting their turn to land, had appeared symbolically beneath the headlines proclaiming the end. Meanwhile, on the deck of the attack-aircraft carrier, the U.S.S. *Hancock*, a newscaster reporting for ABC News had declared with eerie matter-of-factness that this was "the largest single movement of people in the history of America itself."

There was the South China Sea on April 30, 1975. There was the exodus by air, with the Seventh Fleet and the aircraft carriers *Enterprise* and *Coral Sea* providing air support and cover. There was the exodus by sea, a lurching protuberance of South Vietnamese Navy vessels, barges, tugboats, junks, sampans, fishing boats, and other makeshift vessels, all heading away from the coast of Vietnam, toward the Philippines, then, it was hoped, to Guam. Had my grandfather watched Saigon squirm, witnessed these unbreathable sights?

The endless possibilities of what could have occurred occupied me completely. I tried to imagine the progress of his life: had it been chaotic or orderly? Beyond the exterior captured inside the rectangles of faded photographs—the stillness of Baba Quan's startled, demure face; my grandmother's wild, shoulder-length hair; and the landlord's sticky plumpness—I could sense a common subterranean memory, immaculately concealed. My grandfather, a farmer whose bravery had been rewarded with citations of honor from both the province chief and the American commander, stared at me with hard, impenetrable eyes. I could imagine his reproach of his daughter's discreditable behavior. What must he have felt when he thought she hadn't come for him? He had not asked for much. He had hoped for an intact family, but his belief in a simple betel-nut story and his faith in family devotion had failed him miserably in the end.

As my mother made the transition into the complex business of fully recovering, I seemed to be doing the reverse. Almost two months after my interview, I was still hoping and waiting for an answer. Worse, I could feel myself slip into an inverted world, a parallel existence insulated from those around me but strangely connected with the mysteries of April 30, 1975, a day that was, for me, still packed with the tight, coiled force of the unknown, a force with sufficient potency to blow the daily routine off its hinges. This was, perhaps, what an unearthly, nonphysical existence could be like, I thought, a furious connection not so much with the here and now as with some other inexplicable time and place, a world that could only be reached by blasting open the mysteries that hovered in the vicinity. What had happened to my grandfather? What sort of sorrow was my mother living with?

While I asked these unanswerable questions, my mother and Mrs. Bay continued to create a new reality—a courtly, entrepreneurial future for themselves in the here and now of America. They had begun to put on paper their clear-eyed plans, the projected costs and profits, which appeared to be distinctly plausible and remarkably realistic. I had always assumed it was shared memory—the way a ripe tropical fruit bursts through its skin, how a rice field looks after the first hard monsoon—that had hinged them together in this country. But now their voices over the phlegmy hum of Vietnamese opera concerned the solidity of the immediate present—the precision of numbers, the estimate of supply and demand. Until Hanoi could be vanquished and the chaos that would inevitably follow could be resolved, they would have a chaste and secure business plan in Falls Church, Virginia.

One Sunday evening, while my mother was going over the numbers with Mrs. Bay, I let myself wander aimlessly through our apartment. An observer could have mistaken me for a guest trying to make sense of the pattern and arrangement of new territory, a more obliging landscape capable of reflecting touchable lives—a calendar marked with plans for our routine weekend events, a grocery list my mother had put together for our weekend guests. As I shuffled across the floorboards past my mother's bedroom, a quick something told me to stop, a steady pulse that I sensed I'd be able to decipher and appropriate. I stood in the hallway, listening. On the other side of our plaster walls, every sound—a baby's cries next door, raindrops against the glass pane—were bouncing off the bare walls, giving off an unobstructed echo.

I knew what was beckoning inside my mother's bedroom. I was going to do what dead ghosts do, steal sweetmeats and pork buns and sticky rice from their true and rightful owners. Somewhere, in some unknown place beyond the Newtonian space of force, mass, and acceleration, my mother used to say, our ancestors continued to look over us, living out their existence simultaneously through their, and our, lives. Although I had always experienced that statement as a threat, I now saw it as a wish, my wish for the ability to see their lives, unfragmented and intricately webbed, pass themselves through my mother's written thoughts down to me.

I took several steps and made my way toward her dresser. Here was the chest of drawers donated by the nuns our first week in Virginia. Here was a set of fake brass handles incongruously mingled with a different set of pewter fixtures. If I were to count from the bottom up, I was certain the third drawer would reveal a bundle of notepad pages wrapped in a towel, where my mother had recounted numerous lives into the noiselessness of night.

Senseless thoughts played inside my head. Seconds, then minutes passed. The goosenecked lamp shined a weak beam of light on the wood floors, and I told myself that learning about my own and my mother's history could save us both, my mother and me. It need not be an act of betrayal or a lack of trust; it could be viewed as a child's tender gesture, a simple desire to see where life began and ended.

I began turning, turning, turning. I could feel the pulsing of veins that usually precedes entry into a forbidden, private realm. Here, right here, within my reach, was the truth of my mother's many lives, the vivid details that accompanied every fault and fracture, every movement and shift that had forced her apart and at the same time kept her stitched together. There was something about my mother's Vietnam past that I would like to understand, the molten fluidness of the rice fields, the graceful sanctuary of a convent, and the blinding purple of bougainvilleas. I was merely a child trying to understand and save her mother. What harm could there be in that?

Mai is under an illusion of freedom. Unless you create your own circumstances, make your own luck, determine your own fate, forge your own path through uncharted territory, you're not free in her eyes. That is why she wants to leave home to go to college. So she can have a new beginning unrestricted by a past life. There, her eyes will always be glued to the far horizon.

Yesterday, Mai informed me I did not need to attend the parents-teachers meeting at her school. I would not have gone even if she had asked. I nodded. I saw how the honey-colored light cupped her face to reveal the face of a seventeen-year-old, a child in this country, but an adult in many other parts of the world. By the time I turned seventeen, I had already been married to her father for two years. Still, even with a revised appearance and seventeen years of age, she remains a child in my eyes, and I am as mindful of the two of us as I was when we were held together by the same set of nerves and veins. Seventeen years after her birth, I can still feel her fullness inside my body, as warm and heavy as when I carried her at the height of my pregnancy.

The connection goes beyond our shared flesh, beyond what was forged during those moments by the mango grove when the two of us shared stories. I am not ignorant of this fact, and I comfort myself with it when Mai struggles to establish a distance between us. Still, I aim to keep her within the embrace of our household, ostensibly to protect her from danger's reach, but more, I suspect, to keep her to myself and prolong the process of separation.

It will always be there, of course. Even Mai has worked her way into accepting that fact, the fact of our connection, strong and steady like the heart's vascular valves. They call it genetics in this country, but in Vietnam we call it karma.

Mai believes in genetics because her American teachers taught this science to her in school, and I believe in karma because I have witnessed it all my life. Genetics and karma, they're as intertwined as two strands of thread from the same tapestry. If you believe a pebble dropped into a pond makes circles after circles of ripples, you are a believer in the forces of karma.

Why do children resemble their parents? My daughter would describe a process called heredity. She would know about the chemistry of genes, how they're carried by chromosomes located in the nucleus of a cell, how the chromosomes contain codes and instructions—a parent's genetic messages—to be transmitted from the parent cell to the child cell. Eye color, the shade of the skin, the shape of the body, the disposition of emotions, the type of blood, certain strands of diseases are hereditary traits parents give to their children. It would all be right there, every infinitesimal trace, even before the child's birth, and everything in that child's life could turn on a wrenching detail—the randomness of genes and the unpredictability of their combinations.

Mai can lose herself in that way of thinking, the school's way of thinking. In my daughter's reasoning, it is a fact, intangible but scientific, that the child can inherit the face of the parent but not the parent's karmic history. A child carries the preordained width and length of her family's genes, but not the inner workings and dictates of her family's karma. Yet karma, my child, is nothing more than an ethical, spiritual chromosome, an amalgamation of parent and child, which is as much a part of our history as the DNA strands. One is already the face of the other. Even as I write this, the shared facts of our lives continue to thread their way through our flesh. There is no escaping it, the fact of mother and child, as synchronous and inseparable as left and right, up and down, back and front, sun and moon.

This is the lesson you must learn. Have you forgotten the story about the little Japanese girl who was so contrary against her mother that the gods turned her into a stone? When the mother said, "It is such a perfect day for the ocean," the girl would say in reply, "I will go to the mountain." And when the mother said, "All right, go to the mountain," the daughter would answer, "I think I prefer the ocean today." And so, when the mother became ill and knew she was about to die, she told her daughter, "Make sure you bury me by the river after I die," thinking that the daughter would do the opposite and bury her in the mountain, which was where she really wanted to be buried because of the beautiful view she would get to see from above. The daughter, though, repented after her mother's death and decided to do as the mother had asked. She acted like a robot and listened to the mechanics of what her mother said rather than to the true meaning of her mother's heart. And so she buried her mother by the river, rather than in the mountain, not realizing that the yearly flood would arrive to wash her mother's tomb away. Because she did not fulfill her mother's last wish, she was turned into a stone, and in that spot in the village today, a shrine has been built next to a stone shaped exactly like a girl punished for disobedience. In our way of thinking, it is not enough to obey, you must also, as a child, look deep into your parents' wishes, the soul of your parents' souls, and distill the true meaning behind all the outward conversations. A child born from her mother's womb should be able to unlock double meanings.

Yes, for all of our lives, we would have these connections. It already shows in the mouth and hands, and in certain gestures I recognize in myself, the nervous chuckle, the hand-on-hips stance, passed right through me to Mai, a likeness that we parents can only hope will impart some degree of reassurance that here, in us, is a future that awaits our child, a future that is perhaps not perfect but good enough.

I too was an immigrant; at practically the same age Mai was when we first arrived in this country. Before I crossed the Pacific Ocean to join my daughter in the United States, I had already crossed the Mekong River to embark on what would be one of the more furious riddles of my life, wifehood. The year I turned fifteen was the year I left my beautiful school to marry her father, left my village with its green liquid rice fields to go to her father's village, many kilometers away.

My daughter, who was born into a country already at war and sheltered in Saigon, has never known a rice field and the current of grace that runs through it like golden light. She has never known how it is farmed, how it is loved, how a bowl of rice is also a bowl of sweat, a farmer's sweat, a mother's sweat. If she were to ask me, I would tell her about a rice field—its beauty, the way it meanders across the land and carpets the horizon in a bright emerald, the way the slate-blue water along the banks buoys the earth and makes it float toward the sky like a carpet in flight, the way the water swallows the distant coconut palms into its depth like a permanent mirror, translucent rectangles forever framed in the very heart, the very soul of the land. To know a rice field is to know the soul of Vietnam, that's what my mother's husband, my father, Mai's grandfather, Baba Quan, always says. That's why the war was fought in the rice fields, because it was a war for the soul of the country.

I have only fond memories of my childhood in my own village. There, everything turned on the presence of the rice fields, and against their vastness, just about everything seemed either too mild or too small to merit a comparison. Everything took place by the rice fields. It was by the rice banks, where a coolness congregates near a coconut grove, that I took my afternoon nap. Brown vertical trunks absorbed the righteousness of the fields and shot heavenward like sacred pillars of an ancient pagoda. Husky grains dangled from the rice plants, so fragile and awkward they almost looked bashful. Our futures hung on their growth, and all of us, children included, tended to that fact. Boys and girls on water buffaloes' backs shielded themselves under conical hats etched by the hat-weavers with poems and watched the progress of the fields, singing an occasional midday ballad. That, and more, much more—my soul itself—was what your mother had to leave to become a daughter-in-law in another's house.

Our family leased a tiny one-hectare rice plot from Uncle Khan, the richest of all landlords, not just landlords from the province of Ba Xuyen but from all of the Mekong Delta combined. Our plot occupied a compact square nested in a palm of earth on the eastern side of the river. Every morning, we devoted ourselves to our precious little rice field, which my parents had furrowed with gullies and irrigation canals. By the time I was four, I had been groomed for a life of farming and for the recognition that it is the land that carries life. I led the water buffalo we rented from Uncle Khan onward and forward; the animal pulled the plow Baba Quan guided from behind. We followed the directive of virtue, tending our land with a gentleness reserved for one's most precious attachments. We went from one end of the field to the other, with the plow cutting and sifting and pulverizing the soil until, by the start of the planting season, a flat unsorted land would be turned into terraced earth—the only thing besides the distant line of palm trees that broke the overwhelming flatness of the land.

Of course, it is not that there are no rises or depressions in the land. It is just that the illusion of absolute flatness dominates over all and gives one the sense that the only way to go is forward or backward, to follow the straight and precise line of life that favors patience over passion. The way to do things is to do what has always been done, to adhere to the plainness and simplicity of order and tradition, my father advised.

Every night, before bed, Baba Quan, draped under an old blanket the color of mud, would roam the house as a water buffalo and I, a five-year-old buffalo girl, would ride him tall and upright, nudging his belly with my heels, once, twice, three times to command him to stop, or clasping my knees hard against his ribs to order him into a quick trot. In the darkened room, by the light from a kerosene lamp, we would crisscross the house in search of diamonds and gold nuggets—my mother's rock candies—which pirates had hidden since time immemorial. I could feel the muscles on his back struggle as we made our sixth circle around the house. But our job was to find treasure for my mother, and he would submit to my orders with the tenderness of someone who aims only to please.

In July or August, when young rice plants are fat, full-stemmed, and ready, we transplanted them from their seedbed into our plowed one-hectare plot, our bodies hunched and twisted like the sea-horse shape of Vietnam itself. Five months later, we harvested the crop, cutting the ripe, ripe stalks and threshing them, swinging the heads against a wooden lattice, then winnowing the grains in a large flat tray to separate them from the husks. With precise shakes of my wrists, I jerked the grains to the edge of the tray and tossed them to the wind at just the right angle, so that the chaff could be cleanly flung from the basket and blown into the air while the grains landed neatly on a mat that had been strategically placed on the ground. The stuttering of the tiny granules in the air was like constant bird cries that kept our village awake all night.

Our job was to grow, from black earth, the one staple food of the country. And that, for the most part, was what my life was like, season after season, year after year, until the year when I turned ten and the most powerful landlord of the delta, Uncle Khan, whose wife had had another miscarriage, asked to adopt me—not in an official sense, but in every other way that mattered. I can imagine my parents' surprise. My mother, after all, soaked our aluminum pot overnight to soften the hard, inedible crust of rice stuck to the bottom. In the morning, she poured water in last night's leftovers and made us a new breakfast of porridge. My father was the sort of man who hammered parts of our house together with nails salvaged from other people's planks and beams. He was the sort of man who pounded cans into a flatness of tin and wired them into floors and walls. The French called houses like ours bidonvilles, tin-can cities. The landlord's act was wholly unexpected. If they were capable of attracting this powerful man's attention, they were capable of everything. The corrugated roof on our house could fly open and a new life of fortune and luck could be ushered in. Their only child could be sent to school. And that, of course, was what happened. A thousand sticks of fireworks wrapped inside a beautiful candy wrapper, that was what his gift must have been like to my parents.

Uncle Khan later told me that it was his wife who had been determined to adopt me as her own. She had suffered a series of heartbreaking miscarriages, and on the night of her last miscarriage, she had dreamed of an old man with halos of flowers that floated above his head, who stood on a dragon boat as it cut its way through the pond water like an arrow with wings. As the boat reached a cluster of lotus flowers in full bloom and the sky blossomed into a constellation of celebratory red, the old man in the dream stepped to the boat's edge and handed a baby girl over to her. Auntie Khan woke up happy for the first time in years, for the first time since her last baby girl had died, two days after birth; the face of the little baby girl in the dream, as she described it to him, was my face, the face of one of his poorest tenants' daughter, overshadowed, even then, by two long, prominent ears. It was the immaculate face of happiness, Auntie Khan had said when she met me, when she realized it was my face she had seen in her dream.

Out of nothing but the goodness of his heart, and of course the preordained dictates of his wife's dream, Uncle Khan, a man who was so powerful people said he could bring the sun and the moon together, what with the big yellow headlight on his Citroën shining in the dark at night like a bright midday sun outshining the moon, Uncle Khan, whose family had been rich since the beginning of time—since the days when the mountains were first born from the live underground coal of the earth and the oceans were first carved out of the seamless silk fabric of the sky—this very same Uncle Khan stopped by our house the day after his wife had the dream and asked, no, begged and pleaded with Baba Quan to allow him to care for me the way he would his own daughter. Whose spell had made such a thing possible? It was a question the villagers had to have asked. Was it a beneficent spell nurtured by our ancestors' good, obviously very good, karma?

I knew from the way he walked and dressed that he was like no man I had ever met before. Unaccustomed to the heat, he moved slowly. The handkerchief knotted around his neck was always pure white, with corners that flapped in the summer breeze like a pair of white doves. His legs were the color of a weak jasmine tea, his face even more pale, an oyster white foreign to my eyes, a white he protected with a wide-brimmed hat with a red peacock feather pinned in the front. He and his wife came to our house asking for me the way the richest groom would come asking for his bride. They brought tea and candy and a crate of Pinot Noir from the Côte d'Or in Bourgogne. They brought boxes of moon cakes and swallows' nests and bags of lotus seeds. There was meaning in the wife's dream, and the obvious message it carried had to be heeded. They could find their reward right there, under a corrugated tin roof and among four plywood walls. The poor farmer's wife had carried this baby girl for nine months, but she belonged truly with them. And they, of course, would experience the gratitude of those whose deepest desire had been fulfilled.

And so, with all expenses paid in advance, in one lump sum, to the Providence Boarding School, run by a French convent, I was immediately enrolled in this walled compound one day and two hours away by rowboat, where I stayed for five happy years before I met my husband and was chosen by him to be his wife. I could sense, the first day I stood in front of the black iron gates that opened into a brick courtyard with rows of stone benches, each carved with the name of a different city, Paris, Lorraine, Avignon, that a sweet glory would be found among the school's four walls, clusters of it, the kind of glory I or, rather, my ears know usually precedes heartache and sadness, in the same way that the beautiful white light of lightning always precedes the raging, rumbling roar of thunder in the middle of a dark night.

For five years, except for summer vacations and religious holidays, I lived and studied with the other girls and learned to know and love the school, its singular devotion to order, its corridors, a precise formation of alternating black and white tiles, its classrooms, ivory-white walls and an assortment of saints framed above the blackboard, even its window ledges, always dustless because it was my chore to wipe them with a wet rag, as it was also my chore to wipe the polished mahogany benches in the chapel where we prayed from five to six, as the sun began to peek its way into the stained-glass windows that took up one entire wall in the chapel.

We had to be tightrope walkers to please the nuns. I settled easily enough into the ways of the school, the stiff-jawed, erect-postured manners of the sisters. I was touched by the rhythm and dignity of convent life, actually. There was something ennobling about it. And it was easy for me, because I already had the rice cycles running like warm blood through my veins to guide me through the implacable daily routines of a Providence day: morning prayer, the doxology and the book of catechism, reading and writing (my five favorites, Corneille, Racine, Bruyère, Boileau, and Molière), poetry recitation (Paul Verlaine and Alfred de Vigny), two hours of chores, then milk and chocolate croissants with white tablecloths and polished cutlery and fresh flowers, and, on special occasions, Eucharistic rites and First Communion ceremonies performed by priests from the nearby boys' school. I could see beauty in a table with sandwiches they called Croques Mesdames. I could see beauty in the clever mnemonic the nuns gave to help us remember their seventeenth-century writers: "Corneille sur la Racine de la Bruyère boit l'eau de la Fontaine Molière"—*The crow on the roots of the bruyère tree drinks from a fountain called Molière.* If the season was right, the nuns would prepare durian for dessert, having learned to appreciate its creamy flesh and fragrance only after years of initiation into the odors of Vietnam.

Day by day, I learned to understand and love the nuns. They were just like the Ba Xuyen farmers I knew, disciplined, reserved, unpretentious, perceptive in their knowledge of and faith in a higher authority. Both had learned to adopt, despite the vagaries they witnessed, an attitude of contentment that others have labeled fatalistic. I saw it not as blind faith but as dignity, a dignity that comes from the knowledge that uncertainty has no bearing on the deep-rooted faith that life is ultimately good.

At the end of every year, for the five years I was there, I passed all my exams with top honors and would have graduated with a degree, a bona fide degree issued by the headmistress of the main Providence in Paris, had I not met and fallen under the wit and charm of my daughter's father.

A million red ants crawling inside a silk sheet, that was what I should have seen. But I only saw instead the soft artist's hands whose fingers painted secret poems on candy wrappers and banana leaves addressed to me. I only saw, on occasions when the boys' and girls' choirs had performed joint concerts, the thick thatch of hair, long at the top and cropped short along the sides, in a fashion unlike anything I had ever seen. I only saw the smooth, thin face—delicate like one of Uncle Khan's persimmons or rare royal pears—and the single pressed rose or purple bougainvillea slipped in a book of verses he had someone smuggle from the nearby boys' school where he studied, up the iron spiral stairwell, down the black-and-white corridor, straight to my bedroom in a corner on the second floor.

178 · *Lan Cao*

All those little gestures formed but a background to the real art of seduction. I never had the chance to meet him face to face until one afternoon in the summer, when, by pure accident, I saw him as I walked across a monkey bridge in Ba Xuyen. From afar, or even up close, the bridge is nothing more than a thin, unsteady shimmer of bamboo. It could take outsiders, or the uninitiated, by complete surprise, when they realized that this, this uncommanding structure, lacking completely in width and strength, was what they were expected to place their entire body weight on. And, more than that, propel themselves forward and across.

As a child of parents who farm, I have crossed many rivers, narrow and wide, on our monkey bridges, on my way to the market. That is how rivers are crossed by boatless peasants in Ba Xuyen. That is how we leave one village and head for another. The secret of such crossings lies in the ability to set aside the process itself in favor of seeing the act whole and complete. It could be dangerous, of course. But we had no other bridges, and rivers had to be crossed, so why not pretend we could do it with instinct and ease?

My agility must have impressed my future husband, because, as I glided across the bridge, I could see the way he looked at me, like someone who had seen something special. We were opposites: I, who can look at a monkey bridge and see an uncomplicated surface; I, who know every stage in the rice-planting process, from the time the seeds have to be planted in carefully plowed and tenderly watered seedbeds to the time when they must be transplanted into a knee-deep water-filled paddy. And he, who can no more make his way across a monkey bridge than walk on air itself, although he had plenty of other skills that few young men of the time possessed—a love for Rousseau and Voltaire, and an ability to sit perfectly still for hours, his face skyward and sheltered from the sun by a hat, contemplating a perfect philosophy and an even more perfect future to be crafted by human thoughts and human hands.

When we finally met, after I crossed the bridge that summer day, I was as ripe for charm as Baba Quan's one-hectare plot was ripe for a harvest that season. I introduced him to Verlaine, and together we recited a line or two of poetry I had memorized: "Les sanglots long / Des violons / De l'automne / Blessent mon coeur / D'une langueur Monotone." He remembered them still years later and recited them, right in the middle of a fight we had, and that simple but tender act of his once again endeared him to me. By then, the poem had become quite notorious. It was those two lines that the French underground had broadcast over the airwaves to signal the beginning of their campaign of resistance to the Nazis.

Under the influence of his philosophical contemplations and his obviously exceptional intelligence—that summer, he actually seethed with beauty—I began to think of myself as a one-eyed fish that on its own could see from only one side of its body; for perfect vision, the fish had to have a companion to help it see the other side. Mai's father, I thought, would surely be that other half to my imperfect eye. And that was why I opened so much of myself up with him. Our first face-to-face meeting by the monkey bridge was the meeting that forever altered the course of my fate.

How? you might ask. Like a balloon bellied upward by the wind, or a child's kite steered by a northerly rather than a southerly breeze? I would have to say no, not like that, not at all. Nothing so romantic as a kite swaying in the tropical air, because, although my future husband could recite the political philosophy of Jean-Jacques Rousseau, that, all that, was for the world only, not for his wife, once he got his wife into the private world of the home, separate from what he called the "open-air world" out there. I didn't realize it at the time, but who would know more about the world outside the home, an indoor philosopher pale as an eggshell or a rice farmer the color of rich lotus tea, like me? But I didn't question then, and I simply assumed that, if he wanted the open-air world, he should have it. That was how I loved him. I was willing to concede everything to him, and turn over to him the very same world where I had always been before I met him, the open-air world I knew as intimately as I knew the cycles of the seasons.

When we met again, that first week of summer vacation, in Uncle Khan's summer cottage behind the courtyard—for I was by then as much Uncle Khan's as Baba Quan's daughter—it was his passion that dazzled me, passion for a new world he was so sure would unfold as easily as one could unfurl a beautiful banner, passion for the dream of "Liberté, Egalité, Fraternité," for workers and peasants and all the dispossessed of the earth alike. He imparted his vast knowledge to me. He told me about eighteenth-century French peasants in pre-Revolutionary France who had had to endure crushing misfortunes because their crops had been destroyed by wild rabbits that could not be killed because they must be protected for the lord's hunting. He told me about a peasant he saw by the rice fields who had preferred a dirty spiderweb over a bandage and a dab of Mercurochrome for an ugly cut on his finger. And he told me about the exorbitant rent payment our beleaguered peasants had to pay, 45 to 50 percent of their annual rice crop (which, believe me, I, a child of peasant roots, could have told him all about but didn't), to the landlords—his father, for example—from whom they had to lease their land.

As the son of a rich landlord who could see the injustice in our landholding system, he was, as he called himself, ahead of the times. And the times, he assured me, would follow him shortly. "The way you'll follow me," he whispered, and looked at me as if he were kissing the curves of my face and eyes. We never touched, of course, but his eyes, I could feel, wrapped themselves tenderly around me and produced a hot sensation strong enough to pull me toward him, straight into the temptation of his open arms.

It hit me so fast that I had no time at all to think about it. It was faster, more powerful than a wild jungle fire, more unpredictable, even more savage than the flow and tributaries of the Mekong River at the height of a monsoon. The reason, of course, is as clear to me now as it had been unclear to me then. Binh, my handsome, intelligent, and modern-thinking husband, had described the dream of all dreams so beautifully, so convincingly, that I could not have possibly seen it for what it was: a dream that did not include me at all.

And so that was how I, the prized pupil of the Providence, the girl with a mind as ravenous as a periscope, walked into that beautiful dream without suspecting in the least that it harbored as many goblins and demons as angels and other heavenly beings. It started, of course, as it had to for the adopted daughter of a landlord from a family as established as Uncle Khan's, with an elaborate gift-presenting engagement ceremony, the "crossing of the woman's house-gate," as we call it, fitting and proper for the union of two of the most prosperous landowning dynasties of the Mekong region. A good match, the villagers said. Uncle and Auntie Khan outfitted my parents in new shirts and pants of moiré silk and gave them black velvet sandals studded with silver sequins. Fresh red gravel was poured onto the dirt path leading from the bamboo gate to the porch of the villa, set a dignified distance from the main road. Window frames painted a vermilion red and decorated with colored glass were polished over and over. The banquet table was strung with orchids and jasmine and spread with crisply roasted ducks and geese and heaping plates of glutinous rice and quail eggs and bowls of shark fins and swallows'-nest soup in red-lacquered tureens.

As the clock struck the astrologically correct time, the groom's family made their entrance and formally proposed marriage. With a noted astrologer by their side, Uncle Khan and Binh's father went through the chart to pick the most auspicious date and time for the wedding. The correct combination of date and hour could make the difference between a good or a bad marriage and, in some cases, even life and death.

All of us in Ba Xuyen had heard about the tragedy that had befallen a nobleman in the emperor's court during ancient times. With the birth of his firstborn son, the nobleman had thrown an elaborate party for hundreds of guests. The boy was born in the Year of the Rat, the Day of the Rat, and the Hour of the Rat, a very rare combination. By coincidence, the wife of one of the nobleman's servants also gave birth to a son at the same exact moment. The servant was poor, so there had been no celebration to mark his son's birth. But for the nobleman's son, a feast was arranged, and guests were entertained with firecrackers and dragon dances.

The two boys grew up side by side and became close friends. Both received top scores on their university examinations and joined the ranks of scholars. Both were astrologically destined for greatness, but, unfortunately for the landlord, his son became inexplicably ill and died, whereas the servant's son went on to become a mandarin at the imperial court. The nobleman fell into a great depression, gave up all worldy possessions, roamed the country, and joined a monastery to live a life of devout contemplation. There he met a wise man who gave him the answer to the question that had haunted him. His son had been born in the Year of the Rat, the Day of the Rat, and the Hour of the Rat; the commotion surrounding his birth, the crowd, the feast, and the firecrackers, had frightened the spirit of the rat and sent it into hiding, and it could not be retrieved. A wholly different life awaited the servant's son, because his rat had neither been startled nor terrorized.

The date and hour for Binh's and my wedding were meticulously determined by charting our combined dates and hours of birth. Clocks and watches in our houses were synchronized to the second. At the precise moment in time, led by his parents, Binh walked through the

*gate with a tray of betel nuts. Behind him, brothers and sisters and
family friends followed, each carrying trays of tea, sweets, and gifts
that had to be presented.*

*In other parts of the world, the girl's family must present the
boy's family with a dowry. But daughters in Vietnam are not terribly devalued, and so, before a family is willing to part with its
daughter, it must be courted by the boy's family and adequately
compensated for the loss of a valued family member. That day, tray
after tray of betel-nut arrangements were presented, complete with a
set of betel bags, silver spittoons, betel-nut cutters, lime boxes, and
spatulas, all wrapped in a bronze box inlaid with amber and turquoise. There were also rare wine; cakes and candied fruits; dumplings
shaped and flavored like twelve different kinds of flowers; ice cream
made from a chilled mix of milk, rice, and camphor; incense and
joss sticks; gold and jade necklaces and matching earrings and
bracelets—tray after tray paraded before great-grandparents, grandparents, aunts, and uncles of both sides. Binh and I knelt before the
family altar and bowed three times.*

*It was the sort of ceremony that must have let Baba Quan know
in no uncertain terms that he had indeed moved into a wholly different
land. In Ba Xuyen, it was understood that the course to follow was
the straight course, the course of steady patience. And for those like
my father who did not own the land, it was further understood that
tending the fields through flood and drought was in itself a worthy
discipline, for ownership was not a prerequisite to tilling the land
with pride. "The land isn't ours, any of ours, to own, in any event,"
my father used to say philosophically at the end of the day, when
our field lay before us in an utterly flat stretch of luminous green
and we could comfort ourselves with the knowledge that we had
received it with discipline and love.*

*But there he was, on my wedding day, dressed in a black moiré
gown with a red satin sash around his waist. He stood proudly by*

the altar and concentrated on the groom's procession, the broad, unrestrained manifestations of wealth. It was a beautiful wedding, a summer wedding much like the first ceremony, only more. More of everything, more candy, more food, more polite bows, more watermelons and other fruits containing as many seeds, representing seeds of fertility, as possible. Except, of course, more of home, more of Baba Quan and Mama Tuyet, more of Auntie and Uncle Khan, more of my little hamlet, more of the sights and sounds of the Ba Xuyen I had known and loved since I was a baby in my bamboo crib on the dirt floor by my mother's bed. This, of course, was the beginning of my emigration, years before my second one, to the United States.

Ba Xuyen in the summer, I still remember, was mostly an endless rush of noise, as if the land had held its breath all year and finally exhaled to release all that had been suppressed. From my bedroom window in Uncle Khan's house, I could hear the crickets chirp, their sad songs carried through the windowpanes into the house from the vacant fields and the cemetery down the road. I would know from their sounds whether they were what we called charcoal crickets, black and large, or fire crickets, small but quick and nimble. As a child, I used to keep them in a perforated matchbox under my pillow and listen to them at night. Next to the cemetery was a large pond covered with moss and tall grass crowned with silver blossoms. The dampness of the area attracted not just crickets but also frogs and tadpoles, and the noise they made, when combined with the flapping of wings by birds at night, often frightened passersby, who imagined they had heard a lament from the graves. In the evening, as I lay on a rush mat and listened through the thin walls of our cottage for the sound of rice being rinsed, the crackling of sesame seed roasting on a metal pan, the chants of sampan drivers navigating their boats down the river, I used to think how utterly beautiful life could be. I remembered all those sounds—the sounds of my childhood—after I

left my village, after I arrived in Binh's village, where I was im-
mediately taken after the wedding.

We rode together in Binh's car. Crows scattered from a row of
dark trees. The familiar fields fanned out and, absorbed by the ho-
rizon, disappeared into the rearview mirror. Sealed in place by a
thick, lumbering humidity, the heat could be felt on the skin, but
Binh kept the windows tightly sealed. I was, at that moment, sup-
posedly imbued with the female yin force of virginity and required
protection from the intrusive and disruptive male yang influence that
inhabited the reckless world beyond Binh's vicinity.

That was the beginning of my path into exile, a special kind of
exile, the kind that makes you an exile in your own country. Exile
is leaving everything you know and love at the age of fifteen in order
to live, eat, sleep, breathe with strangers you suddenly have to adopt
twenty-four hours a day as your family members, to pretend you
have never known Paul Verlaine or Charles Baudelaire and yet have
always known, the way you know the tips of your fingers and the
pulses on your wrists, the many splendid ways of cooking rice and
boiling water and making tea there could possibly be to know.

That was how I was ushered out of the Providence and into a
whole new life. Just like that, with the ease and assurance of a thing
that was not only commonplace but also predestined. Tran Thi
Thanh. Thanh, my beautiful first name, which means "clarity" and
"brilliance," became Binh. My new husband's name meant "peace."
With one stroke of the pen, one nod of the head from Uncle Khan
and Baba Quan, I, now newly married, took his name and became
Mrs. Nguyen Van Binh. There, hidden behind my husband's gor-
geous gesture of love, was the beginning of a lesson I would realize
soon enough: gorgeous gestures backed by a thousand years of tra-
dition may not be much different from wars and other acts more
stark and obvious in their capacity for violence. Victory bestows
upon the victors certain privileges. Vietnam became Cochin Chine,

186 · *Lan Cao*

Annam, and Tonkin. Rue Catinat, named by the French after one of Louis XIV's marshals, became Tu Do, or Freedom Street, after the French lost and left, and then Dong Khoi, or Uprising Street, when the communists won and Saigon collapsed. Saigon, of course, is now called by its new name, Ho Chi Minh City. That was my transformation, both by name and by deed, only mine had been shrouded in love and accompanied by the sort of beauty that made me believe I could fall and remain in a state of devotion forever.

Is it as difficult as learning a new language or learning a new culture, the way my daughter has learned English and the ways of the Americans? Like Mai, I too have known disappointment, the disappointment of seeing a thing one way and finding out that nobody else has been seeing it that same way at all, so that the dream that was supposed to be a common dream had in fact never been commonly shared. That's what my marriage was like. But mine was a transformation accomplished with a certain muteness and mildness and devoid of obvious tumble and tension. I would have a completely new life that was pleasant enough. Binh would continue with his life wholly unchanged, in a way that suggested its own sense of unalterable destiny. Binh was a man of ideas, a thinker ahead of his times. I could be carried into the future with him. Ours, after all, was not a marriage arranged by a matchmaker or by our parents. Ours was a union of two educated people, a marriage freely chosen. He, the new, the modern, the individual man of a progressive Vietnam, had done the choosing himself, and I had willingly followed because I was in love.

My husband wrote against feudal vestiges and believed in the mission of a modern Vietnam, charged with progress and individual rights, but only individual rights for himself and for those in the open-air world out there—landless peasants, factory workers, tribal minorities whose struggles had been documented in books he read and collected. My life would have been better had he never had a modern idea in his mind. And that is yet another reluctant truth. If someone were to ask me whom I prefer, a modern man or a traditional man, I would have to say a traditional man. One can count on a man bound by tradition to pursue the path of least resistance, to perform the unglamorous tasks of tilling the land and providing the family's livelihood. He wouldn't be the heroic type, but one who would temper his individualistic impulses with old-fashioned Confucian concepts such as responsibility, obligation, and community. He would, in other words, be like Baba Quan.

A traditional man would not have left his wife two days after their wedding to go spread his wings, his individual wings, at the University of Saigon, where he stayed almost ten years while his wife remained behind in a strange village, with a strange family she had to learn to call her own. A modern man, sanctioned by a new philosophy to honor the sanctity of the individual and immersed in books that declared The Rights of Man, would do and did do all of that. For a modern man, in a war between tradition and modernity, between family obligation and individual right, the modern individual would prevail. I know because that was what happened to me. I had imagined it differently: either I would have a traditional marriage, like my parents, or I would have a truly nontraditional marriage, in which all was possible. I never thought I would have an unequal mix of the two, Binh's individual freedom and my old-fashioned obligation.

It happened the very first night we were together. Binh had dimmed the light. Our room was washed in the glow of candles, and I could see a dozen long-stemmed red roses Binh had set in a vase by our bedside table. Binh slipped a white sheet under me as we lay in bed. I was a proper, well-brought-up girl, and my husband naturally got what he wanted to see, three drops of blood, betel-nut red against the white sheet he decided to fold in our bedroom drawers rather than display for his village to see. Displaying a wedding sheet, my husband said disdainfully, is a feudal custom Vietnam can do without. My husband thrived on that, on being a very modern husband to a very traditional wife.

The next morning, that was when my new education began in a big way—a big way because I realized that morning how the little ways in which I had always lived my life would change. In my new room, the morning light, unfiltered by the thick green branches that once screened my bedrooms both at my house and Uncle Khan's, looked startlingly harsh and unforgiving. I missed the clattering noises a longan or a lychee fruit made when the wind jostled it from a tree and made it fall down a slanted roof. Outside Binh's windows, there was only silence, an eerie stillness without the twittering cries of baby birds screaming from their nests hidden among the branches. Binh, I later discovered, was an avid student of astronomy, which was his way of studying the science of the stars in a way directly rebellious of and opposite from what he considered the superstitious ways of astrology. In order to give him an unhampered, telescopic view, he had had every tree by his bedroom cut down, leaving only short, mutilated stumps sanded smooth and improvised into stools to be used for outdoor midnight stargazing.

That same morning, as I settled myself downstairs and was reintroduced by Binh to his parents, brothers and sisters, and every other member of the family ranked above and below, it occurred to me, suddenly, like the rapt fury of a stone against glass, that this would be my new life and it would be lived here, among these people, right in the middle of this large house on a solid but practically treeless piece of land, surrounded by shelves full of Binh's Diderot, Montesquieu, Rousseau, and Voltaire. I could learn to want all that, I told myself. I could forget classics by Verlaine and Molière, and learn to sigh over a line or two by Montesquieu. And I could act as if running a new household was an ambition I could concentrate on and fall in love with.

Monkey Bridge · 189

Binh's parents stroked my hair and told me their home was my home, their family my family, their business my business. It was a big department-store business, the biggest in the province, stocked with everything from aspirin to silk, from one-hundred-pound bags of rice to perfume from France. They handed a set of keys and a book of records over to me. It was an act of trust on their part, and it touched me. The price of every item in the store, the family's code of letters, purposefully irrational and nonsensical—"E" for "1,", "I" for "2," "R" for "3," and so forth—used to record profits in the books, had to be memorized, along with the names of all the regular customers and each customer's family members, so I could ask about them the next time the customers came into the store. From then on, this was my daily routine: I made sure the store's baguettes came out right; I ran my hand along the underbelly of a trout to test its freshness; and at the end of the day, I returned to the house and checked on the progress of the evening meal.

I listened to the servants talk. Through their eyes, I learned the new details of my life: my husband's grandmother and her bad back and the best cure possible for it—a dash of cognac laced in her chocolate Ovaltine drink to soothe the pain; Binh's father and the tick in his left eye, which always meant he was under pressure and should not be disturbed; Binh's siblings and their particular likes and dislikes. Because Binh's older brother, for example, hated his food hot, his rice had to be spooned from the surface of the pot to get only the top, cool part of the rice; because Binh's older sister, on the other hand, liked her food piping hot, her rice had to be spooned from the middle layer in the rice pot, where the heat had not yet escaped.

That was how my new life was lived—in the daily details of things that needed to be mastered by new wives and new daughters-in-law. In that way, perhaps I can be grateful for the way I was incorporated into my new family. There had been no singular calamity that conspired to vanquish me, no remarkable catastrophe that would warrant a battlefield badge or a medal. Rather, there was only an accumulation of changes no different from the changes many women from our village had to undergo. That, I suppose, is what culture and tradition are all about, and at very few points in time would battles be declared and bloodshed conspicuously drawn.

No one in my new family was cruel to me. No one pulled my hair or slapped my face or insulted me. Perhaps, if Mai were to read this, she would ask: Is that all? My daughter, like the American accustomed to hearing about the savagery of foreign lands, might expect much more drama from a life in a country back there. Where's the cruel mother-in-law, where's the rape, the floggings, the bandits and the cannibals, the savage dismemberments? she would ask. What she wants to see is a good exciting movie of adventure set in a foreign land where people are as capable of inflicting brutalities—of the kind no one here could be accused of inflicting—as they are of enduring them.

No, I had had a good house, my new parents called me a model daughter-in-law. But it was an entry into a sort of exile, nonetheless.

And, much to my surprise, I even had moments of believing there was sweetness in the way things had turned out. It wasn't a sweetness I had planned on, but it was a kind of sweetness I had in fact learned to like. I learned day by day to love the simple comfort of always knowing where the canned milk was kept, where the salted duck eggs were stored, how to please my father-in-law. All these things could converge into a single devotion that yielded a degree of satisfaction. A house, even another's house, a kitchen, a country store, each of these things could be made to have its own hidden beauty. That, I suppose, must be what my daughter has learned to see in this new country we have suddenly found ourselves in, a beauty that she finds palpable but which seems to be beyond my reach.

One evening, before the last ray of light had been extinguished by a darkening sky, I decided I would simply ask my mother the question itself. I envisioned her smile, and the long sigh as we gave ourselves over to an honest conversation. I could begin to see beyond the form of her body and the exterior of the flesh, touch the unobstructed emotional core where her written thoughts had been stored. I was yearning for a direct connection, to see my mother's fear and acknowledge her sadness with the freedom of someone who had in fact been given knowledge directly and honestly, not through secrecy and theft.

I could offer a confession of some sort myself—my fear of the wide-open space, my inability to feel connected to the American soil, or even the constant concern I carried in me about being deported—all of which might have eased the way for similar confessions on my mother's part. But all I could manage was a question general enough to ask even a relatively recent acquaintance: "What are you thinking, Mother?"

"I was thinking about the hui and who should be included in the pot," my mother replied. "Mrs. Bay should be more careful about who we make a commitment to. But you know how she is." My mother rolled her eyes. "She can be a bit too reckless. As the administrator, she's considered the guarantor of the pot. If a hui member collects from the pot in the first round but refuses to pay money into the second round, or simply disappears altogether, Mrs. Bay will be the one everyone looks to to make the pot whole again. She should be careful to include only people we know and trust."

I nodded, although I knew Mrs. Bay would have difficulty taking on the part of an implacable disciplinarian. Her strength was her ability to elicit and inspire confidences rather than fear in the people she befriended. She lacked the toughness needed to inform someone she or he would not be allowed to participate in a community money-borrowing scheme.

I twisted the plastic rod and watched the slats in our venetian blinds open. Clean horizontal light from the street lamps entered our apartment. My mother was by the sink, cleaning our set of new dishes from the neighborhood dime store. Next she would begin the ironing for tomorrow's work clothes. She had recently returned to the Mekong Grocery, where she continued to be in charge of managing the store's fresh-produce supplies. Basil, coriander, parsley, and other herbs and spices were matters she would contemplate and monitor. Is this carton acceptable, or is the lettuce too bruised? Are the persimmons too hard and green, or will they ripen appropriately over time? It was she who would have to predict the customer's demand for perishables and calculate the necessary weekly supply.

I looked at the clock on our kitchen wall. In a few hours, my mother would retreat into her bedroom to enter into the unextraordinary state of sleep. But early in the morning, when I peeped in to check on her overall condition, she would have regressed beyond sleep, into a transformed state of early childhood or even infancy. Under the folds of a winter quilt, she could acquire the appearance of a vulnerable month-old baby, forehead damp with sweat, small and curled in a tight fetal position like a question mark soaking in the hot perspiration of last night's dreams. And so my nightmare would remain, night after night: as the bare, whitewashed walls rumbled and closed in on me, the sky would shift, an invisible hand would pull the earth from my feet as my mother cowered in a corner, banging her head into a mass of ruptured blood vessels as she searched desperately, desperately for her father, her mouth pried open, a soundless circle screaming silent screams no one could hear. During those moments, as I stood alone and watched her in the bare and gray early-morning mist, a part of me felt afraid. I was afraid of my mother, and for her frailty.

I asked, "Do you think you're feeling better, Mother? Do you think you should go back to work so soon?"

"I like being back at the store. Mrs. Bay and I take the bus together to and from work every day. There's nothing to worry about, all right?"

You need a precise question if you want to elicit a precise answer.

I looked at her face. "Do you miss Baba Quan?" I plunged in. That was the question I wanted to ask. I knew we were on sensitive territory. Who wouldn't be permanently haunted by the knowledge that she had left her father behind as enemy forces were closing in for the final kill? With the hoard of memories my mother had of her father and of their time together among the rice fields of Ba Xuyen, how could she not be yearning for him, how could she not be agonizing for any bit of news?

"Naturally, I miss Baba Quan. I miss him a great deal. And I think about him a great deal," she said. "But you and I are together, at least. Not every family can say that. The poor boy who came over on a boat—he was in our apartment when the fortune-teller was here—do you remember him? He can't say he's got any family with him, can he? I've learned to be grateful for what we've got."

She reached over and pressed against me with a tenderness that touched. At that moment, I saw my mother's reticence as a simple acknowledgment of the many thanks we could give in our lives, not as a desire to maintain secrets. Yet, even though I couldn't argue with the need for appreciation and grace, I didn't want to be stymied in my explorations.

"Do you have any idea what could have happened that day, Ma?" I asked. My mother had, on occasion, with a certain degree of caution, allowed me to approach the unfathomable subject, but today I would go further.

I could predict the answer, a brisk recounting of that day's events: a darkened sky bisected by the sharp phosphorous white of rocket fire; a car stopping by the fenced-in park, making three or four slow and thorough turns around the spacious perimeter; my mother's unsuccessful attempt to undertake a search on foot—she had been restrained by the other passengers, who feared she would derail their own possibility for escape. I knew the pattern. The story could repeat itself three or four times if my mother became distressed by the immediacy of memory recounted. Still, like the detective who believed that a rehearsal of the same facts would in time reveal a detail that had previously been missed, I continued my desire to probe for a loose memory.

"I have many ideas about what could have happened, but none based on any fact," she replied, rolling a remnant of loose thread between her fingers. "He simply was not where we decided and agreed he was going to be. It is one of those unpredictable turns in life that cannot be explained." She paused and looked toward the ceiling.

"He had papers that Michael had arranged for him that would have granted him entry into the American Embassy. Those papers were worth more than gold then. There are moments when my mind wanders and I fear he could have been robbed. . . ."

This was a new detail. Perhaps she had witnessed the attack on her father but had had to leave in order to catch the designated flight. I could see the metal barrel of a pistol, or the sharp edge of an army knife. A robber (or, worse, a murderer) somewhere in the United States, reinventing himself with my grandfather's identification papers.

"I have our address in Ba Xuyen. I've written, but I've never received a letter in return. I could go on calling after him, but there's not much to be done when no connection exists," my mother stated defensively.

Why couldn't she have waited longer for him by the park? Why couldn't she have done more to find him and bring him with us to Virginia?

My grandfather might as well have walked through the hum of our orbit into a stillborn space where all tangible residues could simply be made to disappear. It was an accruing mystery, but that, in effect, was what an American trade embargo could do, make an entire country vanish like an electronic blip from the living pulses of the world's radar screen. Mail service to Vietnam was not reliable. Packages of monetary significance could not be sent. And telephone connections transmitted from the United States were simply prohibited. There was no getting around the distance of miles and the implacability of an embargo, the fate, it appeared, for countries unlucky enough to defeat the United States in war. For countries that lost, there would be aid and recon-struction—a Marshall Plan, perhaps. What I was fearing more and more was that, if the ordinary channels had become unavailable sources of information, a clear picture of that day in 1975 could not be made to emerge.

Still, I persisted. I glanced at my mother. "Were any of your letters returned because of a wrong address, maybe?" I asked. "He might have just moved."

"Nothing was returned by the post office," she finally answered. A moistness was beginning to collect in the corners of her eyes. "I really tried," she said with a look that seemed to beg for forgiveness.

And there it was, self-evident, a vulnerability that could almost break your heart. But for a moment, it induced in me a desire not to offer comfort, to deny what was, at that brief moment in time, wholly within my power to grant—a kind word or two. I could take this opportunity, I thought to myself, to remember all those moments, however minor, in which I had felt wronged by my mother. Instead I reached out and gave her palm a reassuring squeeze.

My concern, my desire to know, was failing us. Through my questions, I had managed to ensure that she would be reminded of and pained by the continuing absence of news.

"I'm sorry," I whispered. "I did try to find him for you," I confessed. It had been Bobbie's and my affair alone, but now our failed trip to the Canadian border seemed an ap-propriate subject to bring up. Now perhaps our attempt to make a family connection my grandfather called luminous motion could bring her comfort. "Bobbie and I drove, tried to drive to Canada to call Baba Quan," I said with pride.

My mother's face changed color. I could almost see an arrow of sweat work its way down the slope of her nose. "Why?" she asked in a hard-edged voice. "Why?"

After an awkward pause, my mother sighed and placed her hand on my back. "Why take that long trip to Canada? You and Bobbie driving alone. Anything could have happened."

"I wanted to be able to deliver the fact that grandfather was still alive and well to you. I wanted to bring the news that I had spoken with him straight to your hospital bed," I said, startled by the tone of her voice. Her suspicion did not make sense, and in fact struck me as odd.

She stared at me, transfixed. She could have reached over and pressed me to her flesh, or she could have decided to fill the moment with some other equally tender gesture, and we could have easily commenced a more happy conversation about a less complex subject. In a voice perhaps more stern than she meant it to be, she asked, plainly, "And did you talk to him? Was he at the number you called? What number did you call?"

I shook my head. "No," I said. "We didn't make it all the way up to Canada. We . . ."

My mother gave a quick lightning bug of a smile. I might have just imparted to her a bit of good news which somehow had a reassuring effect. I looked at her questioningly, and we both remained in the moment's silence for a palpable and protracted second.

I put the voice of the solicitous child away. "Ma? I don't understand. If we could have, wouldn't you have wanted us to make the phone call? Ma?" I insisted.

For a moment, I imagined the best possible to the worst

possible reply. He's not reachable by phone, he's probably missing, he's made a disappearance into the vast burial grounds of Vietnam and his grave is untended, he's angry and would rather not hear from us ever again. I could have supplied her with those plausible answers. But my mother continued to float in the quiet hum of her own breathing, and I could have left her in the privacy of her own submerged storm. I weighed my options; I was willing to push it to the limit and court her exasperation.

"Someone must know what's become of him," I persisted. This was the time to suggest my plan of action. "Uncle Michael might help us if you asked him." Someone who had once saved an American Special Forces unit may be given some special treatment. With my mother's voice added, I could revisit it with Uncle Michael.

I could feel the blood pump through her chest. I had finally touched a nerve. My mother's face shifted.

"There are ways, still, I think, of getting those with American connections out. Should I call Uncle Michael?" I was in the realm of the wild and fantastic, but for the sake of my grandfather, for the sake of my mother, it felt right to explore even the flimsiest improbability.

"He doesn't have any American connections," my mother declared with finality. The smile on her face revealed a saucily dismissive flash of teeth.

"Not officially, but he helped save an American unit, didn't he?"

I noticed my mother's bony wrists. I noticed the delicate rim of black around her eyes. I noticed the vacant stare that shot through me to focus on some undiscernible spot in the background.

"What did Michael tell you?" she finally asked.

"He told me about his time in the delta. He was stationed near Ba Xuyen—well, you know this—so there were stories he could recount about the place. You know the story about what happened to him by the monkey bridge."

Her face slammed shut. There was no swell of emotion, no tangible reaction I could hold. She was no longer resisting with an opposing force, but leaving me with a soft boneless-ness that could not be grasped. Ancient warriors and Taoist philosophers called it the softness of water, and its formless quality could confound even advanced electromechanical technologies.

"I know the story about what happened by the monkey bridge," she agreed mildly.

"So you know how grandfather was honored with a medal of appreciation," I continued. "Two medals."

She nodded, drawing a rasp of breath as she continued to put forth an unguessable face for my sake. "That was an extraordinary feat of bravery. Your grandfather risked his own life to save Michael. He had a rare sense of personal loyalty."

"Should I call Uncle Michael" I asked.

"You should call him," she echoed. "You should call him. Perhaps he'll be able to discover what's happened to your grandfather and help us do something about it," she con-ceded with affable complaisance. I was too surprised to resist. What else could I urge upon her when she had already agreed to everything I suggested? And yet I felt a hollowness cling inside the space between my bones. I forced myself to look tender, because I could easily have screamed. I could easily have scratched someone's—anyone's—patch of flesh until skin could be broken. And as I put my mother to bed, I could feel a swell of uneasiness make its way noiselessly through the length of my body.

I slipped into bed and pressed my ear against the soft plaster wall that divided mine from my mother's bedroom. The quietness sealed inside her room emanated as an invisible but pervasive hush. As I lay in bed, I actually missed the overt battles of other people's families, the evident, articulated frustrations of the parent and the child. I would have gladly traded my mother's subtlety for voracious rage. Indeed, tonight I would have gladly traded my mother for anyone else's altogether. I turned toward the window and pushed it wide open. It was all I could manage. The rush of night air might do me some good. I thought of tapping on my mother's door. I thought of slipping into bed with her, of squeezing myself between the embrace of her arms and demanding that she become more capable of direct and frank displays of emotion.

Of course I did nothing. Perhaps, in our eager search for shelter and love, we children invest our faith too elaborately in parents who can never humanly meet our exorbitant expectations. Perhaps the sheer distance between what we want of our parents and what we can actually receive can never be truly reconcilable.

After seventeen years with my mother, I was still not accustomed to the peculiar way she revealed her world to me, an austere landscape released the way a Chinese handheld scroll was meant to be unveiled, vertically downward, piece by piece, section by section. It was not the sort of canvas that could be taken in in one easy swoop, and I was beginning to suspect I had been able to see only one corner of a drawing she had yet to unroll.

My own crying woke me one night. Swift, muffled sobs that kept me pinned to the bed and left a hollow burning sensation in the chest, like a fire in the belly of the earth, dead but still hot with infernal ashes and cinders. I lay perfectly still, calmly, calmly reaching for the glass of water by the bedside. One wrong move, one minor mistake, and the world, unhinged, could explode like a fantasy coddled much too long. It was a matter of keeping everything under control. I pressed my hands against both sides of my head, stilling the raw nerves, containing the network of mismatched wires inside. My forehead, clammy and cold, stuck to my fingers like blood. There was only quiet, three-o'clock-in-the-morning quiet, except for the shuffling of my mother's pen sputtering across a cemetery of white pages next door.

It was near the end of April and my mother and I were both occupying a common space, the space that exists during an exact moment in time before ice melts or water freezes. We were both in the space where all things linger, only to turn unpredictably with the exquisite swiftness of a hard flower. We all enter this space when we wait—for motionless shadows to shift with a moment's notice, and hopes to become possibilities. I was waiting for an answer from Mount Holyoke, and my mother, along with the rest of Little Saigon, was waiting for a change in the political fortunes of Vietnam's Communist Party.

I walked the stretch of road from our apartment to the Mekong Grocery. Thawed, the air felt zingy and raw, a twist of lemon on a dry tongue. Spring started officially in March, but really we were still in that dead space between the end of winter and the beginning of spring, where everything seemed to be put on hold. The sun was bright yellow, but the air was still deceptively cold, and I had to remind myself to bring a jacket for my mother just in case.

I pushed open the door and stepped into a transfigured space, distinctly foreign to the senses, where shadows took on different forms and cast silhouettes in an alien way. Here, inside the Mekong Grocery, three different radios tuned to three different stations—the Voice of America, the BBC, and a French station—were being monitored simultaneously. The urgency of recent events had successfully displaced the more conventional routines of selling and buying.

"Where have the Chinese tanks gone?" was the question being asked. In addition to the daily little worries, these were the sweeping imponderables that held their attention. War, rearranged borders, a country assembled and disassembled by forces beyond their control. Here was the ironic otherness that existed in the Little Saigon community. When did our nationalist proclivities get traded for brute anticommunism? People were listening to the latest news about a border skirmish that had begun in February between Hanoi and Beijing. Although there was little chance that it would become a full-scale struggle to end all struggles against communism, people were nonetheless hopeful.

They were, after all, in Northern Virginia's Little Saigon. A world in and of itself, a world that census takers had documented, one hundred thousand and growing. But it was also a world in which every shop was a shop specializing in the business not of numbers so much as of dreams. People here could touch you with their fertile hopes and great expectations, and in their midst you could easily succumb to the sheer seductive powers of nostalgia and single-minded conviction. Right around the corner was a brand-new tomorrow, people would promise, a glorious monument to a picture-perfect past uncomplicated and unimpaired by political realities. I didn't always mind the simplicity of their faith. It could at times be beautiful.

The Mekong Grocery was in a small shopping complex, sandwiched between a 7-Eleven and the Petit Saigon Restaurant. Along the wall in the back, pickle vats and ceramic elephants rested in crates. Finely sculpted and painted a glossy orange, the tusks and trunks jutted out like bright brass horns from the wooden bars. On a Formica table, papier-mâché boxes of ivory combs, tortoiseshell barrettes, embroidered handkerchiefs, and fat-Buddha jade statues waited to be sorted and classified.

All those articles were in a part of the store I wished I could explore. But my mother's spot was in the back back, a distant twenty or more feet diagonally across from the area warehousing the shop's more luxurious items. Because of the vegetable peels and water spills, her corner had had to be roped off after a thief fleeing the store made a wrong turn into the back area and slipped and fell on a carrot peel. The incident had been widely covered in all the Vietnamese newspapers, because the man had sued my mother's boss the following week for negligence.

The American Dream could be worked with ardent criminality. "THIEF Sues and Demands Money!!!" headlined the articles. "Thief" was the operative word. It remained a mystery to my mother, the obscure details of the American system that could catapult themselves into the Vietnamese mainstream to alter our lives. In her mind, it was simply inconceivable that a villager would engage in the unapologetically American mode of conflict resolution. And it was simply inconceivable that a legal system would tolerate and coddle the disreputable confessions of a thief and transform them into a true and actionable legal claim.

"What are you doing here?" my mother asked. "You didn't have to come all this way." She was bent over the sink, her S-shaped spine twisted like a crooked coastline. I felt a spate of feelings—guilt, pity, love—crowd inside my chest.

From a corner, Mrs. Bay nodded at me as if to say, "Good girl." I gave my mother a long hug and got right to work. My purpose in coming was to help my mother stock up for the weekend. I pried open several cartons of bean sprouts, basil, and lettuces and soaked them in a pail of water. Dirt and soil tend to hide under their multiple folds, and so each leaf of the Boston and red lettuce would have to be scrubbed individually. Under the fluorescent light, we took turns washing and packing. Basins and buckets were scattered on the floor next to boxes of plastic bags and rubber bands. Green and purple dotted the water, leaves bobbing like butterfly wings. After an hour, my hands turned limp, like free-swimming jellyfish puckered in little wrinkles and folds along the fingertips.

My mother hummed the first few notes of a French kindergarten song. *"Il était un petit navire, il était un petit navire, qui n'avait ja, ja, jamais navigué."* She rolled each syllable and stilled it momentarily in her throat. There was my nocturnal lullaby. I turned myself over to her voice; we stayed that way for several minutes, linked in prolonged silence by the familiarity of my childhood song.

"Are there sailors who have truly never ever sailed?" I used to ask her with the persistence of a sucking child. In our house in Saigon, my mother had finally been happy, I thought. She edited my father's papers and indexed his research notes. She kneaded noodles, spindly strands of pearls, out of fresh dough, and baked dumplings stuffed with shiitake mushrooms and cellophane noodles. We would give the food she prepared to soldiers in the streets—crab men, as they were called—with flesh-colored plastic that doubled as both fingers and toes. Among the many war-wounded of Saigon, wounds from a kitchen fire, a gloss of scar tissue my mother carried on her face, did not have the troubling quality it had somehow acquired in this country.

I couldn't begrudge my mother her wish to return to a more familiar home. Anyone who'd been through what she'd been through, an exile at the age of fifty-five, about to be utterly abandoned—at least in her mind abandoned—by her only child, was allowed to suffer moments of incomprehensible spells. What good could 4.0 and the English novel do for an exile parent who in all likelihood would much prefer a solid, reliable child with no ambition greater than the parent's own horizon? It was not as if I didn't or couldn't understand, but . . . I flashed her a showy, conspicuous smile. *"Il était un petit navire . . ."* I whispered, and her face registered delight. In my hand, my mother's palm felt clammy, the pulse on her wrist meek and unsteady. The last thing I wanted to do was betray.

I reached up to massage the sinews and tendons of her back. That had been one of our regular rituals in Saigon, when my mother, my father, and I sat in the square perimeter of electric light and turned ourselves over to Channel 11, American television transmitted by satellite to entertain American GIs. Even in the grainy gray of black and white, every vestige of Robert Conrad in *The Wild Wild West* held the promise of a more powerful and reckless rendition of life. I sipped drinks made from Uncle Michael's Kool-Aid mixes and waited for the clutching syncopated beat of the *Mission Impossible* theme song played against the close-up of a sizzling match. My parents and I watched until the very end, hanging on like a cat with claws until midnight, when the station shut down and our house collapsed soundlessly into the armpit darkness of another curfewed night.

"Someone's here for you, Mrs. Bay," a voice called from the front.

"Who is it?" she screamed back with a voice that skittered with enthusiasm.

"Your American GI friend, the one who buys fish sauce. He wants to talk to you."

"I'm coming," she hollered. And to us she said, "I'm going to bring him back here, all right?"

"Don't let him near my corner. I don't want him to slip and fall by his own mistake and then hit us with a lawsuit the next day," my mother warned.

"Bill? Bill is a good man," Mrs. Bay defended her old friend.

Bill, last name unknown, was a regular among a gaggle of other GI regulars at the grocery. I found this fact to be intriguing, his desire to undertake routine visits to an unglamorous warehouse that doubled as a grocery store. Bill did not subscribe to President Ford's proclamation that the end of the war "closes a chapter in the American experience." Years after his tours of duty, the debris of Vietnam remained. Bill continued to carry an underlayer of precautions mingled with cynicism that clung inside his pores. I could see how he would be prone to suspicion, but with Mrs. Bay he was willing to relinquish all his evasive instincts.

Today Bill came into the store to make an unexceptional purchase, two cans of condensed milk, and to search for the psychic compatibility he seemed to experience only with Mrs. Bay. Her large maternal frame put out a comforting mingle of kitchen scent, a dash of sea salt, a wink of sugar. She had the capacity to minister to his memories, and between them a tender space existed which allowed them to exchange confessions about the turbulence of daily life.

"How are you today, GI?" Mrs. Bay laughed as she and Bill made their way toward my mother and me. It was a name he had insisted upon, GI. The abbreviation stands for "galvanized iron" or "government issue," such as shoes, rations, and other items provided by a military-supply department.

Bill's face turned dim. "I have a funny story for you, Mrs. Bay," he said. "I pulled into a gas station this morning. I'm telling you. We have to do something about this Middle East oil business. The line was so long it stretched all the way down the road. So I thought to myself, all right, I'll just put it in park and try to relax until the line starts moving again."

Mrs. Bay nodded impatiently. "And then?"

"And then this guy tries to stick his big fat car right in front me. So I honked and honked, but he refused to budge. I got out, walked toward his car, leaned over, and just as I was about to tell him I didn't appreciate his cutting in the line, the guy saw my pea-sized insignia button that said 'Vietnam vet' on the rim of my shirt pocket and practically wet his pants." He smiled and glanced at all of us. "To tell you the truth, I'd forgotten the insignia was there, since I almost always wear that shirt with a jacket. For dramatic effect, as the guy backed up and tried to pull his car out, I narrowed my eyes and gave him a deadly stare. 'Next time you do that to me, I'm going to take out my shotgun and blow you to pieces,' " Bill said in a voice that suggested an imitation of psychotic derangement.

"But you look so crazy, GI, even I would think you have a shotgun," Mrs. Bay said teasingly. She reached over and pinched his cheeks. The American public indeed seemed quite willing to believe that men who returned from the original sin and primordial evil of Vietnam had a natural predisposition toward madness, and the assumption was natural enough to require no further exploration or investigation.

Mrs. Bay laughed. She sensed a continuing connection with the American soldiers who visited the store, for the simple reason that a common base, she believed, existed to connect us exiles, on one point, to these lost men, on another point of the American triangle. We were all trying to make our way from the bottom base toward the unreachable apex, and along the two equal sides of an isosceles triangle; the slope we would have to climb would be a difficult one. But she also genuinely liked him, I believed. Here, in this store, she could offer him momentary solace and protection. Here, in this store, he would bring his little piece of a big history with him, and even though it was not the same as ours, we were in fact parts of a shared experience. We were like two distinctly different shapes that would come together to form an amalgamation of common and at the same time competing truths.

Mrs. Bay rolled her eyes at Bill. "They're stupid. What can you do?" She shrugged and took a big gulp of a McDonald's chocolate shake. She had a tendency to project outward rather than absorb inward. Nothing would be allowed to fester inside her skin. The skill to propel and externalize was one I could say I truly envied.

"I suppose they no longer find this government issue to be of much use," he sighed.

Mrs. Bay shrugged, picking off a twig from his jacket collar. "Have you seen the Jane Fonda movie?" she asked.

"Don't get me started, Mrs. Bay. Don't get me started," Bill grumbled, his eyes wide and unblinking.

"She's a good actress. Why shouldn't she play any part she likes in a movie?" I interjected. It was supposed to be a small question about an ordinary movie, and I did not intend it to carry any hidden version of war. But I should have known that, where Jane Fonda and the war were concerned, there would be no intellectual remove. She seemed to be a perennial and inexhaustible point of focus in the Little Saigon community.

"She can play any part she wants. But why does Hanoi Jane have to be given the lead in a story about a vet's coming home?" Bill protested.

Although he was a frequent customer, I had no real relationship with him. "I only mean to say she's a good actress," I quickly retreated. The terrain they had mapped was one that required absolute unambivalence, and any exploration that demonstrated hesitation on my part would be considered hostile. I would have had to adopt the required posture of unambiguous indignation. "Maybe she's moving on completely to a nonpolitical life, a new moviemaking life," I said in a light, cordial tone.

"A double life, maybe," my mother added. "Like this?" she asked. It was all the opening she needed to work her new double-lifeline life into our conversation. "Come look, Bill," she urged, proffering him her arm. "I have a new lifeline," my mother repeated. She did, in fact, have a shadow of a line, running like a long, shallow arc, parallel to her lifeline.

Whether she had always had two, or whether one had only recently appeared, as she claimed, I didn't know. The additional lifeline was not deemed a cause for concern, although, more often than not, my mother had cursed the fact that she was still walking among the wreckage of multiple lives, as she called it. "A human being can undergo only so many changes and take in only so many experiences. My pores are full," she once said.

My mother, however, was taking this new lifeline as a sign of rebirth—not rebirth into the cycle of birth and rebirth the Buddhists pray to escape from, but true rebirth, nirvana itself.

"The new line also forks off from the old one," she emphasized. She looked at us and traced the curve with her finger. It seemed to flow south through her wrist toward her heart, like a tributary going back to its source.

"If I were a fortune-teller, I would say it means you're going off in a new direction," Bill noted with seriousness.

"A new business, yes?" Mrs. Bay laughed. "A new life as entrepreneurs?" Since their decision to use hui money to start a baking business, their favorite English word was "entrepreneur."

My mother gave Bill a flashy smile. Moments like these worried me. I looked at my mother and I saw that I was slightly afraid of her, her promises, her collapsed expectations, the unintegrated present and past she had forced together. I closed my eyes. If it happened to her, it might in fact happen to me too.

I did not want a strobe light shone on our lives to reveal that mine had been, like my mother's, an amalgamation of incompatible odds and ends. I had new grounds, already staked, that must be reoccupied. What my mother didn't know was this: all it took was one slip, one step backward across the boundary, and the entire apparatus of American normality could fall right out of sync. The luxury of seamless, unsuperstitious order, after all, did not come without a price.

All four of us stood together in a circle and watched a faint chiseled line run the full length of my mother's palm. The three of them made an unlikely but nice little congregation in their pool of common space, a coalescence of assorted shapes that fit snugly in their common contagion of nostalgia. I knew I had no choice but to simulate well-manneredness and join them. As my mother's eyes and mine met and locked for a brief moment, I was afraid I knew what she was thinking: among the four of us, it was not Bill, but I, who would be considered the outsider with inside information.

From my bedroom down the hall, I could hear the faint sound of an argument in the kitchen several rooms away. A few whispered words could be heard through the plaster walls, and I strained myself to make out as much as possible the focus of their disagreement. I could hear the underlined syllables in Mrs. Bay's sibilant whispers. "Your father," she emphasized. And "Mai." "Curious." "Just tell her."

I held my breath and hoped that their fight would escalate into an audible pitch. Although it quickly subsided, what I was able to catch was sufficient to arouse suspicion. For weeks, I had begun to suspect that the pieces were not adding up, that information was being withheld and much had been left unsaid. Bad news of some sort was being forgotten by my mother. There was something inconsistent about the story of my grandfather and his life, like an inexplicable blemish, a smudge of gray appearing on a vast and pristine horizon.

It was not a complete surprise, my realization. My mother's silence, the awkward attempts to sidestep, the continuing resistance to my suggestions that more be done to locate my grandfather. Perhaps he had indeed, as I feared and fantasized, died a violent death, his body slumped while a straight line of blood leaked from an unplugged hole in the brain and thieves rummaged his body for precious departure documents. Perhaps my mother had had the misfortune to witness it the day of their rendezvous and had had to leave him unattended. Perhaps she had been overcome by fear and had remained a safe distance away, unable or unwilling to risk her life to help her father fend off danger. The possibilities were unending. Uncle Michael had said almost as much.

"It won't do your mother any good to have this unknown past brought up in front of her," he had declared with unwavering certainty in our last telephone conversation. "To raise her hope unnecessarily would be unforgivable. Especially when there is not much hope at all that we can do anything from this end to get him out."

I could see him shaking his head with sadness. What danger could there be in trying? Yet even Uncle Michael insisted on offering me threats of harm instead of assurances that all would be well.

"But more than a million people have managed to leave already, so how hopeless can it be if so many have left?" I asked. I had read about the perilous journey in small boats across the South China Sea to Indonesia or the Philippines, or, alternatively, across the Gulf of Siam to Thailand or Malaysia. Both were equally dangerous. The estimate was that at least two hundred thousand had died at sea.

"And many don't make it," he replied, information I already knew. It was precisely his failure to sweep me into his normally generous circumference and the finality with which he had made his declarations about the supposed unknown that alerted me to the strangeness of it all.

When I suggested again that the government might have

tangible proof of my grandfather's valor, a file that could be used to prove the requisite American connection for departure from Vietnam and entry into the United States, the answer I received was "I doubt the government still has a file on him."

"The decision to take the steps necessary for escape has to come from those over there themselves, sweetheart. It's not something that one can say to someone over the phone, even if the telephone were a possibility—'Have you thought about leaving?' or 'Make your escape plans, will you?'—unless one wants to get those over there imprisoned or killed. It's not a matter of our buying them a plane ticket either, offer them an itinerary and say, 'Come over, we'll pick you up at the airport at noon.' The file, if it exists, may help once your grandfather is in Thailand or Malaysia, but it's irrelevant before that."

Perhaps he had not meant to be as implacable as he had sounded. Perhaps the phone lines had made his voice more harsh than he had intended. He could have been equally frustrated by our helplessness. He was correct, of course. Everything he said was the truth. My grandfather's fate rose and fell with political realities.

But still. "I would be surprised if someone like your grandfather would even want to leave his homeland," Uncle Michael continued. These were all imponderables, I had thought. Who could truly know the answer until the question was asked or the necessary action undertaken? "Your mother is recuperating so gorgeously. We don't need to solve his whereabouts or produce his voice to speed up her recovery," Uncle Michael had tried to reassure and convince. But this was a desire of the heart, no more, no less, I wanted to explain—not an argument about the causes and origins of my mother's illness, not a subject to which logic and symmetry could be applied.

After my conversation with Uncle Michael, I had gone to the library and flipped through the card index for books on Vietnam. They were classified under "Vietnam War" and were all written by Americans. Most had been written at the height of the American involvement in the war, when more than five hundred thousand American troops had been sent. It was only four years since the war ended, and there was nothing about Vietnam after April 30, 1975, and nothing about my current preoccupation, the boat people and their methods of escape from the new communist regime.

"Come taste some of this food for us," Mrs. Bay hollered from the kitchen. Her summons almost broke my heart. She seemed to have replicated perfectly the cadence of my mother's own voice. "Hurry, Mai," she called with more urgency.

My mother and Mrs. Bay had been fussing in the kitchen every evening this week to accommodate the ritual of feasting that continued to be held every weekend in our apartment.

"This looks wonderful," I told them. What were you arguing about? I wanted to ask.

The weekend feasts hosted at our apartment were events I looked forward to with real enthusiasm; I liked to watch Mrs. Bay and a few Cao Dai women prepare the meals while I did my homework. From their long elaborate periods in front of the stove, we would have pork filet stewed in a carbonated coconut juice that came in a can, or stir-fried watercress with hazelnut. For dessert, we would have an innovative version of mango ice cream, which Mrs. Bay made by scraping the sweet golden flesh of a ripe mango into a blended mix of milk, cream, yellow rock sugar, and vanilla ice.

But nothing I had witnessed so far could prepare me for the extravagance of this particular culinary event. Something new was being prepared every day, and our kitchen was becoming a place of limitless possibilities. Lists of items to be purchased, methodically enumerated, appeared on our refrigerator door. Swallows' nests were softened in pots of warm water. Marinated meat sizzled in a frying pan. Slabs of dough lay covered under a gauzy fabric, waiting to be pummeled and mauled by Mrs. Bay. And even though I had no role to play in my mother's elaborate preparations, I was part of something immaculate and sweet, a domestic order that comforted and consoled. From our sparse apartment, a daily warmth could be made to exist. My mother hinted, when asked about the special occasion, that she might invite our non-Vietnamese neighbors, Bill and Mrs. Bay's other American vet friends, and even the Catholic nuns who had sponsored us in 1975. It would be a remarkable party, and already our apartment was acquiring a quality of exaggerated and unrestrained festivity. I could tell. The air itself was imbued with the glory of anticipation.

On the counter were trays of pigs' feet and tripe stew and an assortment of less subversive dishes. Diced lemon-grass chicken in a stew of fresh coconut juice, beef in a spicy broth of hot pepper and cilantro, and a large pot of sweet-and-sour fish soup flavored with the tanginess of ripe tamarind occupied all four burners of the stove. There my mother could still produce an exquisite meal devoted to the pleasure of the palate. A tender slice of sweet memory. We could have been in our ordinary Saigon kitchen, where my mother had flipped eggs and rolled half-moons of croissants stuffed with Meunier chocolate, where sticky rice with steamed peanuts and roast-pork buns were routinely removed from a hot steaming oven.

We could have been in our brick courtyard in Saigon some time before April 30, 1975, and I could have been surrounded by an intact family: my mother, my father, and my grandfather, on one of his rare visits to the capital city to celebrate the fifteenth day of the seventh lunar month, when the heavenly gates are unbolted and spirits descend the earth to be commemorated. Inside the meshed steel fence that surrounded our house, I, along with school friends and neighbors' children my parents had invited, waited for one of our favorite annual rituals. As the three adults made their way upstairs and onto the second-floor terrace, we children labored below. Against a lavender mist, our wrought-iron balcony, with its intricate curlicues, floated weightlessly, like an aerial chariot, in the sky. We jostled for the perfect position and waited for the adults to perform.

As they tossed "spirit money" from above, a scattering here, a scattering there, we scampered across the courtyard and chased after the silvery medallions. Real currency was used for the evening's ritual. We would do it more by feel than by sight: rush headlong into the voluptuous tumble and chaos of coins dropped by the fistful. No one was thrifty on a festival night; extravagance was called for. For that one night in the lunar calendar when the moon was at its biggest, it was assumed that we children were manifestations of our ancestors' spirits. We would be catered to, honored. Grace would be raucously bestowed from above. I could feel it along my spine. I was certain that the moon, vertiginous and round, shone for us. I believed that money could be snapped from a shirtsleeve. We were those fortunate spirits whose living family members continued to await us. Our transition to the other world continued to be marked and remembered.

The moon hung like a silver coin, a white molten medallion that watched with exaggerated abandon from the sky's height.

When it was all over and we children turned our pockets inside out and shook our collection cans to hear the profligate sound of coin against metal, a true feast would begin. My father sliced open a square of sticky rice wrapped in banana leaves. A thin line of steam escaped from the cut. My grandfather nodded approvingly, placed three cups of tea in front of my grandmother's photograph, and sat cross-legged, in several minutes of silence, among trays of grilled shrimp wrapped around sugar cane and fish stewed in clay pots. This, after all, was the true reason for the celebration: commemorating the luminous link that binds the dead and the living. My mother lifted a square of skin from a red, roasted pig whose head and tail spanned the full length of a hot log. Roasted to a perfect crispness, the skin crunched to the touch of a knife but melted in the mouth.

My mother, after all, had once been a person fundamentally devoted to the celebration of food and the nourishment of family. Her cooking was an extension of our days, and significant events in our lives were marked by the feasts she concocted. I could tell the seasons of the year from her food: three bowls of plain white rice, three cups of tea, a hard-boiled egg. Simple food even I could have prepared, but it was this meticulous arrangement, with the rice bowls here, the teacups there, exactly where they should be, that I always remembered. It was what my mother had placed on the family altar when my father died.

There was the altar, with its gilded borders and red sheen that absorbed the glazed white bowls and cups. There was the simplicity, death and its suggestion of permanence, that was almost too severe and stark for human eyes. I could feel it even now, not as a memory to be pulled by the thread from a past into the present, but as a palpable surge, an immediate aliveness that completely defined the moment.

Around us, an immaculate whiteness had been erected. My father's body, in a mahogany casket, was covered in a white shroud, his face hidden behind a white silk square. A white fabric twisted into human form lay by his side to receive the soul. He had somehow become separate, beyond our reach.

The code of conduct for the day's ceremony had been laid down in books my mother seemed to know well. My mother dressed me in a funeral garb of white gauze. We were part of a ritualistic column of swaying white. The color of mourning floated in the haze of the morning sun. A mere seventy air-miles or so away, a major battle was being conducted in the province of Phuoc Long. Here we were, less than six months before Saigon's collapse. South Vietnam was sailing into approaching darkness, its capillaries bleeding a slow red. We could hear the steel-treaded roar of the North's multiple infantry divisions, its overwhelming artillery and tank-supported assaults. Out of the more than five thousand soldiers from the South who had taken part in the battle, fewer than nine hundred would survive. We could hear the eventual loss of an entire province and the eerie silence, the absence of reaction this loss had provoked, from the Americans. The United States had pledged it would react vigorously to a violation of the 1973 Paris Peace Accords, and the North Vietnamese Army assault units that attacked the province had suddenly come to a temporary halt, to gauge U.S. reaction.

That morning, as the funeral procession walked toward the cemetery, it was the ether of silence and an absolute expanse of absence that we heard and felt. Before me, a two-meter-high hearse painted in a patina of red carried the casket, and around us, musicians sounded a tune of extravagant sorrow. I could hear the minor chords. I could see the mouthful of air pulled into the brass trumpets and released as a gelid moan that meandered and froze in the feverish heat. Despite the grieving chants and prayers of monks and the lament of a lone harmonica, the predominant sound lodged in my chest was the sound of turbulent silence, the silence of Phuoc Long Province and the silence in my own body.

As our procession came to a sudden halt at the cemetery, by my father's freshly dug grave, I could see a collection of straw figures, a bamboo house, and votive paper money folded in sheets of silver and gold. We would burn them and my father would have company, shelter, and wealth. My mother had consulted a geomancer, and, based on his astrological calculations, a precise plan had been drawn up. My father would have this particular plot; his grave would be dug just so; his casket would be laid in this exact direction. A meticulous adherence to the plan would ensure that my father would be put to rest in the propitious center of a dragon's wide-open mouth.

Through the incensed smoke of burning papers, my mother whispered in my ear, "Our mourning will last for three years. For three years, we will light incense every day and a candle will be lit at every meal." As my mother and I threw several handfuls of dirt into the grave, plates of sticky rice steamed in banana leaves, grilled shrimp, and fish stewed in clay pots waited for my father. But my mourning for him promised to be everlasting. To this day, I continued to follow the route of his hearse into a withdrawing space beyond this earth.

Here was my mother again, recuperating from a head wound and a stroke, standing erect in the kitchen in our apartment, impersonating an old abandoned self as Mrs. Bay stood by her side. Our kitchen submitted quite amenably to their demands. Huge hunks of dough humbled into delicate star-shaped dumplings, a complication of intestines and goose liver baked into precise loaves of pâté, four distinct types of dessert—hand-whipped chocolate mousse laced with Chantilly cream, caramel custard inspired by my mother's Providence School days, lotus-seed pudding in a rock-sugar concoction, and the most delicate dish of all, a porridge of rare swallows' nests. In less complicated days years ago, nests spun from regurgitated bird saliva would sound no more, no less perverse than snails simmered in butter and garlic sauce.

I stood in front of the window and took in the glare and shimmer of the afternoon sun. I'd suddenly become a child whose mother cooked. There is no denying the beauty of new dreams.

Over the rustling faucet and the constant hum of the fluorescent light above the stove, I could hear Mrs. Bay and my mother's laughter flow like a flute through the rooms of our apartment. My mother's cure-all mixture of tiger balm, orange peel, and chopped lemon grass, boiled in a pot to steam open the pores and rid the body of toxins, had settled under the plaster, hugging every curve of the apartment with proprietary ease. My mother called it her special formula for decongesting the body, and the mind. Weeks after she first turned our kitchen into a steam bath, I could still feel the aftershock of the concoction, a sharp smarting sting like Japanese horseradish stuffed in my nose.

Mrs. Bay was speaking loudly, flailing her arms in wild gestures. She was all energy again today—molecules colliding in a superexcited state against my mother's more cautious deliberations.

"How many times do you want me to say I was wrong? I've said it multiple times. I was wrong and you were right. And I'm glad I listened to you and did not allow that woman into our hui," Mrs. Bay said with feigned humility. And to me, she whispered in a conspiratorial voice, "She can be a true tyrant when she's right, your mother." It appeared that my mother's suspicions had proved to be well-founded. According to the Vietnamese papers, one of Mrs. Bay's hui candidates had a record of "hui-breaking" in Orange County, California, where she had been charged by the authorities with multiple counts of fraud.

I ran my hand over the huge jars lined up like oxygen tanks on the kitchen counters against the walls. They were my mother's reserve of security and composure, these containers in which she marinated her mustard greens and daikons in a mixture of ginger-and-chili pickling liquid. In other jars my mother had stacked in the cabinets, small pearl onions, hot red peppers, and sprigs of cilantro suggestive of her herb garden in Saigon gathered in miniature clusters.

Instead of the baking business, which, according to my mother's and Mrs. Bay's calculations, might be more costly than they could at present afford, they had decided on a simpler, more even-tempered venture—supplying pickled vegetables to restaurants like Petit Saigon and stores like the Mekong Grocery, which lined the length of Wilson Boulevard, the main thoroughfare in the heart of Little Saigon. The right, predictable mix of anise and cinnamon in a bowl of Hanoi beef-noodle soup, the precise balance between the sweet and the sour in a tamarind-based broth, the authentic blend of spices and vinegar to ensure that the cabbage and carrot retain a crisp texture—those were attachments Little Saigon considered most profound. Anyone with the right know-how and patience could massage the bittersweetness of nostalgia into hard cash.

"We have enough stocked up to start a business tomorrow if we want," my mother conceded. She was in an easy, buoyant mood, and everything was possible tonight.

Mrs. Bay nodded. Already, I could see her bare-armed, hand on hip, directing the show. She had canvassed the A & P's frozen-food section, with cassavas and pigs' ears factory-sealed in airtight, ziplocked packages, which seemed to be a big sell to Old World exiles suddenly educated in the modern, pristine language of the FDA. I was happy to see that she appeared to be conscious of the inevitability of licenses, permits, FDA inspections, and other bureaucratic complications of business American-style.

Other exiles had not been as well versed in the demands imposed on a small business. Most seemed to believe that anyone could peddle exotic wares by setting up a business at any street corner by the mere act of staking out a patch of cement. A year ago, one of the Cao Dai women had decided to convert her apartment into a café by planting a picnic table in the living room and serving her specialties to friends, who were willing to pay twice what a restaurant charged for her unmatched sugarcane shrimp and Hue noodle soup laced with tomato paste and hot red peppers. By word of mouth, it quickly became a popular place for fast home-cooked food for American-busy exiles—that is, until it was closed by a health inspector, who promptly fined her for operating a food business out of her home without a license.

Ours would be a different fate. Mrs. Bay had enlisted the help of her GI friend. Bill would do the necessary research, navigate the multiple agencies, take care of the American end of the business. My mother and Mrs. Bay would do what they did best. Already, our apartment had been scoured clean—"in case the health inspectors drop by without warning," my mother had explained. Ours was becoming a flawless space in which every object had its rightful place. During the past two weeks alone, she had embarked on a cleaning frenzy that rivaled the cleaning ritual of Tet itself, when ushering in the new year meant paying past debts, shedding the old, and bringing in the new. The space behind and under the couch was swept and mopped. Floor moldings and windowsills were dusted and wiped. Grime hardened around the stove's edges was scraped off with a knife. Even a new ao dai had been ordered for this particular weekend event. There was a new gleam and glitter to our lives, and the sight of our apartment could give one the sense that order, not randomness, was the fundamental state of nature.

The ritual of food, the virtue of a clean beginning. I stood over the sink, listening to the rasp of Mrs. Bay's and my mother's voices, steady sounds of people who belonged one to the other—and I suddenly feared at that moment the simple loneliness that seemed to pervade my life. I was on the verge of getting what I wanted, a college existence away from home. But here, right here, at this moment, was what

I had suspected all along. Unlike my mother and Mrs. Bay, whose familiarity with one another predated their American connections, I had no emotional attachments that carried the length and depth of time and space. I would continue to go through life looking for goals to be met, but would I fail to make an essential human connection that would truly sustain?

And for a moment, as my mother and Mrs. Bay laughed in unison, I stood there in my separate space of remove and detachment and pondered other people's lives. I wondered if they too experienced the panic of insecurity or the occasional moments of doubt about whether or not they had in fact overstretched their capacity to achieve. I wondered if other people too could find themselves in the tangles of lives inclined to deliberations of the sort that asked more questions than they could answer. And I wondered if I too would have to have all of that as well.

Dear Mai, my daughter:

As I sit in bed writing to you, the wind is blowing furiously outside, and the rain that has been beating against our windowpanes reminds me of the monsoon that sweeps across the flat rice fields of Ba Xuyen. Of course, Ba Xuyen monsoons have a terminal quality that spring showers in this country lack, but in my imagination, the full force of the monsoon is already upon us, with broad sheets of water that descend from the sky, scour the earth, and eviscerate old residues.

By the time you read this, you will have discovered the truth about your mother's life. You will have discovered that, like the monsoon that brushes through last season's fields and obliterates the landscape beneath a sea of foam, I too have tried to extinguish the imprints of my life and create alternate versions that suit my imagination and heal my soul. The new world that I tried to create is the world I left in a drawer for you to find, the world I wished I could have handed to you as the unhidden truth of a mother's life. I wish I had that legacy to turn over to you, but the history that has melted into the very walls of our veins is a long history filled with the disappointments of two full generations before.

How could I have told you that Baba Quan, the man I call Father, is a Vietcong from whom I am still trying to escape? How could I have revealed his true identity, when the world of Little Saigon is a world inclined toward the passion and fury of anti-Vietcong sentiments? And so how could you have known that there had been no rendezvous by a fenced-in park, no car that would have scooped him up to deliver us to an American plane? While you imagined your grandfather as a phantom figure lingering in the shadows of a black statue, waiting to escape from a country on the verge of collapse, he was in fact part of a conquering army whose tanks blasted through the barricades and stormed down Saigon's boulevards with predatory fury on April 30, 1975. The thunder and rumble of that tank remain with me to this day.

As I sit here and look at your picture on my night table—the only baby picture of you that I was able to take with me to America—I can almost feel your baby flesh and touch its softness with my hand. There are so few words I could have said while I was still alive that could have explained my heart to you. Though I have often thought of revealing that hidden world for you, I also wanted to protect you from the phantoms and apparitions that come with it. In the end, my conflicting desires have left you with an invisible silence that slides like a soft whisper beneath the double shadows of our lives. As often as I tried to touch you, as often as my heart collapsed whenever I failed to reach you, I also fretted each time I thought of telling you the truth. And I knew I couldn't do it. How could I when I had spent most of my life shielding you from it, from the smoldering ashes of prior generations? How could I when the false lives I had summoned and conjured were finally beginning to acquire a weight that could convince me that they were, imagination and all, mine to hold?

On those long nights when I lie awake, I think about you as I contemplate our fate, my fate that I fear can become yours, and I wonder how I can save you from this terrible truth—the long, deep line of karma carved by a world which precedes you—the truth of sin, illegitimacy, and murder. I have sometimes felt your distance, your discomfort with our lives in Virginia. And although it pains me to feel your withdrawal, it also gives me a strange sense of faith, the faith that the distance slowly edging its way between us might help separate you from the fate of our family and in the process allow you to recede from the shadows of our family's karma. The silence I feigned does not mean you are not in my thoughts. What worries me perpetually is how to best love and protect you from the karma that divides and subdivides like a renegade cell in the malignant darkness of our lives. What I think about incessantly is how to shine a torch of hope through the turbulence that has settled like dust in our lives.

What do you know about your mother, Mai, about the emptiness that has occupied my heart like a persistent squatter hovering in the brooding silence of our lives? When did it all begin—this vision of a thousand red spiders and giant rats chewing tin cans and crawling rhinoceros beetles each as big as a black fist, pounding, pounding, pounding every side of my head like a sledgehammer striking into a coconut shell?

In the lives I constructed for you, Baba Quan was a devoted husband, a father dedicated to an uncomplicated life among the green terraced fields and fresh plowed earth of Ba Xuyen, a farmer who tilled the land with patience and dignity. That was the nature of my longing, and so he was all that and more in my fictional re-imaginings. But the truth was, beneath the seemingly harmonious exterior of a man who tends the burial grounds and sweeps the village pagoda, my father, your grandfather, is also a husband fully capable of asking his wife to prostitute herself to a rich landlord known in the Mekong Delta as Uncle Khan and, in the process, set in motion a sequence of events that continues to loom large in my heart today.

For years, behind the bamboo thickets and hedges that insulated our village from the world beyond, under the seemingly imperturbable tranquillity of country life marching a green straight line across the fields, your grandmother and Baba Quan concealed a secret that I discovered only by accident on the day of my wedding. Plagued by drought and flood, they had had difficulty paying Uncle Khan his share of the family's harvests. After four years of failed crops, the plot of earth they leased, a vacant field of hard brown earth, was slipping irrevocably beyond their grasp.

While your grandmother watched the barren land recede into the bones of the earth, Baba Quan sank into the sourness of despair and sought solace in the pungent heat of hard liquor. While your grandmother practiced a mating dance to appease and seduce the landlord, Baba Quan began to nurture a murderous rage, which he continued to harbor silently year after year, setting in motion a terrible karma that I am still trying to shield you from today.

On nights when I made my way across the floorboards of the bedroom into the bathroom, where I spent the night hugging the toilet bowl, I would have to ask myself this one question: how had it come to this? How did a girl born with a set of long, generous ears end up the way I've ended up: an old woman with a napalmed face and a sin as great as the act of creation? How did this woman end up with all the signs of a ravaged battlefield on her face, a face of war I had to explain to you, my own daughter, as the face of a random accident as innocuous as a kitchen fire?

I would have to go back to the time when it all began, at the moment when I was first conceived, when your grandparents passed their sin down to me through their blood and bone, tissue and flesh. I was conceived, not on a plywood bed on the dirt floor of our two-room scrapwood house, but instead under the plush French-lace bedspread of Uncle Khan's mahogany bed in the middle of an opulent bedroom I would later visit as the adopted daughter of the richest landlord in town. Not that I knew any of this. I grew up believing that Baba Quan was my father. I grew up learning to live with his bouts of depression, his unuprootable attachment to alcohol. I used to watch your grandmother pry the empty bottles from the knots in his twisted sheets while he breathed noisily in a corner, his body coiled in a tight fetal position, soaked in a sheen of sweat.

In the morning, when the roosters shrieked their wake-up call and your grandmother and I and every other villager headed to the rice field along with the yellow wasps and the black mosquitoes that had nested all night in the swamp grass behind our house, Baba Quan would still be slumped over in bed, unbudgeable as a sack of rice. "Your father has not been feeling well," your grandmother would sigh as she placed a cool towel on his forehead. Successful farming requires equilibrium between sun and rain, drought and flood. Rainy days could mean exposed roots, soggy fields, or plows that drowned in the mud and muck. Dry days could mean lower water levels, parched fields, and brittle roots that you could snap with a twist of the thumb and finger. Baba Quan, especially in the later years, could barely muster the exacting patience that is demanded of a Ba Xuyen farmer. Year after year, fortune, for us and for others in Ba Xuyen, lay unmoving and flat, its face ground against the hard land.

Your grandmother and I would do most of the work in the morning, and we would see him only in the late afternoon, after the hard midday sun had retreated behind the coconut groves, by the rice banks, where he would display a collection of unicorns and dragons sawed from raw wood and chiseled into intricate carvings of good fortune—majestic animals with wide-open mouths, exaggerated fangs jutting from thick red lips, all-powerful charms on constant guard, he said, against evildoers: trespassers and spirits jealous of our tiny one-hectare holding of land.

I suppose there might have been rumors. Of course, nothing wild or extravagant would have survived Uncle Khan's wrath. But later on, when I discovered the truth, it was as stark and irreducible as the numbers in the book of debts hidden in Uncle Khan's wine cellar, a book as thick as the village records of births and deaths. I knew people must have wondered and I knew they must have known. The mere fact that a landlord like Uncle Khan would have paid any attention to my family at all, the mere fact that I was put through the most expensive French Catholic school and that an entire room was redecorated in his villa as a bedroom for me, complete with Marie Antoinette chairs and wall-to-wall shelves of leather-bound books and porcelain dolls, that alone would have been enough for people to believe that ours was not a relationship of such random serendipity as a mere dream about a dragon boat and a wise old man.

On my wedding day, to escape the pounding heat, I wandered down the staircase into Uncle Khan's wine cellar. I wanted a moment of solitude, and the stone walls held a coolness that provided relief from the terrible stinging heat above. There, in the book of debts, as it was called on the cover, I discovered the truth about my life, hidden in a three-legged caldron decorated with a monster mask in the front and an etching of two dragons facing each other in profile in the back. From beginning to end, the book contained lists of names and dates that went as far back as twenty to thirty years. Uncle Khan was a landlord with a relentless passion for raw, hard numbers. Like rent paid to other landlords in the area, the rent paid to Uncle Khan consisted of half a tenant's rice crops, several days of free labor each month, routine offerings of the firstborn goose or the first harvest of fish from a tenant's fish pond. But unlike other landlords, he had little patience for and little faith in second chances.

Some of the names I recognized as our neighbors. Mrs. Bay's parents had been among the very first group evicted. All had been crossed off by a line of red ink drawn ruler-straight across the page. In the columns set next to their names were multidigit numbers recording debts still outstanding and finally, in the last column of the same line, the verdict: eviction. Everyone had been evicted, except your grandmother and Baba Quan. All became landless laborers with one stroke of the pen, except your grandmother and Baba Quan.

I stood in the dark, breathing, the veins along my neck thumping their hard, quick beats. I could feel the suspense intensely, heavy and full like a wet rag on a warm, humid day. As I suspected, this extraordinary goodwill only began one year after the year of my birth, the year your grandmother and Baba Quan ceased being mere tenants with rows of black digits by their names. Suddenly, the fact of your grandmother's sacrifice revealed itself as I stood in the cellar with the book of debt before me. That was how your grandmother and Baba Quan had managed to transform themselves into people who had given the landlord what his wife couldn't give him, a child. That was why a landlord like Uncle Khan made offerings of roast ducks and steamed rice to one of his poorest tenants. Baba Quan and Mama Tuyet had acquired a sudden shift in status, an unexplainable promotion that could be explained only by the illegitimacy of my birth.

It wasn't until years later, when we moved from the village, from its endless rice fields and the familiar burial ground we all took turns tending, that your grandmother confided the whole story to me. By then, our lives had irrevocably changed. Once we relinquished the village earth from the tips of our fingers and felt its absence as we crossed the village border into an exterior world none of us could comprehend, we became, in a palpable way, a people who were neither alive nor dead. Your grandmother believed we had indeed lost our souls. She was lying in a bed that was not hers, a few days before her death, in a village that was not a village at all but a concrete-cement lot called a "strategic hamlet" constructed to protect us from the hazards of war. In that unreal village, in which delta residents had been transported to keep us away from both the nightly terrors and the recruiting sessions of the Vietcong as well as the free-fire zones and the search-and-destroy missions of the Americans, in that strategic hamlet, your grandmother began to peel away the layers that had accumulated in our lives. There, my own history cracked wide open. There, I saw my life and the lives of your grandparents rush past me in hard, backward sequence.

"You do what is necessary to save your family," your grandmother explained, her thin body floating inside the brown cotton pajamas. Another failed crop, she explained, another month of sucking on rock sugar for breakfast, lunch, and dinner, another year of slaving on other people's rubber and coffee plantations, and she believed Baba Quan would have died. It was Baba Quan who first came up with the idea, although your grandmother hastened to add that it almost killed him even to have to suggest such a deed.

And so that would be the surprise of her life. Named for snow although she had been born in the humid tropics, your grandmother had expected surprise of an infinitely different kind. "I became a concubine instead," she whispered sorrowfully. And that of course was the beginning of the far-flung web that I'm still caught in today. That was the beginning of Baba Quan's passion. It had always been about possession all along, not the land but his wife and his daughter and, later on, you, the darling grandchild. The thought of reclaiming what had been wrongfully wrested from him began to sough through every fevered fiber of his being. Even my mother became a little afraid of him then, of this inexhaustible passion that he managed to hide behind the cold, calculating doctrine of class warfare between landlord and peasant. Although the history of Ba Xuyen, you see, was about sweeping, generational wealth, unanswered passions, coveting but never owning, Baba Quan's desires were wholly personal ones, and the world, for him, narrowed and converged into the one dark shaft of revenge.

How did your grandmother end up on a deathbed in a strategic hamlet of corrugated tin, black asphalt, and cement blocks so far from the luminous motion of our ancestral land? It happened one year after you were born.

After five miscarriages, I was able to give birth, finally, to a healthy baby girl. Your father, who only visited three or five times a year for a few days at a time, came back from Saigon, where he had been acquiring an armload of advanced degrees in French political philosophy. I had learned not to hope and not to mind. I had your father's parents to take care of, I had the store to tend to, I had my own mother and Baba Quan to visit at the end of every week, which pleased me because it gave me a chance to return to my village and the rice fields and the river of my birth.

By the time you were born, we had lived through years of suffering from waves of local bandits and Japanese occupation and famines so terrible that we had to storm a number of Japanese granaries to recapture grain the Japanese had made us store for their troops in case of an Allied landing. And when the war was over, we had all thought: Finally, peace at last. But the French came back and wanted to reestablish their Indochinese empire, and the Vietminh and other groups opposed them, and we never had peace. Saigon after the war was even worse off than the Mekong Delta, and I had to worry about your father, caught in a city everyone was fighting over—French paratroopers and Foreign Legionnaires, Vietminh, Cao Dai, Hoa Hao, Trotskyites—French flag, then Vietminh flag alternately hoisted, then pulled down, then hoisted from rooftops again, with strike after strike called by nationalists emulating Gandhi's fight only a few countries away.

Saigon itself, we heard, was paralyzed, everything shut down, electricity, water, trams, and rickshaws. Even the powerful French residents had to shut themselves in the old Continental Palace Hotel to hide from the gunfire and mortar attacks unleashed by the Vietminh and other noncommunist nationalist forces. By the time the French lost at Dien Bien Phu, their troops and the Vietminh had devastated almost every city and even parts of the Mekong Delta, where we were constantly harassed, our villages burned, our bridges destroyed, our markets pillaged.

And so it was natural that your grandmother would think it had to be the war raging outside that had disrupted nature's balance and invited demons and devils from the netherworld to create mischief and cause miscarriages. To counteract this curse, I had to wear a small mirror around my neck as protection, because evil spirits are frightened by the sight of their own faces. But I knew even then that it was not an evil spirit but my own fears that had turned all my children into a collapsed mass of cells to be expelled from the body of their mother. I knew even then that I was the antithesis of most normal mothers, whose inclination it was to protect, not expel, their children from the safety of their wombs.

Motherhood, I was told, comes with a reliable array of unconscious but continuing instincts. As your grandmother reassured each time I became pregnant, maternal intuitions take over to create mothers out of even the most ill-equipped. But instead of giving my babies life, I did everything I could to take it away from them. I knew deep in the bone of my bones that it was my own unhappy heart, not a curse, as your grandmother feared, that had killed all my babies, before they even had the chance to grow. Their mother's dark will, her damaged heart, had prevented them from becoming anything more than blood clots I would expel unflinchingly from the depths of my body. It did not take long for me to recognize the signs: the little beads of sweat around my mouth, the quick palpitations of the heart that made me see black fire, the sudden attacks of panic that pinched my stomach and threw me into dry-heaving fits so violent that every baby in its right mind would do everything it could to escape. It was as if I already knew, even then, the nightmare that would descend upon us. It was as if I had to do everything I could to save their souls from a fate that would surely be theirs if they were to become my children. And that was why you were such a miracle baby, hanging on to your mother's womb until the very last moment, to be born to me at an age when I didn't think I would be pregnant again, overwhelming my will with yours the way you still do.

And of course your grandmother was right. She was absolutely right about the love that takes over, a love that is exquisite and terrifying at the same time, a love that inhabits a mother's heart completely and sets it in a tangled and frantic motion the moment her child is born. You became that most tender part of me, the part I didn't think could possibly exist, and my primary concern became your well-being and your safety. Will she be well? Will she be safe when I am not there to throw my body over hers in a moment of crisis? Life takes on a new dimension, and I prayed every day after you were born for an end to the war, not just the war outside, now an altogether new and different war between the North Vietnamese and the Vietcong on one side and the Americans and the government on the other, but also the war inside, the war that still eats, like savage locusts, shred by shred, the very tissue and flesh of my heart. But as it turns out, in the same way that my life itself always turns out to be the very opposite of what I want, the war that was to come, the war of the flea and the war of the elephant, was a war like no other we had ever seen. It was a war that essentially sliced the soul of our village in two; it was a war that disrupted the luminous motion of the earth itself.

How did this terrible war start? It started with the weight of goodness, when the Vietcong and the Americans both decided they wanted to own the soul of the villages and the villagers of Ba Xuyen.

I still remember how this quest for our hearts and minds first began, very innocently, with nothing but a crate of brand-new stoves. And even though I didn't know it then, it was the beginning of a long nightmare Baba Quan would throw over us like a giant black cape, exactly one year after the men first came to your grandmother's village, with grins on their faces and stoves in their arms to distribute to every peasant household.

I could see them as they made their way up the rocky hills. They were very young American men in their tropical jungle green, a little frightened, perhaps, because everything must have looked and smelled as new to them as their country, fourteen years later, looks and smells to us. They had learned to bow the Vietnamese way and immediately gave your grandmother a deep and respectful bow when they came by her house. As a matter of fact, I had brought you over for a visit at Grandmother's that day, when the first Americans arrived in our village.

They were going from house to house, handing out goodwill: free modern stoves that were supposed to emit much less smoke than the ones we villagers had been using. The stoves were made of polished steel and looked impressive, a portable box with an oven below and pot-holes on top. Everyone wanted one. But after the men left to go to another village, it only took us less than one month to realize that the stoves, the epitome of perfection, were in fact useless. They were too good. Landless peasants like us had thatched, not corrugated, roofs. Hardly any smoke was discharged, and no fumes had circulated through our thatched roofs. Termites and other pests that were once exterminated each time we cooked had suddenly thrived, causing damage not just to the roofs but even the foundations of houses.

And so, when the men came back for another visit, they were surprised to see their stoves blackened and abandoned like carcasses along the roadside. These poor people must not have understood that smoke can damage their lungs, the soldiers must have thought. Or perhaps they thought we hadn't appreciated these particular presents, because the next day they began to shower us with more presents— soap, candy, hydrogen peroxide, and Mercurochrome—as they embarked on one of their new projects, setting up nutrition and personal-hygiene classes in the town school. They even wore black or brown pajamas and, to keep the sun from beating against their heads, began wearing our straw conical hats as if they were natives of the soil. They accepted the occasional sweetmeats and rice buns your grandmother gave them, politely, with both hands. The children liked them. You loved to swing from their wrists like a monkey on a branch, tying the hair on their arms into yellow knots and tugging at them like grass in the fields. That was how they became a presence in your grandmother's village, as easy and simple as the first thread of yarn looped around a knitting needle.

But just as you can't have a top without a bottom, or a sun without a moon, you can't have Americans without Vietcong, not in those days, and so, within one week of the day when the Americans first appeared, trudging like awkward elephants haphazardly across our fields, sitting cross-legged on our floors to sample our chrysanthemum and jasmine tea, the Vietcong too began their sundown visits, like swarms of invisible fleas, the very minute the day ghosts, as the Americans were called, left the village for the night. And suddenly there were Vietcong study sessions we were forced to attend, and fund drives we had to contribute to. Rice had to be supplied to the Collective and Purchasing Committee of the Front, in exchange not for cash but for promises of payment and receipts redeemable only after the revolution. There was even a rice-bowl policy, so that everyone had to set aside a designated portion of rice every night for a Vietcong soldier, the way you would for a dead family member.

After a few months, the night ghosts, as your grandmother called the Vietcong, began encouraging, and then ordering all of us tenant farmers to stop paying rent. They intimidated the landlords by stringing dead ducks through wire lines and impaling pigs' heads on metal spikes staked around a landlord's house, their protruding animal tongues pulled from the depths of their throats like banners mocking the earth, the sky, the landlords, even Heaven itself. "Land for the landless," the night ghosts would moan over and over, until the tenants themselves knew the phrase by heart as well, so well in fact that for some the phrase became as common a mode of greeting as a casual nod of the head.

The Mandate of Heaven, the night ghosts whispered, no longer belonged to the landlords. Under the revolution, the fields would no longer be muted by a silenced passion. Peasants would own their land (until a dictatorship of the proletariat stepped in and owned it for them). The virtuous sword of a new Son of Heaven, they said, had been passed to a different generation of revolutionaries imbued with divine authority. This message they carved with a dagger into every tree in the village square, so that even the trees became the equivalent of an unearthly mind, the medium through which Heaven conveyed to the village the heart print of the sacrosanct mandate ordered from above.

It was no more than a few months before landlords in every part of Ba Xuyen began their exodus from the villages into the city. Even Uncle Khan, the greatest of the great landlords, who had refused to budge although wine bottles and broken glasses smeared with human feces had been scattered across the gate into the main courtyard of his house, had had to give up in the end. We were there when he received the message from the village diviner, a mandarin who performed the ancient Chinese ceremony on a flat, polished bone drilled with a small hole in one end and scratched with a question in the other. Should a dragon have to leave the cloud and the mountains and the river of his land? the holy man asked. And the answer, when the diviner torched the hole with fire to produce a pattern of cracks in the bone—a message from Heaven decipherable only by the diviner himself—was a clear and inevitable yes.

The day ghosts of course could not allow the night ghosts to win without retaliation and retribution. After all, the day ghosts were big like elephants and the night ghosts were only fleas that could be easily extinguished. The American day ghosts decided they needed something swift and clean and absolutely decisive in order to show us who were really in control. After the last of the landlords left, the hygiene teachers and the special forces of soldiers handing out soaps and stoves and candy also disappeared from the village, replaced suddenly by truckloads of soldiers in flak jackets, helmets, and steel-plated boots.

These new men did not bow to your grandmother or to the elders. They refused our food, preferring their own packs of canned beans and canned fruit and freeze-dried stew they would mix like cement, in well water purified with tablets. They kept to themselves and hid their faces behind a coat of jungle-green paint. They trampled our rice crops, ripping through the village with what we called their thousand-meter stare—scanning one thousand meters into the distant horizon for each footstep taken—their eyes checking every bush, monitoring the fields in front and the fields behind, turning their heads to the left, then the right, before putting one foot before the other. They stared so hard we thought they could shoot fire and burn the shrubs and carve a trail with their eyes alone. And of course they could. They possessed the power to summon a combustible constellation of sizzling orange flames and lolloping comets that sent all of us scurrying for cover.

Once, when your grandmother and I were picking mangoes from our fruit grove behind Baba Quan's house, I saw a young boy, his face beaded with sweat and his skin redder than a ripe red plum, kiss his rosaries as he inched step by step across a field, stopping every now and then to listen to sounds even my ears couldn't hear, and my heart, my heart almost broke in two for him. The sight of him clutching rosary beads made me want to cry, and it was then that I realized how attached I had been to a convent's life. It was as if he were kissing my life, my old life once upon a time at the Providence, and I, ignoring Baba Quan's screams, ran toward him, trying to touch a bit of my Providence past. Halfway across, I stopped, though, because I saw the way he froze and dropped to the ground, flat like an upside-down jellyfish trapped in the sand. He was scared—of me—and I suddenly of him. His rosaries dangled loosely from his neck, and all I could see was the giant rifle in front of his face and the coils and coils of ammunition around his body. I wanted to say, "I'm not against America. I'm not against your people." But I could tell he couldn't distinguish me from the enemy. It was Baba Quan, as a matter of fact, who had to leap across the field, zigzagging like the flash of a warrior's sword, dodging invisible arrows, knowing just where to turn to deflect undetectible danger, to scoop me up and bring me back into the safety of the house. I had no inkling then that he was already a Vietcong agent. His intimate knowledge of the dips and bends that define the earth's curves could be easily explained by the fact that he was a native of our soil.

Most of the time, though, these new men did not travel by foot but in military jeeps turned into armored tanks, fortified with sandbags from top to bottom and left to right. The cars would cut right across our seedbed and kill the plants before they had a chance to grow. Baba Quan would stand on his brick patio, beating his chest, screaming that they were worse than the worst drought, more unforgiving than the fiercest flood. But that was before your grandmother thought of using American military cars to help thresh our crop. She would spread ripe stalks of rice on a mat laid across the road so that their giant wheels would tread over the heap and loosen the dry grains from the stalks, in the end saving us at least a day's worth of arduous threshing work in the hot sun.

One summer day, even the fragile calm of the earth broke loose and exploded like a violent underground mine. By this time, I had decided to send you off to be with your father's parents, who had moved into the center of the city along with Uncle Khan and the rest of the landlords. I was visiting Baba Quan and your grandmother, and if ever there was a time when I knew as well as I knew the shape of my own ears the danger that was to befall us, that day was the day.

An American jeep pulling off the main road suddenly flew in the air and flipped into a somersault like a salmon flying up-current. The blast was so loud and the fire so bright I could see the flames and feel the tremors in the earth from my end of the village, which was quite a few rice fields away. But that wasn't all there was to make the elephants unleash every grunt and cry, every stampede and bit of firepower they had been saving like secret weapons until that day, discreetly in check deep inside their trunks and tusks and giant padded feet, so nobody, not even the fleas, would be able to see. What happened was something else altogether, a discovery so startling that the war of the fleas and the war of the elephant had to come to a final and crushing crescendo.

First there was the crushed jeep and the driver with the sheered toes and fingers and splattered face, then the booby traps and feces-smeared bamboo spikes that inflicted terrible puncture wounds on the four Americans running across the field toward the crushed car. And then, finally, there was the incredible maze of tunnels running from one end of the village to the other. I had never seen nor had I once suspected there was such an underground network of villages right under the soil of our own village. Inside the narrow shafts covered with a wooden trapdoor, the American day ghosts discovered a tangle of paths, each with its own road signs, depots of grenades and pistols, makeshift hospitals with syringes and bags of penicillin and half-burned candles, barrels of rice grain filled to the rim, and even a red altar with plaster statues of dragons and Buddhas. So narrow were the tunnels and so delicate was the maze that only the smallest of the elephants could crawl through the system.

Though they might have been too big to crawl underground, they were big enough to destroy our village the next day. They were, after all, elephants. Not the elephant that had predicted the birth of the Buddha, or the kind that dwelled on the Gold Mountain and had six tusks, each one corresponding to the six dimensions of space—upward, downward, forward, backward, left, and right. No, these were different elephants. Instead of the six sacred tusks, these elephants had bullets, machine guns, mortar shells, the constant wop wop wop of chopper blades, and automatic rifles blasting all day and all night, toppling every tree, even the hundred-year-old banyan tree, which had always been indestructible, always indestructible, that is, up until that day, because hanging from its thick and shady branches are roots that have always been able to multiply into new and sturdy trunks that spread across the fields.

But even that, even the dead banyan tree, hadn't been a sufficient show of force. The elephant had yet to spread its ears or trumpet its loudest, most ominous battle cry. In their final and deadliest charge yet, the elephants rolled out drum after drum painted with orange stripes and sprayed our crops overnight with a special kind of poison, a mixture so powerful that it could command even the most majestic of trees to prematurely drop their leaves. The young men we once saw crouched and frightened every time they walked our roads had become fire gods, thunder gods, and lightning gods with enough power and rage in their breaths to denude our land, maul our trees, and turn the green of our rice fields into the dead dead brown of stone. As a gush of sourness bellied from our earth, sumac bushes, papaya trees, jackfruits, everything and anything that could hide the enemies withered into a deep, slow burn of ash and cinder overnight.

We would have left the village for good. But everyone knew the story of the betel nut by heart, and no one wanted to lose her soul or turn into stone-cold lime or betel-nut trees or betel-nut vines. So we decided to stay and rebuild, to keep watch over the burial grounds of our ancestors and answer the call of the earth. And we did what had always been done. We plowed and harrowed, weeded and watered, and we fertilized and refertilized our fields. Beyond our village gate, we realized, the world was vast and incomprehensible. But here, in the geometric landscape with its many bright hues of green, among the lush and condensed groves of mangoes and coconuts, there has always been a continuity that we understood, and we wanted to salvage and preserve what we had inherited from our parents and our parents' parents.

Some of us who had a cash reserve ventured into the city to buy miracle rice of the kind used in India's Green Revolution. Despite our continuing efforts to resurrect the earth, the village soil remained dull and dead, an ungenerous gray that could easily keep raw ashes smoldering and hot but could neither keep nor sustain life. There was only a flatness of dry rocks and dead trees, brown leafless knobs that collapsed into an inert, suppurated mass of poison that was beyond resuscitation. Nothing, not one blade of grass, not even the sturdy betel vine that had mythically survived even the most calamitous drought in the history of the country, could grow from dead soil. Not even the rice fields, the soul of the country itself, could be revived. Everything we did was, ultimately, in vain.

Earthworms, after all, do not lie. As a final test, it was Baba Quan who ventured into a village several kilometers away to dig for a handful of earthworms. He brought them back and burrowed them in our village soil, the moistest, most humid, most fertilized soil we could find. And every day, your grandmother and I and the rest of the villagers would wait by the spot and watch the earthworms, and together we would pray for their survival. "Are they going to make it?" someone would ask. "I see something moving," others would cry, hoping against all hope that life could be borne from the bone-dry wasteland of our soil. But in the end, all our earthworms died. And so it was, on our second and third and fourth attempts. The earthworms, our litmus test, could not live in poisoned soil. And neither could we.

That was how the second half of our nightmare began, with the death of our village soil. Soon thereafter, leaflets were dropped from the sky to warn us that our houses would be doused with petrol and burned to the ground so that the Vietcong could no longer be harbored in the village and hidden from view. We were told to pack up and move across the river to a village of concrete surrounded by barbed wire and trenches as deep and wide as the gulf in my own sorrowful soul.

"This is the end," I thought to myself as we crossed the river and stepped into a sun-soaked expanse of hot, black tar. And of course I was right. In this terrible and desolate landscape across from our old village, your grandmother, as I expected, gave up the will to live, and it took but a few days for her to pass away like a slow, hissing sigh.

They called it a strategic hamlet, this concrete lot where we came to live so that our old village, a Vietcong stronghold, it appeared, could become a free-fire zone where the enemy could be searched and destroyed with impunity. Inside the safe circumference of our strategic hamlet, an enclosure reinforced by double coils of concertina barbed wire, stood an endless crawl of houses sheeted by corrugated-tin roofs painted with giant red crosses easily visible from a plane above. Here, among the unmoored lives of villagers who had once anchored themselves by the roots of the earth, your grandmother and I and Baba

Quan were told to navigate our way into a new life. I remembered feeling the strange hardness of cement beneath my feet as I held your grandmother in my arms. We were in a barracks, one among many identical barracks. On a table were two tin pots, a can opener, and a carton of canned sardines issued by the government. Tacked on the wall was our schedule for the week, lectures on civic duty, lessons on the art of uncovering Vietcong agents, seminars on village au-tonomy and economic self-sufficiency.

There was a certain degree of calm in this concrete lot, but inwardly none of us felt calm. Across the expanse of water, beyond the barbed-wire enclosures, the war continued to rage with unremitting fire and fury. You were still with your father and his family in Saigon, and although I knew you would be safer there than in the strategic hamlet with me, I could not help worrying about you every day. I would run my hand over my belly, and imagine that I was still carrying you in my womb, your form and shape pressed solidly against the embrace of my flesh. The slow, unsteady pulse of our village could still be felt, especially by the elders of the village, who pulled their chairs to the edge of the river and looked blindly out at the slate-gray water toward our village until the last ray of sun threaded its way into the dark horizon beyond.

It was one week after we arrived in the strategic hamlet that your grandmother died a death both sudden and unexpected. Although she had been in good physical health, her death, our barracks neighbors proclaimed, could not have been avoided. She died in the late after-noon, on a makeshift bed, while Baba Quan was supposedly engaged in self-defense maneuvers designed to train villagers to protect them-selves from Vietcong attacks and propaganda. Because Baba Quan was nowhere to be found, I knew I would have to take matters into my own hand to preserve your grandmother's soul, to nurture it back to the land of its birth before it could make the move into a non-earthly, everlasting peace.

Even though our old village had been declared a free-fire zone, which meant that any moving thing caught in its vicinity could and would be shot, I knew I would have to find a way back there, back to the graves of my ancestors, back to the sacred land where my mother's placenta and umbilical cord had been buried and where her body would have to be buried as well. She would have to die where she was born, and I would have to construct this circle for her, a beginning and an end that converged toward and occupied one single, concentrated space. And so I persuaded an old boatman by invoking your grandmother's spirit and playing on his notions of filial duties to lend me his livelihood, a tiny vessel which he used to ferry people a safe upstream ride toward a market situated in the opposite direction from our old village.

By the time I hauled your grandmother's body onto the boat and stocked the boatman's craft with as many buns and dumplings as the neighbors could give me on the short notice I gave them, it was already late in the day, and I had to hurry to make it across the river before the sun went down. It was a lonely journey, and I had to make sure I remained undetected as the boat edged along the gray shadows of the burned coconut groves. The unmistakable force of your grandmother's presence stayed with me throughout the entire trip. Once you've touched a dead person, you carry her with you for the rest of your life.

There were warnings everywhere along the riverbanks. "Free Fire Zone," "Unexploded Mines." We were borne by the current, the river swelled with broken bottles, cigarette butts, and other rubbish. I tried to row as little as possible, listening carefully for the slightest pull against the oars, which would signal underwater trip wires or bamboo stakes and metal spikes that could rip the boat in two. A slight clearing in one part of the banks seemed like a possible landing spot, and I quickly navigated the boat through the weeds, grateful because I realized that it was a part of the river that faced south, where the village graveyard, like all tombs and graveyards and pagodas, was situated, toward the southerly direction, where it is believed all the dominant and active forces of life, fire and summer and the lucky color red, dwell along with the Son of Heaven.

I moored the boat and ventured inland, leaving behind your grandmother's body, which I had wrapped inside a quilt. The area by the riverbank was thick with mud, and all around us, collapsed trees with hollowed trunks and roots that rotted in a pool of brown juice covered the sodden earth. I knew I would have to locate an unobstructed path from the river to the village burial ground before maneuvering my way through the sediment and undergrowth with your grandmother's body on my back. And that was when I saw it, the act that continued to haunt me to this day. In the lavender light among the gray-hued tombs of our ancient burial grounds, three ghostly figures hovered among the markers. A lavish arrangement of betel nuts, kumquats, plums, and persimmons was displayed on a tray placed before a gilded picture of Uncle Khan's mother. I realized it was the anniversary of the death of Uncle Khan's mother, and he had returned from Saigon to pay homage to his mother by her grave.

At first I thought Uncle Khan had arranged a gathering by the tombstone to commemorate his mother's death. But I saw the truth soon enough. Through a faint stream of light cast by a kerosene lantern, I could make out the red-smeared face of Baba Quan. While another man pinned Uncle Khan to the ground, Baba Quan plunged a knife through Uncle Khan's throat. Right there, on sacred earth, our village burial ground, a murder was being committed before my eyes, a slow-burning rage that had begun years before, finally released with the deadly precision of a knife's edge.

"Don't you have something to tell him?" a man's voice asked as Baba Quan dug his knife into a tangle of veins. "Let him know. Crimes against the people cannot go unpunished. Land to the Landless."

"Believe me, he knows, comrade, he knows the way he knows the beat of his own lustful heart exactly why he is being punished," Baba Quan sobbed. Here was the man, he must have thought, whose hands had once touched his wife's naked body. The three sticks of incense before Uncle Khan's mother's tomb—my grandmother's tomb—gray and dusty like our poisonous soil—flickered, three red dots dead in the swirling gusts of wind.

I watched as they dragged Uncle Khan's body to the water's edge and dumped it into the river, next to a warning sign covered with weeds. There was the legacy that coursed through the landscape like a slow but steady rush of a death foretold. I watched as the corpse floated into the undulations of the dark-gray current. "It'll look like he tripped on a punji stake," Baba Quan whispered.

And I watched as they disappeared, slipping from the surface of the earth like a pair of eels darting into an underground of tunnels the day ghosts had yet to discover—a network of passages lying inside the belly of the earth like a shadow village to our own village above. And that was when everything made sense to me. That was when I realized the raw, untamed anguish of a man who had lived his life like a clenched fist, a man who had dreamed of turning a cool hatred into a tormented howl for revenge—against a landlord who had turned his wife into a concubine and taken from him a child who should have been rightfully his. I understood it clearly as I stood by the river's edge, this thumping, messy rage, tightly wound and simmering like a hissing fury—funneled and unburdened decades later as nothing more than a pristine lesson in class warfare.

What could I have done? A part of me died forever by that river's edge, and I have never been able to touch it since, that most wounded part that still lies inert beyond my grasp, like the sorrow on my face, seared by a fire dropped into the free-fire zone from a plane as I fled from the cemetery toward the safety of the boat. Everything was on fire. I will always remember that moment as the moment the earth screamed its tormented scream. From the ground where I was lying face-up, I could see the gathering red that poured from a lacerated sky, the red of fire bisected by a black, black smoke as far away as the untouchable line where heaven meets earth.

Someone had seen movement in a free-fire zone, and surely, just as we had been warned by leaflets dropped from the sky, the village would once again be pacified. Clusters of bright-yellow flames burst through a high-explosive mix of gasoline and jelly to stick to my face and burn spider holes in my skin. I felt it the way you would feel the quick, unexpected splash of boiling water against tender skin.

When I finally came out of a full six-month coma, lying in a metal bed in a hospital in Saigon, I was told I would have to be reconstructed, as the doctors euphemistically phrased it. After the fifth and final operation, in which my skin had to be stripped through the flesh and down to the bone, I learned that my mother's body, your grandmother's body, was never found and must have remained exposed, soulless, forever hungry and forever wandering by the waters of the Mekong where I had abandoned her. That is why the grave I have for her is only an empty grave, a hollow pit inside the earth that I can only cover with sorrow and shame.

What more can I say after I've said everything I have to say about the karma that has pursued our family like a hawk chasing its prey? What more can I tell you about Baba Quan, a man I continued to call Father until my last day in Saigon? He was a man who tried to drink his despair away, a man consumed by a resonating anguish, a deeply personal passion that always curls back into the reflection of its own anger. The basic building block, the atoms and molecules that mattered to him, was not the certainty of conviction but the raw messiness of faith and retribution. That was what motivated him to risk his own life to save Michael from the riddles of a minefield he himself had designed. Love and hate rivered through his veins and blasted through his flesh, and he could as easily murder his enemy, the landlord Khan, as he could save an American Special Forces unit. He saved Michael, and Michael in turn saved us. I comfort myself with the hope that, after this harvest of the heart, perhaps amends had indeed been made.

Years later, in a room far away from Ba Xuyen, I can sit in my bed, close my eyes, and still hear the wails of ghosts and the cries of demons submerged in the blood and flesh of my body. In theory, a different course, the course I imagined and left in a drawer for you to find, could have been possible. Baba Quan could not unknow or undo the fact of his wife's unacceptable deed or his complicity in it, of course. But if he had been able to do what your grandmother was able to manage, till the land, follow the particulars demanded by parenthood—change the diapers, prepare the food, ease a crying fit—a different, less ravaged truth could have been produced. Tonight, as I sit in bed to write this last letter to you, I can still feel the uncauterized burn against my face as sharply as I first felt it almost seventeen years ago. Karma is exactly like this, a continuing presence that is as ongoing as Baba Quan's obsession, as indivisible as our notion of time itself. Our reality, you see, is a simultaneous past, present, and future. The verbs in our language are not conjugated, because our sense of time is tenseless, indivisible, and knows no end. And that is what I fear. I fear our family history of sin, revenge, and murder and the imprint it creates in our children's lives as it rips through one generation and tears apart the next.

This is how your mother loves you, Mai. This is how I want to shield you from the misfortunes of our family, to keep you from living and reliving your grandmother's and mother's multitudes of lost lives. In that way, motherhood is the same in every language. It touches you, exaggerates your capacity to love, and makes you do things that are wholly unordinary. It calls for a suspension of the self in a way that is almost religious, spiritual. The true division in this world, I believe, is not the division founded on tribe, nation-

ality, or religion, but the division between those of us who are mothers and those who aren't. Those of us who are on this side of the divide would revert to animal instinct and plunge headfirst without a moment's thought into the barrel of a rifle to shield our children from a bullet's deadly path. And so I can only hope that my act of sacrifice will give you the new beginning that you deserve, far from the concealing fields and free of a destiny that should never have been yours.

In 1963, in an act that stunned the world, an elderly Buddhist monk stepped calmly from a car into the street, crossed his legs in a serene lotus position, meditated himself into a contemplative state, and watched in silence as a group of monks and nuns encircled him, dousing him with gasoline and lighting him on fire. As passersby threw themselves reverentially on the ground, the monk performed the ultimate act of sacrifice and pressed his palms in prayer, a sermon of fire, his body in an erect, uncollapsible lotus position, while flames, burning, burning, orange and ocher, the color of his saffron robe, enveloped and consumed the flesh he offered as an act of supreme devotion.

I'm already a dying person, Mai. This soil is as poisonous to my soul as the poison that once turned our village into dead earth. Years ago, I followed your grandmother into that phantom world by the river's edge, across from the dead world of our village, and I have never found my way back. But as I am sitting here writing to you, I feel something that I haven't felt in a long time, an unburdened sense of tranquillity palpable enough that I can almost run through it with my hands. And for the first time since our arrival in Virginia, I can almost feel the geometric shape of the shimmering rice fields outside, a rebirthed expanse of flat, flat green, answering the call of my heart.

The legacy that I leave you will inevitably include the leanness of your father's body, the thickness of his hair; it will include the angular structure of your mother's facial bone. But besides the work-ings of the cells and the replication of our DNA structures, you will also have a different inheritance, an unburdened past, the seductive powers of an American future, a mother's true memories of Ba Xuyen—its warm breast, a lone water buffalo amid a shimmer of liquid green, a solitary leaf turning its belly toward the direction of the full sun. When all is done, it is all yours, the nerve tissue of your family's past, the labor and loop of your mother's life, and the blood that pumps its own imperishable future through the chambers of your heart.

In the meantime, the feast of swallows'-nest soup, the lotus pud-ding, the tripe stew and pigs' ears, the chocolate mousse, and the caramel custard, this is the funeral feast I have arranged for both your grandmother and myself. It is exactly the feast I would have prepared for your grandmother years ago had we not been caught in the cross fire between the elephant and the fleas.

It wasn't until years later that I learned there was a name for what my mother was—a depressive, someone not with supernatural ears but ears that heard voices of despair urging her on.

What kinds of private thoughts did she have? I never knew she had a whole separate language of her own until after she died, when I discovered it in a letter she wrote to me, not the gorgeous fictional reimaginings of an improvised life—the life she wished she had—but the real one. She had passed out by then: the effect of multiple sleeping pills mixed with half a pitcher of vodka had been much swifter than she had anticipated.

My mother hadn't seemed any more undone than Mrs. Bay or any of the people I knew from Little Saigon. In one way or another, my mother and her friends were not much unlike the physically wounded. They had continued to hang on to their Vietnam lives, caressing the shape of a country that was no longer there, in a way not much different from amputees who continued to feel the silhouette of their absent limbs. Years later, they continued to deny the fact that some tender and unexpendable part of them had been exiled into a space that could not be reached, and so they would continue to live their lives, like my mother, in a long wail of denial.

Would it have been different had I been more perceptive? Could I have understood a week-long four-burner feast to be a death mask or a funeral arrangement, a happy face to be a face of despair, a double lifeline to be a single line of imminent death? Could I have guessed that behind my grandfather's caresses were fingers that committed murders and designed a labyrinth of underground tunnels and mines?

I had believed my mother would get better and better, that she would always live forever. I had answered in the affirmative, "Yes, mother, of course," when she had asked, "Do you love me?" But a simple, unprompted "I love you," that was what I hadn't said, even though I had had years to say it, when saying it would have mattered the most.

She had lain face down on the mattress with the rigid flatness of someone who had been held up by robbers pointing guns into the naked bones of her back. Something is terribly wrong, I immediately knew, the same way I knew my knees had turned as watery as her favorite jasmine tea. The windows had been shut tight, the blinds pulled all the way down, the darkness final and complete.

It was the face I had found most shocking, not the green vomit that leaked from her nose, but the imperceptibly calm face, a dead face, blue like the tender middle of raw meat. She had vomited in her coma, and it must have blocked her lungs, turning her face a hard, morbid blue. How did this happen? I wanted to ask. But it was too late, and my body had felt nothing except its own lead-heavy movement fleeing out the door, down the stairs, into a place I could not say where.

Afterward, how or when the ambulance and the police

and Bobbie and Mrs. Bay arrived I no longer remember. My mind had turned tight and motionless like a metal clamp, the screws sharp and relentless, a factory-driven screw pressing everything downward, toward a hard and tightly sealed bottom not even I knew existed inside my body. I had not cried at the funeral, sitting with my arms neatly in my laps, next to Bobbie, feeling nothing while I watched her cry, her face as white as the funeral white she had worn along with a black patch of mourning the size of a thumb Mrs. Bay had pinned to her lapel. The funeral had been paid for by my mother's and Mrs. Bay's hui members, whose first community-financed project turned out to be, inauspiciously, a funeral service. The air, smothering with incense fumes, was filled with the meaningless and overpowering sound of wooden clappers beating all through the service; all around us, faces of people from Little Saigon and wreaths from mourners who had worked with my mother at the Mekong Grocery; everywhere a vast uninterrupted expanse of white as stark and endless as the white of a hospital hall.

A few more minutes and it will all be over. Keep calm, simplify, simplify, everything will be all right. I kept my eyes focused on nothing but the mindless gray of dead space inside, glancing only once at Bobbie through a mist in my eyes. You're not going to have to see any of these people ever again once you leave for college, so everything, but everything, will be just fine. A brand-new slate, that was what my mother had supposedly given me, a slate unmarred by any undercurrents or tremors of Saigon or even of Falls Church, Virginia. Control, everything is order and control. One wrong move, one wrong move, and the entire mess can just disarrange itself and collapse like a hundred pieces of flying metal for the whole world to see.

It was as if everything had been negotiated years before, planned ahead of time, just in case. My adoption papers, handing me over to Uncle Michael, had been signed years before, before I left Saigon on the Pan Am flight out of Tan Son Nhut Airport with my father's best friend. The adoption, Mrs. Bay told me, had never been revoked, even after my mother arrived.

The night before college was to begin officially, as I lay in my bed in Farmington, a new dream—not the three-o'clock-in-the-morning dream I had learned to expect, but a different dream—came to me. The pillow was wet and sticky with sweat. Don't look, keep it in, keep it in, I whispered, trying to sound the warning, my hands squeezing the blanket, clutching it like a child hanging on to the narrow armrests of a plane preparing for irrevocable takeoff into the sky. I kept my eyes closed, breathing even breaths, one in, one out, one in, one out, bracing for the worst.

What I saw was a beautiful ladder, the same one my mother had described many times before, guarded by a secret creature with an inner light glowing through its skin, a light as faint and dormant as the faint flame of a candle glowing through a screen of silk. The creature, my mother once said, always lies with its head cradled on the first rung, waiting for a human soul to pass by to infuse it with an inner life. As the passerby makes her way up the rungs, the creature would slowly stir, following the passerby the way it has followed hundreds upon hundreds of pilgrims generations and generations before, its translucent skin becoming more and more luminous the higher it and the passerby get, making their way up each step. The creature would approximate perfection, its skin would turn lustrous, its light would shine a

brilliant shine the closer it gets to the top, but only at the very top would it achieve perfection; only at the very top of the ladder would the climber cast no shadows and achieve what every seeker seeks through all the ages to achieve: nirvana itself.

A climber who cannot make it all the way up would have to come back down, and the creature, the creature, my mother whispered, would have to give up as well, reverting once again to the pale, lightless creature it once was, its moan as it makes its way back down a low, mournful moan sadder than the cry of a silkworm spinning its last thread of silk. According to my mother, the creature has made it up to the top only once. In my dream, it would make it up a second time, with my mother leading the way, step by step, into perfection.

This was the first time since the funeral that her death had seemed final, final enough for me to imagine her climbing something like a ladder toward Heaven. I could feel a part of me, the part that had always wanted to break loose from my mother, make a sudden turn in reverse to rush backward into the folds of my mother's womb. We had inhabited the same flesh, and as I discovered that night, like the special kind of DNA which is inherited exclusively from the mother and transmitted flawlessly only to the female child—the daughter—a part of her would always pass itself through me.

A sharp, irrepressible sob broke loose as I stared at the ceiling, a funeral-white ceiling Uncle Michael had mercifully remembered to paint over with pink. Careful, easy does it, slow down. There is always order to tend to, chaos to push swiftly away. I held myself against the bed, keeping the tears I didn't know I had in, inside, safely invisible behind the eyes. Across the room, on my desk, a glossy color brochure promised us incoming students the openness of an unexplored future and the safety of its sanctuary. "A college for women, the challenge to excel." I could walk right into it. Next to the brochure, a pamphlet addressed to the Class of 1983, its cover the yellow of our class color, ticked off a helpful list of suggested items for dorm living: a desk lamp, sheets, towels, a flashlight. I would follow the course of my own future. The acceptance letter from the Admissions Office whispered a starlight of reassurance.

Outside, a faint sliver of what only two weeks ago had been a full moon dangled like a sea horse from the sky.